"Quirky characters, a darling small-town New England setting, and a plucky heroine. I thoroughly enjoyed this puzzler
of a mystery. Reilly cooks up a perfect recipe of murder and
mayhem in this charming cozy."

—Jenn McKinlay, *New York Times* bestselling
author of *Assault and Beret*

"You had me at deep-fried haddock and malt vinegar. This
is a terrific book—smart, sassy, and a little bit scary. Everything a good cozy should be!"

—Laura Childs, *New York Times* bestselling
author of *Egg Drop Dead*

More Praise for Linda Reilly

"Reilly's debut uses her expertise in title searches to create
a pleasing mystery with some interesting twists."

—*Kirkus Reviews*

"Sure to attract cozy fans." —*Library Journal*

"I had the pages turning so fast that I was almost afraid of
setting the book on fire. I loved the characters and can't wait
to see them again very soon." —*MyShelf.com*

Berkley Prime Crime Titles by Linda Reilly

FILLET OF MURDER
OUT OF THE DYING PAN
A FRYING SHAME

A
FRYING
SHAME

LINDA REILLY

BERKLEY PRIME CRIME
New York

BERKLEY PRIME CRIME
Published by Berkley
An imprint of Penguin Random House LLC
375 Hudson Street, New York, New York 10014

Copyright © 2017 by Linda Reilly

ISBN 9780425274156

First Edition: April 2017

Printed in the United States of America
1 3 5 7 9 10 8 6 4 2

Cover illustration by Dan Craig
Book design by Laura K. Corless

For Nanna and Pop:
I miss you every day.

ACKNOWLEDGMENTS

As always, I owe my deepest thanks to all the wonderful folks at Berkley Prime Crime. Editors Michelle Vega and Bethany Blair—you are a joy and a pleasure to work with. Daniel Craig, not only did you design another fabulous cover featuring Bo the calico cat, but you captured details of the story that I know will delight readers.

To my agent, Jessica Faust, my eternal gratitude for planting the seed that sprouted into the Deep Fried Mysteries.

To John White, retired captain, Massachusetts State Police, a tip of the hat for your excellent advice on the use of court-ordered tracking devices. If I made any errors, they are mine alone.

And to my husband, Bernie, for patiently listening to me chatter about murder and mayhem while he's trying to eat dinner.

Most of all, I am grateful to my readers for expressing such interest in my characters, both two-legged and four. It has made all the difference.

STEELTOP FOODS

First Annual Cook-Off & Bake-Off

SAVORY CATEGORY:

NORMA FERGUSON
(flaky-top chicken stew)

HARRY SUMMERS
(tangy tamale casserole)

CRYSTAL GALARDI
(home-style meat loaf)

SWEET CATEGORY:

VIVIAN LAVOIE
(spiced ginger cookies)

TALIA MARBY
(miniature deep-fried apple pies)

DYLAN McPHEE
(cinnamon-swirl brownies)

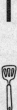

As if a rogue summer wind had suddenly swept over the cobblestone plaza, the door to Fry Me a Sliver flew open with a bang. A pctitc woman with a full head of meticulously dyed blond curls rushed inside. In one beringed hand she waved a large plastic disk.

"Talia, did you get your Flavor Dial?" Crystal Galardi rushed up to the speckled turquoise counter. Behind a pair of ruby-colored eyeglasses that lent her a slightly feline look, her kindly brown eyes beamed. "UPS delivered mine a few minutes ago! Oh, I can't believe I entered this contest. Maybe I had a mental lapse that day. Do you think?"

Talia Marby, owner of an eatery that specialized in deep-fried delectables, wiped her hands on her blue Fry Me a Sliver apron. She scooted around the edge of the counter into the dining room. "Crystal, you're a marvelous cook. You have nothing at all to worry about. And yes, UPS delivered mine about a half hour ago," she said with a grin. "Mine has all different spices. Let me see yours!"

Crystal was the co-owner of the Fork and Dish, the cooking supplies shop that had opened three months earlier across from Talia's eatery. Tucked between the Clock Shop and Time for Tea, it was one of six specialty shops in the Wrensdale Arcade, a cozy shopping plaza that resembled an old English village. The seventh and largest shop—a vintage lighting store—had remained empty nearly a year after its owner's life had been brutally snuffed.

The dial in question was a round of clear plastic about a foot in diameter. At least eighteen spice-filled windows marched around the wheel. Each window had a push lever at the top for easy dispensing of the chosen spice.

"Look at this." Crystal aimed a shimmery blue fingernail at her wheel. "Marjoram, mint, oregano, parsley . . . Oh, I'm going to love having all these herbs in one easy-peasy wheel! Okay, it's official. I am really excited about the contest. Not to mention nervous. Aren't you getting nervous?"

Talia laughed. "A little bit. But it's too late to back out now."

Truth be told, Talia was more than a little nervous. Crystal had talked her into entering a contest sponsored by Steeltop Foods, a Midwest-based conglomerate rumored to have ties to the Berkshires. In the town's weekly paper, a chatty article quoted Steeltop's chief operating officer as saying, "The stunning backdrop of the Berkshires is the ideal locale for the trial run of our competition, and to introduce our new Flavor Dial, which we predict will be a huge seller. If successful, we'll choose a different venue every year."

The contest was split into two categories—sweet and savory—and entrants had to choose one before entering.

Talia had chosen sweet, but now she was worried. Were her deep-fried mini apple pies really good enough to be entered in a contest? For weeks she'd been testing them on everyone she knew. So far, no one had given her a thumbs-down. Her boyfriend, Ryan, said they were the cat's whiskers, and her mom claimed that if she served them to enough people they could bring about world peace.

Nothing like biased loved ones to give you an honest opinion.

She had to admit, though, the award money—a cool twenty-five grand—was nothing to turn up her nose at. In the unlikely event that she won, she planned to use the prize money to pay off the loan she'd taken this past spring to renovate the eatery.

The competition was going to be held the following Sunday at Wrensdale's annual summer festival. The festival always took place in mid-August, at the local sports stadium on the outskirts of Wrensdale. Vendors of all sorts peddled fun in the form of games of chance. Others hawked the kinds of edibles designed to expand the average waistline. After the competition was over, the Wrensdale police and fire departments would battle for the win in their annual softball game. It was an event to which everyone in town looked forward.

Talia glanced around. It was midafternoon. The eatery was in a lull. Her only customers, two teenage girls, sat at a corner table thumbing away at their smartphones. Excusing herself, Talia strolled over to the pair. "Anything else I can get you? More soda?"

Both girls shook their heads and smiled. "We're good," they said in unison.

"I wouldn't mind an iced coffee," Crystal said, plunking

herself down at a table. She loosened the neckline of her sleeveless tunic and fanned herself with her spice wheel. "Although I have to say, our air-conditioning is a bit better than yours. Either that or I'm having a hot flash."

Talia knew it was the latter, but she didn't say it. "It might be a degree or two warmer in here than it is in your shop. Remember, we fry food all day."

Behind the counter, Martha Hoelscher, one of Talia's two employees, set aside the batch of coleslaw she'd been preparing and poured out a glass of iced coffee. Talia smothered a smile. No doubt Martha had been eavesdropping on their conversation. The woman had the hearing of a bat and didn't miss a trick.

Martha went over to Crystal and set the cold drink down in front of her. At sixtysomething, she wore her gray hair in a chin-length bob. Today she sported a short-sleeved beige blouse over lightweight yellow slacks. "Okay, I've seen Talia's wheel," she said, sounding unimpressed. "Now let's see yours."

"We sound like grade-schoolers, don't we?" Crystal giggled. "I'll show you mine if you show me yours."

Martha fixed Crystal with a look and took the wheel from her. Her sharp gray eyes roaming the device, she shook her head. "I'll tell you the same thing I told Talia. It's a gimmick, pure and simple. You got more spices in here than you'll probably ever use. You could accomplish the same thing with a couple jars of your favorite spices and a set of measuring spoons. Plus, once the novelty wears off, these things will be clogging landfills all over the US of A. Besides, where're you gonna store the thing? It takes up way too much space." Speech over, she set the wheel down on the table.

Crystal diffused Martha's sermon with a kind smile. "Now, Martha, you have to admit it's a rather clever gadget.

And I promise you, if I ever get sick of using it, I'll see that the plastic is properly recycled."

"By the way, how's Audrey doing?" Talia asked Crystal. "She's been lying a bit low lately. Is she excited about the contest?"

Crystal's business partner, Audrey Feldon, was the marketing guru of their cooking supplies shop. The two had vastly different personalities, yet the partnership seemed to work. In a way, they reminded Talia of her twin aunts, Jennie and Josie, who ran a successful greeting card business in Malibu.

"No." Crystal stuck out her lower lip and rested her chin on the heel of one hand. "She has no interest whatsoever in the contest, or in the festival. She's being a real booby-head about all of this."

Interesting, Talia thought. Something was definitely up with Audrey. About five years Talia's senior, she was a friendly soul who liked everyone she met. But lately, Talia noticed, Audrey had been testy and temperamental. Not her usual self at all.

"Plus," Crystal went on, "she's busy helping Molly get ready for school. Her senior year at UMass, can you believe it?"

Molly was Audrey's daughter, a bubbly young woman who was working part-time at her mother's and Crystal's shop, at least until school started. Talia hadn't known any of the women all that long, but the Fork and Dish was proving to be a fine addition to the Wrensdale Arcade.

The door opened, and a face peeked inside. A pair of pale brown eyes framed by a fine-boned face homed right in on Crystal. "I thought you might be here."

"Hey, Audrey." Talia smiled, detecting a hint of tension in the woman's voice. "Crystal was just showing me her flavor wheel. Would you like some iced coffee?"

Audrey closed the door and stepped inside, her small san-daled feet crossing the blue-and-white tile floor in delicate steps. Even with the mercury hovering in the high eighties, she looked cool as a Popsicle in a pink floral top over a pair of white capris. Her thick French braid, the color of paprika, trailed around her right side and rested just below her breast. "Thanks, Talia, but I've already drunk enough lemonade today to float me all the way to the Atlantic. I came to ask Crystal if she's seen my notebook."

Crystal sighed. "I'm right here, Audrey. You don't have to talk around me."

Audrey tensed. "Sorry." Her gaze drifted to the spice wheel and her lips pursed.

"And no, I haven't seen your notebook," Crystal said softly. "Don't you usually leave it on the left-hand shelf in the supply room? Incidentally, who's watching the store?"

"Molly is," Audrey huffed. "You don't think I'd leave the shop unattended, do you?"

Whoa. Something was definitely up with the pair. The ten-sion was thicker than a fresh batch of Talia's sweet batter.

Crystal's cheeks flushed pink. She gulped down the rest of her iced coffee. "Thank you for the drink, Talia. Pay you later? I didn't bring my purse with me."

Talia smiled at her. "My treat today, okay?"

With a nod of thanks, Crystal grabbed her wheel, rose from her chair, and left. Audrey gave Talia a quick wave and scooted out the door behind her.

Talia picked up Crystal's empty glass and carried it into the kitchen. Martha shot her a look. "What's up with those two?"

"I haven't a clue, Martha." Talia absently dumped out the ice cubes and stuck the glass in the commercial dishwasher. Skim-ming her gaze over the kitchen, she still couldn't believe how much larger it felt after the renovations she'd done this past spring. With Martha's help she'd redesigned the floor plan. The kitchen had gained an extra twenty-four square feet of work space, while the sleek new chairs and fresh paint in the dining area gave it a roomier, more open look.

Martha measured out three tablespoons of chipotle paste and mixed it into the slaw. "Like I said before, that shop is cursed."

"Now, Martha, you know that's nonsense. Just because . . ." Talia's thoughts drifted off, and she gave an involuntary shiver.

"Because the last proprietor was murdered? When she'd been there barely a month?"

Talia gave Martha a stern look. "That doesn't mean the shop is cursed. Crystal and Audrey have done a wonderful job with the Fork and Dish. Besides, there's no such thing as a curse." She went over to the worktable, where she'd left her Flavor Dial. Was Martha right? Was it simply another half-baked idea designed to entice the public to spend?

She picked up the wheel with her left hand and with the fingers of her right hand skimmed the names. Cardamom, cinnamon, cloves . . . on and on through the alphabet until she reached vanilla bean. With the exception of lavender, they were all spices she kept on hand.

With a sigh, Talia set down the wheel. Okay, maybe Martha was right about the Flavor Dial. She'd use it for the contest, but after that it would probably get shoved out of sight on a top shelf somewhere.

But she wasn't right about the curse. Audrey was having problems, that's all. Who didn't have personal problems?

But curses? That was just crazy talk.

Wasn't it?

2

By eleven on Sunday morning, the softball field was bustling. The sky was a cloudless blue, with the temp hovering in the high seventies. Rainstorms were predicted for later in the week, but today the weather was sheer perfection.

"We couldn't have asked for a more perfect day, could we?" Ryan Collins grinned, his smile wide as he strode beside Talia and his dad, Arthur Collins, toward the massive tent. The roof of the open-sided tent stretched across the area beyond the outfield. Beneath it, long tables and folding chairs had been set up. Checkered tablecloths, the disposable kind, covered each table.

"Here's a good spot," Talia said, slipping her arm through Arthur's. She steered him gently toward one of the tables, and he sat down in one of the folding chairs with a broad grin. "Thank you, my dear. Oh, I've so been looking forward to this! I haven't attended in a few years, you know."

Ryan squeezed his dad's shoulder, a pained expression crossing his pleasing features. Arthur lived at the Wrensdale Pines, the assisted-living home where Talia's mom, Natalie Marby, was the assistant director.

"Well, we're going to have a great time," Talia said. "Of course, I'll have to leave you when it's time for the contest."

"I just know you're going to win," Arthur said softly, and then his brow creased. "What did you say you were making again?"

"Deep-fried apple pies, miniature ones."

"Of course." Arthur nodded. "I knew that."

Talia glanced toward the right-field wall, beyond the bleachers. A podium had been set up atop a makeshift stage. Above the stage, a humongous red banner bore the message STEELTOP FOODS. FIRST ANNUAL COOK-OFF & BAKE-OFF. Behind that, stretching toward the exit to the parking lot, six temporary cooking stations had been constructed. The stations ran back-to-back, three on each side. Talia had already stashed her provisions and her portable deep fryer in her assigned spot. Wrensdale Appliances had generously supplied each station with a mini-fridge, a portable burner, a microwave, and a convection oven. All would be donated to local families in need after the contest was over.

"Okay, what does everyone want?" Ryan said. "Hot dogs? Onion rings?"

"Can I help you carry stuff?"

The offer came from Lucas Bartolini, Talia's part-time employee and delivery person. She turned to see his lanky form standing behind them, one stray lock of blond hair dipping over his forehead. "Lucas, you made it! I was wondering where you were."

" 'Course I made it!" He grinned. "I was just over at Queenie's Variety. They have the coolest new book covers. One of them has the periodic table of the elements, which is perfect since I'll be taking chemistry this semester. Anyway, I bought a bunch of them." His blue-eyed gaze skimmed the field.

Talia knew he was looking for Molly, on whom he'd developed an obvious crush. If Molly was aware, she hadn't let on. She was older than Lucas by a few years. Talia suspected she viewed him only as a friend.

"Believe it or not," she said, in a mild attempt to distract him from thoughts of Molly, "I was pretty good at high school chemistry. I liked doing the lab experiments best, although the Bunsen burner scared me a little."

Lucas laughed, and his eyes twinkled a bit. He was such a great kid—although at twenty he was technically an adult. "Where's Martha?" he asked. "Isn't she coming?"

"She's here," Talia said. "She's been dying to mosey among all the crafts tables. Remember, this is her first festival. I think she's been looking forward to it more than she admitted."

"Well, then." Ryan rubbed his hands together and smiled at Lucas. "Let's you and I make a food run."

The two dashed off toward the food stands just as Crystal and Molly came along with their burgers and onion rings and joined them. Molly looked adorable in a slinky pink tank top and cutoff denim shorts that showed off her shapely legs. Her long hair, darker than her mom's, was wound into a loose French braid. The braid was a style both mother and daughter favored. Which reminded Talia—where was Audrey?

"I took a bunch of pictures," Molly said, holding up her phone. "This new iPhone is awesome!" She and Crystal grabbed two chairs and sat down.

"Hey, everyone!" The voice came from Suzy Sato, the owner of Sage & Seaweed—the bath-and-body boutique on the Wrensdale Arcade. "Let's sit here," she said to her husband. "You know all the ladies, right, honey?"

Kenji Sato, a quiet, slender man, greeted everyone with a round of hellos. He pulled out a chair for Suzy, and she sat down next to Talia.

"Where's Kimberly?" Talia asked, eager to see their darling baby girl.

Suzy pushed a titian curl away from her face. "Ken's mom is watching her. We were going to bring her, but she's really still too young. With all the noise and confusion, we thought it would be too much."

Ken sat down and beamed at his wife. "We just celebrated her one-month birthday, didn't we, sweetie?"

Suzy touched his cheek. "We'll bring her next year. We promise." She glanced around and smiled. "Looks like this is the Wrensdale Arcade table. Maybe we should dub ourselves the Arcade Brigade! It's the name of one of Kimberly's books."

"Sounds good to me," Talia said.

"Hey, where's your friend Rachel?" Suzy asked. "I thought for sure she'd be here."

Rachel was Talia's longtime friend—and the significant other of the town's police chief, Derek Westlake.

Talia pointed at the area near home plate, where portable screens had been set up just beyond the pitcher's mound. "She and Derek are giving batting lessons to some of the smaller kids. Derek is pitching, while Rachel does the grunt work—chasing stray balls."

"They sure make a cute couple, don't they?" Suzy grinned slyly. "Just like you and Ryan. And speak of the devil—"

Ryan and Lucas returned juggling hot dogs, grilled burgers, and mounds of fragrant-smelling onion rings, along with bottles of cold drinks. The others sought out their own goodies, and soon the scent of fried food wafted around them. It reminded Talia of how lucky she was to own a deep-fried eatery. And how much her life had changed over the past year.

Lucas grabbed the chair next to Molly's. Every time she smiled at him, his cheeks flamed like a barbecue grill.

Martha spotted the group and ambled over to the table, a tattered straw hat with a McGovern button shielding her eyes from the sun. She sat down opposite Lucas, dumping a hot dog, onion rings, and a soda bottle on the table in front of her.

"Where'd you get that?" Lucas asked her. He pointed at the oversized umbrella dangling from her wrist.

"There's a guy selling them over behind the cotton candy machine," Martha said. She held it up for everyone to see. The tip of the umbrella was a carved wooden duck, so large it almost looked like the real deal. Its webbed feet had rubber soles, so that the umbrella doubled as a cane. If she walked down the street with the tip down, it would appear she was taking a stroll with a duck.

Some good-natured teasing made the rounds. Martha finally said, "Go ahead, poke fun at it. But someday when you're all out there in a hurricane with your cheap portable umbrellas, I'll be the one staying dry." She winked at Lucas.

"By the way," she said tartly, "did you all see who set up a booth near the entrance?"

Talia swallowed a bite of hot dog and nodded. "Bruce Ferringer," she said, rolling her eyes.

"Ferringer the ferret?" Suzy wrinkled her nose.

Her gesture mirrored Talia's thoughts. Ferringer was a member of the local Select Board. Four years ago, when he was first elected, some ugly rumors had sprouted. His opponent had accused him of ballot-tampering, a charge Ferringer vehemently denied. No one could prove anything, so Ferringer got in. Now he was running for state rep in the fall election and was desperate to project a spotless image.

"I'm with you, Suzy," Crystal said around a sip of cola. "Can you imagine wanting to slash taxes by cutting out music classes in the schools? I mean, I'm all for lower taxes, but—" She shook her head in disgust.

"It's worse than that," Molly said darkly. "Instead of funding renovations to the animal shelter, he wants to tear it down so one of his developer buddies can build a luxury condo complex."

Talia hadn't been following local politics very closely, but she had heard of Ferringer's proposal to close the shelter. "But the other area shelters won't be able to handle the overflow!"

"That's right." Molly forcefully squirted a packet of ketchup onto her onion rings. "It makes far better sense to expand the shelter we have, not close it. The man is a buffoon."

Talia glanced over at the area near the entrance where the Ferringers had set up shop. Skirting their oversized table was a red, white, and blue paper apron. Crepe-paper flowers in the same colors lined the bottom, while a banner with the message GO FAR WITH FERRINGER! stretched across the front. Jodie Ferringer, her husband's junior by at least a dozen years, stood behind the table with a brilliant, cherry-lipped smile. A large blue cooler rested on the table in front of her, and she was pulling out brochures and shoving them at anyone unlucky enough to pass within range. Talia couldn't help chuckling at the oversized cooler. Was the woman trying to keep her precious brochures from getting too much sun?

"She tried to give me one of those brochures," Martha said. "When I shook my head, she slapped it into my hand anyway. I had to take it so it wouldn't drop on the ground." She reached into the pocket of her cotton slacks and dug out the wrinkled pamphlet. Frowning, she sniffed it and then tossed it onto the table.

Crystal snatched it up. "What gives him the right to campaign here, anyway? Isn't this supposed to be a fun event for everyone?" She scanned the brochure, and her brown eyes flared. "Look at this. A picture of him, his blushing bride, and his adorable little Pomeranian. Are we supposed to get the message that he loves animals, in spite of wanting to shut down the shelter?"

"Some people will fall for it," Molly said sourly. She looked up. "Oh, here she is—"

An earsplitting squeal from the podium made everyone jump. "Uh, sorry, folks." A young man tapped the microphone. "There's, um, three cars parked near the entrance that are blocking access. Can the owners please move them? Thanks. The, um, tag numbers are H-G-7 . . ."

The young man rattled off the first two plate numbers and was announcing the third just as Audrey Feldon approached their table. Unsmiling, she closed her eyes. "Shoot, that one's mine," she said quietly. Her shoulders slumped.

Molly hopped off her chair. "I'll move it, Mom. Give me your key."

"Thanks." Audrey pulled her car key from the pocket of her drawstring capris and tossed it to her daughter.

Talia's gaze slid over to the Ferringer table. Bruce Ferringer was handing his car key to his wife. Jodie Ferringer looked extremely put out as she stalked off toward the parking lot.

Audrey sat down next to Martha, her face pale and drawn. "Looks like you've all eaten," she said.

Avoiding eye contact with Audrey, Crystal said nothing. Whatever had caused the rift between the two, Talia hoped they would work it out soon.

"Ms. Feldon, can I get you something?" Lucas asked her, his young face looking pained at her lack of food. "A burger or some rings?"

For the first time since she'd arrived, Audrey smiled. "That's sweet, Lucas, but I'm not very hungry. Thank you anyway."

"Hey, there's my girl!" The familiar voice boomed behind Talia, just as a pair of bulky arms wrapped themselves around her in a bearlike hug. The arms squeezed for a moment and then withdrew, allowing room for a Chanel-scented cheek to press Talia's face.

Talia turned in her chair and gave her mom and dad a huge grin. "Hey. I wondered where you guys were. I was afraid you weren't going to make it."

Natalie Marby gave her husband an affectionate roll of her dark green eyes. "Your father couldn't decide what to wear—can you believe it? And they talk about women!"

"Well, I *could* have decided," Peter Marby quipped, "if my spouse hadn't forgotten to wash my lucky polo shirt.

Instead I was forced to choose this"—he wrinkled his nose—"T-shirt I've had since the dawn of time."

"You both look terrific," Talia said, recognizing the dark blue tee. If memory served, he'd been wearing it since she was in high school, and it was one of his faves. She couldn't imagine how it'd held up over all these years.

"You know everyone, right?" Talia said.

Hellos made the rounds, and Peter offered a hearty handshake to Ryan's dad. "Professor Collins," he said. "Always good to see you."

Arthur beamed. "And you as well, Peter."

Ryan and Talia exchanged pleased looks, and Ryan winked at her.

"Can you squeeze in a couple of chairs and sit with us?" Ryan asked.

"Aw, don't worry about us," Talia's dad said. "We're fine. We're sitting at a table over there with some of our condo neighbors." He dipped his full head of lush white hair at a table on the opposite side of the tent.

"We'll catch you later, honey," her mom said. She lowered her glossed lips to Talia's ear. "We'll be cheering for you," she whispered.

The two Marbys waved their good-byes and hustled off to join their neighbors.

"Your mom and dad are so lovely," Suzy Sato said, a look of sadness filling her eyes.

Suzy, Talia knew, had been estranged from her family for a lot of years. In college Suzy had gotten involved in a sorority hazing that had ended with the death of a young pledge. Suzy claimed she'd tried to stop it from happening, and a judge had sentenced her to community service. The

rift it created in her family had never been mended. Suzy
missed her folks something awful. Talia was glad Suzy had
a terrific husband and a sweet baby girl to help fill the void.

Molly returned and gave Audrey her car keys, squeezing
into a chair beside her. A comfortable silence fell over the
group as everyone enjoyed their lunch. Crystal seemed edgy,
no doubt because she was nervous about the contest.

"I . . . I'm sorry," Crystal said, "but I have to find one of
those portable, um, restrooms." She glanced all around, her
face turning red.

"There's one right at the edge of the parking lot," Molly
quietly told her. "I saw it earlier."

Crystal sighed. "Okay, thanks. I guess I'll have to use it."

"Wait a minute," Suzy said. She reached into her tote and
dug out a packet of baby wipes. "Take these. I never go anywhere without them."

Crystal snatched up the wipes. "You're a lifesaver. Thank
you!" She struggled off her seat and rushed toward the parking area.

Poor Crystal, Talia thought. Her nerves seemed to be
getting the better of her.

Talia was biting into an onion ring when she saw a stylish
blonde in a revealing halter dress saunter over to their table. The
woman's makeup, while expertly applied, was a tad overdone
for Talia's liking. Her pink-painted fingernails were ridiculously
long. With a haughty tilt of her chin, the woman fixed her gaze
on Audrey. "Audrey," she said, by way of greeting.

Audrey's face blanched. She stared at the woman for a
long moment and then said quietly, "Hello, Sandra."

The woman seemed to be waiting for an introduction,
but Audrey remained mute. Out of courtesy, Talia started
to introduce herself, when the microphone squeaked again.

Sandra—whoever she was—did a fast pivot toward the source of the sound. A craggy-faced man, at least six feet tall with short, dark blond hair, stood behind the podium holding a mic. Without another word, Sandra raced off toward the makeshift stage, her feet struggling to navigate the uneven ground in her wedge-style espadrilles.

"She's a local Realtor," Suzy explained. "Married to Handsome Harry. Wait till y'all see him."

The man with the mic spoke in a low, silky voice. "Good afternoon, everyone. My name is Wesley Thurman, and I am the owner and chief operating officer of Steeltop Foods. First, I want to thank the kind folks of Wrensdale for your hospitality today. I am more than thrilled to be back here in the Berkshires to host our first annual competition."

Back in the Berkshires? So he did have local ties, Talia mused.

With a "down home" kind of drawl, Thurman went on to explain how he'd started his company from an old metal-roofed building on a remote road in Iowa. He grew Steeltop Foods, literally, from the ground floor up, transforming it into the thriving food conglomerate it is today.

"Blah, blah, blah," Suzy quipped. "Do they all have to make a boring speech?"

Crystal returned and quickly took her place next to Molly. *Thank you*, she mouthed to Suzy, returning the packet of wipes. Audrey shot Crystal a cold look, then pretended to study her watch.

The bad vibes between the two were making Talia uncomfortable. She wished she could help, but she had no idea what their gripe was about.

Thurman lavished praise on Wrensdale Appliances for setting up the temporary cooking stations and for supplying the equipment. Then he went on to thank the contestants for their marvelous entries.

"It was a tough job, but we've narrowed it down to six finalists. By now you all know who they are, but I'm going to introduce them anyway." He grinned, and his gaze homed right in on their table.

"He's looking at us!" Crystal tittered.

Talia smiled at her. This contest meant so much to Crystal. Talia was almost hoping she would end up the winner. Almost.

Thurman summoned the six finalists to the stage.

Heart pounding, Talia pushed back her chair and rose. Ryan gave her a thumbs-up, and the others wished both her and Crystal good luck with their entries.

Molly swiped a napkin over her lips and hopped off her seat, iPhone in her hand. "I want to get some shots of the contestants. Back in a flash."

Her stomach in a knot, Talia followed Crystal toward the stage. She hadn't felt this jittery in a long time. She fell in step next to a striking man with jet-black hair, stunning green eyes, and eyelashes to die for. Vivian Lavoie, a local busybody and a friend of Talia's, was already on the stage. Plumping up her soft pewter curls, she cozied up next to Wesley Thurman as if she'd just been crowned queen.

The only other male contestant, Dylan McPhee, slouched next to Vivian. Talia had never met him, but she knew he worked the early shift at the local diner. While his desserts were rumored to be the stuff of dreams, most of his patrons felt his personality could use a packet or two of sweetener.

The remaining contestant, a seventysomething with stringy gray hair, was the last to step onto the stage. Her mouth twitched nervously, and her eyes darted back and forth. Pinned to her flowered cotton dress was a GO FAR WITH FERRINGER! button the size of a hubcap. She looked ready to bolt.

"And now for the introductions," Thurman said. "In the sweet category, the finalists are Vivian Lavoie for her spiced ginger cookies, Talia Marby for her miniature deep-fried apple pies, and Dylan McPhee for his cinnamon-swirl brownies. If you'll step up, one at a time, I'll give you your official instructions." Thurman grinned at the trio, highlighting the dimple on his right side. He was attractive, Talia decided, in a rugged sort of way. His deep voice added to the allure.

Vivian went first. She plumped up her curls again and waved at the crowd before accepting her instructions. Talia was next. Smoothing her linen slacks, she walked to the podium. She thanked Thurman quietly as she took her written instructions from him, then moved aside to stand next to Vivian. The last "sweet" contestant was Dylan McPhee. Instructions in hand, he strode, unsmiling, to stand beside Talia. Talia glanced over to wish him luck, but he was staring straight ahead with a closed expression.

"In the savory category," Thurman continued, "we have Harry Summers for his tangy tamale casserole, Crystal Galardi for her home-style meat loaf, and Norma Ferguson for her flaky-top chicken stew."

The man with the gorgeous eyes walked up to the podium and accepted his instructions. Was he the Handsome Harry that Suzy had mentioned? Crystal was next. She accepted the sheet of paper with an anxious smile and then scuttled over to stand beside Harry.

Norma Ferguson went last. On worn leather sandals, she trudged toward the podium. She twisted her wrinkled fingers as if she were braiding a rope. Talia watched as the woman stumbled toward Thurman. In the next instant, Thurman's friendly visage morphed into one of sheer revulsion. His eyes hard and blazing with hatred, he almost shoved the instructions at her. Norma clutched them timidly and then scurried away to stand next to Crystal.

Whoa! That was strange, Talia thought. The man clearly had a problem with Norma. But surely he'd known she was a finalist, hadn't he? Why had he acted so shocked to see her?

Thurman recovered instantly, but his tone had a crisp edge when he dismissed the contestants.

For a moment no one moved, as if they couldn't decide who should go first. Finally Talia made a move to leave, and in that moment she saw someone else giving Norma the evil eye.

Dylan.

His thin lip curled, and his eyes were fixed on the elderly woman in a way that looked almost menacing. When he saw that she wasn't making eye contact with him, he got up and stalked off the stage, but not without shooting one last hostile glance in her direction.

Ferringer's wife, Jodie, stood about ten feet from the edge of the stage. She beamed at Norma and clapped. "Go, Norma!" she squealed, as the elderly woman trod down the short steps to the ground.

Norma gave Jodie an odd look and then shuffled away, in the direction of the parking lot. Was she bailing on the gig? Had the expression on Thurman's face—and Dylan's—frightened her enough that she was pulling out of the contest?

Talia didn't have time to worry about it now. Forging a trail in front of the others, she headed toward the cooking stations. On the way she passed Molly. Standing stock-still, Molly stared at the makeshift stage. Her expression was odd, as if she was trying to remember something. Talia waved at her, but Molly apparently didn't see her.

Talia hurried off to her own assigned station, the other contestants trailing behind her. She had exactly one hour to prepare her entry, and then she was done.

She was starting to get the nagging feeling that entering the contest had been a very bad idea.

3

Talia placed the last mini-pie on her tray, the scent of cinnamon and deep-fried pastry swirling around her. During her trial runs, she'd tested out several types of apples. She'd ended up settling on Cortlands, which were juicy and slightly tart. Blended with the right combo of brown and white sugars, the result was near perfection.

If she did say so herself.

And she *had* used the Flavor Dial, although she could have accomplished the same thing with a couple jars of her standby spices. Still, she was obliged to use the wheel for the contest, so she'd followed the instructions to the letter.

After tucking a layer of foil loosely around the pies, Talia stepped out of her cooking station and headed toward the judges' tent. The judges' identities were unknown, but the contestants had been assured that they were all from surrounding towns with no loyalties to Wrensdale.

She was about twenty feet from the entrance to the tent when her toe caught the jagged tip of a large rock. She pitched forward, and in that single moment had a vision of her delicious pies flying off the tray and hitting the ground.

Nooooo . . .

In the next instant she felt a powerful hand clutch her arm in a vise, keeping her upright. Still grasping her tray for dear life, she turned to see the man with the gorgeous eyes. He kept his grip on her arm, while in his other hand he balanced a casserole that gave off a tangy aroma. "Don't worry. I've got you," he said in a soft voice.

Talia regained her balance and smiled at him. "Oh gosh, thank you. For a second I thought these pies were goners."

His smile was timid, but his eyes lit up. "Oh heck. Then I'm glad I was here to help. We don't need any culinary disasters right before the judging, do we?"

"We sure don't." Talia laughed, instantly liking this man. "You're Harry, aren't you?"

He nodded. "And you're Talia. I've heard so much about your wonderful eatery." His smile faded. "A number of times I wanted to try it out, but my wife won't eat there. She says the fried food will wreck her diet. Or her figure. Or whatever."

Talia started gingerly toward the tent, careful to watch where she placed her feet. "Well, if you ever decide to try it on your own, I'd be glad to let you sample some of the goodies before you pick what you want."

"That's very kind," he said.

They walked the rest of the way together until they reached the tent. A bright-eyed senior with a blond bun accepted their entries, then checked off their names on her clipboard.

"Good luck, Harry," Talia said.

He wished her the same, and they parted ways. Talia saw him glance toward the now-empty stage. At the foot of the stage, the woman named Sandra—who she assumed was Harry's wife—was standing close to Wes Thurman with her hand on his arm. If Wes was pleased by her proximity, his face sure didn't show it.

If anything, he looked anxious to get away.

"So how did they come out?" Suzy squealed.

Talia grinned and reclaimed her seat next to Ryan. "I tested one, and I think they came out pretty good, although I almost lost them." She related how she'd nearly taken a tumble, only to be rescued by Harry Summers.

"So, Handsome Harry came to the rescue, huh?" Suzy winked at Talia.

"Suzy," her husband said quietly.

"Oh, I was just teasing," she said.

Ryan squeezed Talia's hand. "So when will they announce the three finalists?"

Talia looked at her watch. "Anytime now. Yikes."

Right on cue, Wes Thurman stepped back onto the stage. The spring in his step that he'd sported earlier was gone, and his wide smile looked pasted on. Though he stood at something of a distance, Talia saw from his flat expression that his enthusiasm had waned.

Wes tapped the mic a few times, and the crowd quieted. "I'm happy to announce," he said in his low voice, "that the judges have narrowed their choices down to the final three. After I call your names, please step up onto the stage and take a seat." He indicated the three folding chairs that were set up behind the podium. "As I speak, the judges are consulting to choose the first-prize winner. We'll have their decision shortly."

Arthur looked at Talia with an eager smile. "Oh, I do hope they call you," he whispered.

Thurman began reading from the sheet of paper in his hand. "Crystal Galardi, for her home-style meat loaf . . ."

Talia looked around. Where *was* Crystal?

"Dylan McPhee, for his cinnamon-swirl brownies," Wes went on. He hesitated for several seconds. "And last of all," he said through clenched teeth, "Norma Ferguson for her flaky-top chicken stew."

A tiny *zing* of disappointment shot through Talia. Not that she'd counted on winning, but it would have been nice to be a finalist.

Ryan leaned over and hugged her. "As far as I'm concerned, you're still the best cook *and* baker in the world."

"Thanks." Talia grinned. "Hey, look, it's not a big deal. Crystal made it to the final three, and that's fabulous!"

Molly smiled. "She must be so excited."

Audrey pursed her lips but said nothing. Instead, she stared out over the bleachers with a faraway expression.

"Hey," Molly suggested, "why don't we all trot over and get closer to the stage? It's hard to see everything from here."

"Good idea," Ryan said. He took his dad's arm, and they all strolled across the field toward the staging area. A few stray clouds blotted the sky, and a warm breeze kicked in. People were moving closer to the stage, moms and dads gripping the hands of their little ones and teenagers shoving one another good-naturedly as they thumbed away at their phones.

A sudden gust ruffled the cap sleeves of Talia's lacy blue tee. A pale green slip of paper, caught by the wind, danced across the grass in front of her. She rushed to snatch it up before the wind took it again, but Audrey came from behind and jolted her aside, beating her to it.

"Sorry. I didn't mean to bump you like that," Audrey said, her cheeks pink.

"That's okay." Talia smiled, a bit baffled by Audrey's behavior. "What is it? Is it important?"

"Heavens, no. It's just my to-do list for later today. I have a lot on my plate right now, and if I don't write it all down, I'll end up forgetting something."

"I know what you mean." Talia glanced around and finally spotted Crystal scurrying across the field toward the staging area. "Oh, look—there's Crystal. I wondered where she was."

"The bathroom, probably," Audrey said, with a distinct roll of her eyes. "When she gets nervous, she goes every five minutes."

More than Talia needed to know, but she was relieved to see Crystal hurry toward the stage and mount the shallow stairs. Chairs had been set up, and she plunked down on the one next to Dylan, her face looking flushed.

Norma trudged along last. She climbed the few steps shakily, as if she'd been sentenced to death by guillotine and was heading toward the blade. Her thin face wore a look of alarm as she took the seat next to Crystal.

"Why, that poor elderly woman looks terrified," Suzy said. "Think she has stage fright?"

"Maybe," Talia said doubtfully. More likely the woman was afraid of Wes Thurman, who was studiously pretending she was invisible. Or was she afraid of Dylan? At this point it was hard to tell.

Wes spoke for a bit longer, his words clipped and toneless. His earlier zeal for the event was clearly gone. Finally, he thanked everyone again for participating and then turned his attention to a teenage girl with an auburn ponytail who was striding up to the stage. With a brilliant smile and a wave at the crowd, she went over to Wes, handed him an envelope, and then scooted back down the steps.

"It appears the judges have made their decision." Wes ripped open the envelope and pulled out a slip of paper. His expression stormy, he spoke into the mic. "Ladies and gentlemen, the moment we've all been waiting for. As our third-place winner, the judges have chosen Dylan McPhee, for his cinnamon-swirl brownies. Dylan, would you stand, please?"

Amid a round of clapping and a few cheers, Dylan slowly rose from his chair. His face was a mixture of surprise and dismay. After a quick nod, he sat down again.

"He's bummed," Suzy said, stating the obvious.

"Thank you, Dylan. And in second place," Wes went on, his expression growing stormier, "is Crystal Galardi for her home-style meat loaf."

Crystal clapped her hands to her chest and jumped off her chair. She pranced over to Wes and took the mic from his hand. "Oh my, thank you. Thank you all! This is such an honor."

"Yeah, an honor that doesn't come with twenty-five grand," Martha muttered.

"But it's still a feather in her cap, Martha," Talia said. "Be happy for her."

Talia, too, had been cheering for Crystal to win the big one. Crystal seemed pleased with second place, but she had to be at least a teensy bit disappointed.

Crystal returned the mic to Wes and sat down. She whispered something to Norma, who looked as if she wanted to shrink into the temporary staging and disappear.

"And first place"—Wes ran his hand over his chin—"and the twenty-five-thousand-dollar prize, goes to Norma Ferguson for her flaky-top chicken stew. Norma, would you please step up and claim your prize?"

Someone off to the side squealed out a loud "Yay," but Norma didn't get up. She sat, frozen, shaking her head. Crystal nudged her gently, and finally the woman rose from her chair. Head down, she went over to Wes and accepted the prize money.

"Oh my, Mr. Thurman doesn't look too thrilled, does he?" Suzy said.

No, he doesn't, Talia thought. *Nor does the winner.* It was all so bizarre.

Some weak clapping and a few fake-sounding cheers erupted from the crowd. Norma didn't seem to have much of a fan base. Wes posed for a few unsmiling photos with her and then stalked off the stage. Norma continued gawking at the check as if someone had just handed her a packet of poison.

After that, the crowd dispersed. People started moving toward the bleachers. The softball game was scheduled to begin at four, and everyone wanted to grab the seats with the best view possible.

Jodie Ferringer, meanwhile, had woven her way through the throng and was headed up the steps to the stage, the magenta ribbons of her floppy hat trailing behind her in the breeze. A huge grin on her face, she went over to Norma and hugged her. Talia watched curiously as Jodie squeezed Norma's shoulder with a bejeweled hand and then led her off the stage. The whole scene smacked of drama—a lame act written by a bad playwright.

At least poor Norma had one friend, Talia thought. Her FERRINGER button had apparently earned her the devotion, whether sincere or not, of the candidate's wife.

Talia was glad the contest was over, but she felt bad for Crystal. It had finally struck Crystal that she hadn't won. She looked sadder than ever as she wended her way toward them.

"I feel like such an idiot," Crystal whined, "grabbing the mic the way I did when I was only second place. I really thought my meat loaf was going to make it. Of course, Dylan and I will each get a five-hundred-dollar gift card toward Steeltop Foods products, but still . . ."

"Five hundred?" Lucas gasped. "That's, like, a fortune!"

Crystal smiled at him. "I guess it is a pretty nice consolation prize. I thought Mr. Thurman was going to announce that part, but maybe he didn't have time."

Didn't have time? Talia thought. How long would it have taken to make such an announcement? Thirty or forty seconds at the most?

Molly leaned over and gave Crystal a long hug. "We're all proud of you, Crystal. Second place is nothing to sneeze at!"

Wes Thurman reappeared on the stage, but at that point no one was paying attention. Was he going to make an announcement?

Talia watched as he stood there, hands on his hips, his gaze skimming the thinning crowd like that of a hawk on the prowl for an unwary mouse. He turned to his right, the hard line of his jaw outlined against the bright blue sky. Something about his profile made Talia's pulse quicken. What was it?

Then his eyes swerved suddenly to where she was standing. She got the weirdest sensation that he was staring directly at her. Until she turned and saw Audrey Feldon threading her way through the stragglers.

"Where's Mom going in such a hurry?" Molly said, strolling along next to Lucas.

"I don't know," Crystal said with a sigh. "I've all but given up trying to figure her out." Her face drooped. "Hey, look, does anyone mind if I skip the game? I'm not much of a sports fan anyway."

"Of course we don't mind," Molly said distractedly.

"Go home and relax," Talia said to her. "You deserve it."

Everyone murmured in agreement. Crystal said her good-byes and left.

"I feel so bad for her," Molly said. "I think she was really counting on first place." She lowered her voice. "Truth be told, I think she needed the money, too."

Talia squeezed Molly's shoulder. She loved the way Molly looked out for Crystal, who had no kids of her own. Divorced, Crystal lived with her aging mom in the two-family home she'd grown up in. Audrey had mentioned once that Crystal's ex had left her with a ton of debt. She'd had to borrow a sizable sum to get her and Audrey's cooking store up and running.

"I think Ken and I are going to leave, too," Suzy said, clasping her husband's hand. "We're not much for softball, and Kimberly gets fussy if we stay away too long." The Satos waved good-bye to everyone and went across the field toward the parking lot.

Martha blew out a breath. "I hate to jump on the bandwagon, but I like watching softball about as much as I like cleaning the grease trap in the kitchen. Actually, I'd *prefer* to clean the grease trap in the kitchen."

Talia laughed. "I'm glad you came today, Martha. Take good care of that umbrella."

Martha tipped her ragged straw hat at the group and shuffled off.

The game was scheduled to start in about ten minutes. Talia was just slipping her arm through Arthur's when she spied another slip of paper on the ground. It looked similar . . . no, exactly like the one Audrey had lost earlier. She bent and picked it up.

The paper was actually a sticky note with the words *Steeltop Foods Corporation* imprinted across the top. In bold block letters, someone had written, WE NEED TO TALK.

Interesting. Was this the same note Audrey had pocketed earlier? If so, then Audrey had lied about it being her to-do list. Talia slid it into her own pocket.

"I'm going to cheer for the police," Arthur said. "How about you, Talia?"

Talia chuckled. Over the past year she'd had a few unpleasant encounters with the police. Mostly because of huge misunderstandings, but everything had eventually worked out.

She winked at Arthur. "I'm with you, Arthur. Let's grab a seat on the bleachers so we can root for the police."

"Ms. Marby?"

The roughened voice came from behind Talia. She turned to see a powerfully built man wearing a clay-colored shirt and beaming at her. A FERRINGER button was pinned to the shirt's collar. Though his eyes were hidden behind aviator sunglasses, his smile was a brilliant flash of white.

"Mr. Ferringer," she greeted, forcing a return smile.

"Please, it's Bruce," he said breezily. He extended a beefy arm, displaying muscles taut and bulging from daily workouts. Talia reluctantly took his hand, and he squeezed hers heartily. "First, I'd like to congratulate you on making the top six. Not an easy feat in a town with so many good cooks."

"Well, thanks, but the better woman won. I was honored to be a semifinalist."

He grinned. "Now, Talia"—he instantly switched to her given name—"from what I hear, you're being far too modest.

Fry Me a Sliver was mentioned yet again as one of the best eateries in the Berkshires."

"Really? Where was that?" Had Talia missed a recent news clip about her place?

Ferringer chewed his lip thoughtfully. "Well, now that you ask, I'm not really sure. But I did see it somewhere. . . ."

Arthur glanced over at the man with a deep frown.

"Anyway," Ferringer went on, "I don't want to take up too much of your time. I can see you're enjoying this gorgeous day with your loved ones." He flashed a smile at Ryan, who was eyeing him warily. "But I do have a favor to ask. One that stands to benefit the both of us."

Oh really? she thought dryly.

He cleared his throat. "My campaign manager and I would like to have a brainstorming luncheon with some of our top supporters. Your restaurant is perfect for it—quiet, cozy, private. If we could schedule a date . . . perhaps the Sunday after Labor Day weekend? We would want the entire restaurant to ourselves, of course."

"I'm sorry, Mr. Fer . . . I mean, Bruce. The restaurant is closed on Sundays, so it really wouldn't be—"

"But that's precisely why a Sunday is perfect," he insisted. "We'd be your only customers, and believe me, these people are excellent tippers. All told, there'd be about a dozen of us, and—"

"Bruce, you really will have to excuse me. The softball game's going to start anytime now. Maybe we can talk later in the week?"

"Of course!" he boomed, looking a bit nonplussed. "I'll have my campaign manager give you a call." He leaned in closer and winked at her. "She's a woman, you know. Bright little thing. A whiz with numbers."

His token female employee, no doubt. Talia resisted the urge to shake her head. Was she supposed to be impressed that he had a woman on his staff?

Ferringer must have sensed he'd worn out his welcome. "Anyway, right now I have to figure out where my beautiful wife has disappeared to. We'll chat soon, Talia. Have a good time at the game, all!"

After he strode off, Arthur said quietly, "That man is a pretender. I will definitely not be voting for him."

"Nor will I, Dad," Ryan said.

"Me three," Talia added.

All she had to figure out now was how to get out of hosting the man's political luncheon.

4

After Ryan and Arthur helped Talia retrieve her supplies
from her cooking station and they'd stashed them in her Fiat,
they found a prime bench on the bleachers and settled in for
the game.

"Hey, I've been looking for you, lady!" Rachel whipped
off her zebra-print sunglasses and threw her arms around
Talia.

Talia laughed and returned her friend's hug.

Wearing an animal-print tank top that enhanced her
curves, Rachel was definitely in jungle mode today. Even
her lush brown hair was pulled back and secured with a
leopard scrunchie. "Yeah, well, I've been looking for you,
too," Talia scolded. "I thought you were going to sit with us?"

"I was," she said with a slight edge, "until Derek com-
mandeered my help with the kids. One of his cop buds was
supposed to do it until he claimed he hurt his back yesterday."

Then her face softened. "Batting practice was kind of fun, though. The kids love Derek. He's a good role model for them. Hey, I managed to catch the awards announcements. I'm sorry you didn't win."

"I didn't mind," Talia said truthfully. "I only wish Crystal had taken first place instead of second."

Rachel greeted the others and then sat on the bench next to Lucas. Lucas stared at her, swallowed, and then mumbled, "Um, hello, Ms. Ostroski."

Talia smiled to herself. Lucas never failed to get tongue-tied in Rachel's presence. He sometimes forgot that while she looked like royalty, she was as sweet and down-to-earth as anyone could be.

The game started, and in the first inning the police department squeezed two hits out of the first three batters. Then Derek was up. He smashed a line drive into deep right field, sending half the crowd into an uproar and the other half into groans. Rachel jumped up and gave out a "Woot, woot!"

The wind had picked up since earlier in the afternoon, and clouds began moving in. Molly rubbed her bare arms and gave a slight shiver. "Mom told me to bring a sweater, but I didn't listen to her." She giggled. "Not that I ever listen to her."

"Molly!" Talia chided.

"I know, I know," Molly moaned. "It's just that . . . well, lately she's been so uptight! Like, weirdsville, you know? Loopy-land."

"I have a sweater in my car," Lucas said, with an adoring look at Molly. "Be back in a flash!"

Before Molly could protest, Lucas leaped off the bleachers, nearly tripping over his own sneaker.

"He's so sweet," Molly said. She looked a tad guilty. "I

don't want to lead him on, though. He's a bit, you know, young for me."

In a way, Talia had to agree. Molly was mature beyond her years. And while she hated to see Lucas get his heart broken, it wasn't her place to interfere.

By the time the third inning rolled around, the police were leading by seven to three. Talia glanced at her watch. "I wonder what's taking Lucas so long," she said to Molly.

"I was thinking the same thing. Not that I'm desperate for the sweater, but it's not like him, is it?"

Talia told herself to chill. Lucas probably bumped into a friend and got waylaid talking. Or something. She turned her attention back to the game. Derek was on deck, taking practice swings. All at once she saw a familiar form rush out onto the field and straight over to Derek. The expression on the woman's dark-skinned face was grim.

It was Detective Patti Prescott of the Wrensdale Police. Talia knew her fairly well, both from the detective being a regular at the eatery and from their mutual involvement last December in catching a killer.

Prescott spoke urgently to Derek for only a moment. Then he tossed his bat to the ground. Derek summoned his fellow officers to follow him, and every player on the field sprinted off toward the area where the cooking stations were set up.

Murmurs of confusion rose from the crowd. "Hey, what happened to the game?" someone brayed.

"What's going on?" Molly said.

Talia wasn't sure, but Prescott's presence made it clear that whatever it was, it wasn't good.

Prescott narrowed her eyes and searched the bleachers. When she spotted Talia, she stopped and made direct eye contact. The detective's face was unreadable, but Talia was sure she saw a flicker of sorrow in those nutmeg-colored eyes.

Talia felt her stomach sink to her knees. Something bad was going down.

In the next moment, Prescott pulled her gaze away and jogged off the field toward the cooking stations.

"Well, Ms. Marby, we meet yet again. It seems wherever you go, murder follows."

Sergeant Liam O'Donnell of the Massachusetts State Police, Homicide Division, crossed his arms over his broad chest. They were seated together at one end of a now empty bleacher bench, O'Donnell wearing a look of sheer exasperation.

After two ambulances and five police cars had screeched into the parking lot, the bleachers had emptied quickly. No one was allowed to leave before giving their names and contact info to the police—a process that took well over an hour. Ryan had provided his name and numbers, along with Arthur's, but Talia had been detained. She'd promised to call Ryan later with an update, once the police got through with her.

Now both ambulances were long gone. One of them had screeched out of the parking lot with the siren wailing.

"That's not true," Talia said, responding to O'Donnell's implication that murder seemed to imprint itself on her. "And it's definitely not fair."

Actually, it was *kind* of true, she reflected. But it certainly wasn't fair. Was it her fault that she'd stumbled into murder twice since she'd returned to Wrensdale? She rubbed her arms against the chill in the air. The wind had picked up considerably, sending bits of debris from the earlier festival skating across the field.

"And I told you, Sergeant," she went on, her patience wearing thin, "I never met Norma Ferguson before today. I certainly have no idea who'd have wanted to kill her."

Unless it was Wes Thurman.

Norma Ferguson, Talia learned, had been found dead in her cooking station. O'Donnell was being evasive about who'd found Norma's body, saying only that it was a local teenager.

Lucas, no doubt. That was probably what had detained him. The poor kid had probably heard her scream or something and dashed into her cooking station to help her. Talia could picture him right now, being interrogated by the police.

O'Donnell had refused to reveal the manner of death, leaving Talia to imagine the worst.

That poor woman, Talia thought. She'd looked miserable from the moment she'd first stepped onto the staging area. Wes Thurman had added to her angst, with his hateful glare and his bad attitude.

"I hope you're going to question Wesley Thurman," Talia said. She related everything she'd witnessed, including the way Thurman had shoved the prize money at Norma as if he'd wanted to push her off the stage.

"Mmmm." O'Donnell chewed his lip.

"I notice you're not writing any of this down, Sergeant." Talia didn't want to sound snappish, but he was annoying the beans out of her.

"Believe me, Ms. Marby, your words are engraved in my head. Tell me what you know about Crystal Galardi. I understand she sat at your table during the festivities."

Talia's heartbeat sped up a degree. "What do you want to know, Sergeant? Crystal is a friend and a fellow shop owner on the arcade. Why do you ask?"

It struck her right then, of course—Crystal was a suspect. But why?

They went on like this for another twenty minutes or so. For some reason, O'Donnell seemed fixated on Crystal. Finally, he slapped his hands on his knees and rose. "You'll need to give us a written statement at some point," he said tersely. "In the meantime, Detective Prescott needs to speak to you."

The Wrensdale police detective had been so quiet that Talia hadn't noticed her padding softly toward them from the adjacent bench. Avoiding eye contact with Talia, O'Donnell trotted down the bleacher steps and hurried off in the direction of the parking lot.

Prescott's lovely eyes were clouded. Her dark close-cropped curls looked askew, as if she'd been running her fingers through them repeatedly. She lowered herself onto the bench. "Talia, I'm afraid I have some bad news."

"It's about Lucas, isn't it?" Talia blurted. "He must be the so-called teenager who found Norma. He's not really a teenager, you know. He—"

Prescott shook her head. "No, a kid who worked for Wrensdale Appliances found the victim. He'd been packing up the appliances to get them ready for transport when he found Norma on the floor. Poor kid tossed his lunch, but at least he waited till he was outside."

"Then what is it?" Talia prodded. "What aren't you telling me?"

"We're not totally sure what happened, but we think Lucas might have confronted the killer in the parking lot."

Bile rose in Talia's throat. "Oh God . . ."

"He was struck from behind with a hard object—we're not sure what yet. He sustained extensive bleeding and was rushed to the hospital. They have a level-three trauma unit there, and he's getting the best care possible."

Talia choked out an anguished cry. "You make it sound like . . . like he's not going to make it. Do his folks know?"

"They're with him now, but we don't want anyone contacting them. This wasn't just a life-threatening injury, Talia. This was a vicious crime against an innocent young man."

Talia couldn't hold it in any longer. She burst into tears, her shoulders heaving so hard she thought her ribs would crack.

Prescott dug into her back pocket and pulled out a pack of tissues. "Here," she said kindly.

Talia blotted her eyes with three of the tissues. If only she had something to absorb the pain in her heart. "Can . . . can I go visit him?" she said shakily.

"Absolutely not. Aside from certain medical personnel, only his parents and selected police officials will be allowed in his room. We're not taking any chances."

Talia sniffled. "I understand."

Prescott gripped Talia's arm. "Listen to me, Talia. Don't go getting any dippy ideas about finding Lucas's attacker. Whoever hurt him is desperate and will stop at nothing to silence him. If you start poking into other people's business, you'll be putting yourself and everyone around you in danger."

Talia jerked her arm away. "Who said I was going to do anything?"

"I know you, Talia. You're too darn nosy for your own good, so I'll warn you once more. If you start pulling one of your Nancy Drew routines, I'll have your butt in the pokey so fast it'll make your head spin."

"On some trumped-up charge?"

"Oh, it won't be trumped up. Obstruction of justice is a serious matter, as is interfering with a police investigation. Think about it. You won't be eating any of your delicious fried goodies in jail. Only stale bread and lukewarm tap water—get it?" Prescott's eyes twinkled with a touch of humor, but she got her point across.

"Okay, I get it." Talia swiped at a stray tear. "Could you at least get the bread from Peggy's Bakery? And add some ham and cheese and mustard to it?"

Prescott leveled her gaze at Talia. "Funny girl, huh?"

"Wrong. There's nothing funny about any of this."

The detective lowered her voice. "Look, Talia, you got lucky twice. But take my word for it when I say the third time won't be the charm. So I'd better not hear about you sticking your nose into things, okay?"

"I promise, Detective Prescott, that you will not hear of me sticking my nose into things. But you have to promise me something, too." Talia's voice cracked. "You have to promise that you'll find the person who hurt Lucas. And who killed Norma."

Prescott nodded. "You have my word on that. There are a few more things I need to tell you, but first I have to run them by Sergeant O'Donnell. I'll stop by to see you tomorrow at Fry Me. Maybe at the end of the day?"

Talia nodded, feeling fresh tears beginning to sprout.

"Come on, I'll walk you to your car. It's mass confusion in the parking lot."

When they reached the lot, they had to weave their way among the clutter of cars, most of which were police vehicles.

A crime scene van was parked crookedly behind the cooking stations. Bands of yellow tape had been strung around the perimeter of the scene. So many people had been in the parking lot during the day, Talia wondered how the police would filter through everything for any real evidence.

They were thirty or so feet from Talia's turquoise Fiat when a noisy, blubbering sound caught their attention. Bruce Ferringer stood next to a metallic gray Avalon, the rear bumper of which boasted two GO FAR WITH FERRINGER! stickers. One brawny arm was draped over the shoulder of his wife, who was crying bitterly into a knot of pink tissues.

Ferringer acknowledged them with a brief nod, then went back to comforting his wife. Jodie Ferringer's stylish hat now sat cockeyed on her head. Her eyes looked swollen and her face blotchy.

In spite of Jodie being a complete stranger, Talia felt an overwhelming urge to rush over and console her. The woman looked positively devastated. For whatever reason, Jodie had bonded with Norma Ferguson. Talia wondered if Jodie had been Norma's only friend.

Talia started toward the woman when she felt a firm hand encircle her arm. "Do not discuss anything with anyone," Prescott hissed in her ear.

Talia nodded and went over to Jodie. Feeling her throat clog, she said, "Mrs. Ferringer, I am so, *so* sorry about Norma."

Jodie sucked in a horrendously noisy breath. "Th-thank you," she gurgled out. "She was such a dear woman. Not to mention a dedicated volunteer. In the short time we knew each other, we really bonded, you know? I swear, we were almost like mother and daughter." A choked giggle escaped her. "Plus, she truly understood my husband's platform, and cheered him on in every way. I'm going to miss her so much."

Bruce Ferringer looked pained. "We both will, honey," he soothed. "But I have every faith the police will find the killer, and very soon." He looked at Prescott. "Detective, will you be assisting the state police on this one?"

"I will," Prescott said. "And I can assure you, the authorities will be working around the clock."

Ferringer squeezed his wife's shoulder. "Come on, dear, let's go home and let the police do their job. That's the best thing we can do for Norma right now." He nodded and escorted his wife into the Avalon's front seat. Even with all the windows up, Talia could hear the poor woman wailing.

Talia was grateful when Prescott finally left her alone, mostly because she needed to cry again. Inside her Fiat, she started the engine and cranked the AC. She sobbed until her chest hurt, then finally headed home.

The sight of her darling bungalow, once her nana's home, normally made her smile. But today all she could think of was Lucas fighting for his life in a trauma unit.

The second she unlocked the door, a furry calico ball launched itself at her. Talia scooped Bo into her arms and pressed her face into the cat's fur. Bo clearly sensed something was amiss because her purring ceased. The cat rubbed her whiskers against Talia's cheek, a soft pillow of comfort.

"Oh, Bo," Talia mumbled over her sniffles. "I just thought of something. How will I ever tell Martha?"

5

Martha slammed the knife into a thick head of cabbage, sending a loud *thunk* reverberating from the cutting board.

Talia cringed at the sound, but she knew Martha's heart was aching. No doubt her employee was picturing the poor cabbage as the neck of the lowlife who'd hurt Lucas.

Finally, Martha set down the knife. She looked at Talia through red-rimmed eyes. "I can't take it anymore. Can we try calling again?"

Talia suppressed a groan. They'd been taking turns calling the hospital, trying to get a handle on Lucas's condition. Each time they'd been referred to a police representative, and each time they'd been told nothing.

Nothing useful, anyway. Instead, the responding officer had asked why they were calling and insisted on taking their names.

"They won't tell us anything, Martha. We'd just be torturing ourselves." Talia went over and squeezed Martha's shoulder. "I know it's hard, but we have to be patient. For Lucas's sake." *And his safety,* she thought to herself.

The morning paper had reported that Lucas, the apparent witness to Norma's brutal murder, remained in critical condition. Just seeing that word—critical—had sent Talia into another crying jag.

For the remainder of the morning, they made it through the usual tasks of peeling potatoes, preparing mushy peas and coleslaw, and whipping up the batter variations used for the different menu items. It was Lucas who usually peeled the potatoes. With his large hands, he made short work of the task. Talia smiled, remembering when she'd first hired him as a part-time employee. His peeling technique had been clumsy at best. Every day he'd dropped at least three potatoes. Once he got the hang of it, though, he could do it in his sleep.

Oh, Lucas, you have to get better. Talia sent him the silent message, along with a prayer to every deity known to the human race.

At eleven thirty, Talia unlocked the door and opened for business. After only a minute or so, Crystal came rushing inside. Her petite face was blotchy, and her eyes were puffy behind her ruby-tinted glasses. She whipped off her specs and with one fist scrubbed at her left eye.

One glance at Crystal's forlorn face sent Talia over to give her a hug.

"Have you heard anything?" Crystal said through her sniffles.

" 'Fraid not." Talia shook her head. She knew Crystal was referring to Lucas.

"Molly is a mess." Crystal plunked herself into a chair at one of the tables. "She blames herself for what happened to Lucas. If she hadn't said she was cold, he wouldn't have gone for a sweater. And then he wouldn't have . . . have . . ."

"Crystal, don't go there," Talia said. "The only person to blame for Lucas's condition is the creep who hurt him!"

"I know. I told Molly that, and so did her mother. Poor kid, she still feels like it's all her fault."

Talia blew out a sigh. In truth, she'd probably have felt the same way if she were Molly. Why was it that the innocent always wanted to take the blame for the guilty?

"Just a heads-up," Crystal said, her voice taut. "The police have been questioning me repeatedly. They"—she swallowed—"they think I might have had something to do with the murder."

"What? But . . . why? That is such nonsense!"

"I know." Crystal looked away, her gaze unfocused. "They've already gotten a warrant to look into my finances. Which, I'm afraid, are not in the best shape."

"Everyone has debt, Crystal. Besides, why would killing Norma—" Talia broke off, instantly answering her own question. "They figure you were second in line for the prize money, don't they?" she said quietly.

Crystal nodded miserably.

Talia placed her hand over Crystal's beringed left hand. "But that's so crazy. It's just . . . grasping at straws!"

"I know, but what can I do? I answered their questions as best I could, but . . ." Crystal slid her fingers underneath her glasses and blotted her eyes.

Talia grabbed some napkins from the speckled blue counter and shoved them at her. "Here, use these."

"Thanks." Crystal snatched up a handful. "And of course Audrey's acting weirder than ever," Crystal lamented, dabbing at her eyes. "I can't even talk to her anymore!"

"I'm sorry to hear that," Talia said. Not knowing what was going on with Audrey, what else could she say?

"I actually came over to pick up some lunch for the three of us," Crystal said at last. "Not that Molly and Audrey are hungry, but I told them they have to eat. As for me, that's what I do when I'm worried: I eat."

"It's a natural reaction to stress," Talia said, "so stop beating yourself up. Eating is good for the soul."

With Martha's help, she whipped up an order of fish and chips for Crystal, along with a selection of deep-fried appetizers. Talia knew Molly loved the eatery's batter-fried meatballs with marinara sauce. She prepared an extra half dozen of them and stuck them into the take-out bag with Crystal's order.

After Crystal left, lunch orders started to pour in. Talia hated having to refuse delivery, but with Lucas out of commission she had no choice. Her customers, fortunately, were more than understanding. Everyone expressed their good wishes for Lucas's speedy recovery.

If *he recovers,* Talia thought glumly.

An elderly woman with soft white curls tottered up to the counter with her order. Her already rouged cheeks grew even pinker. "I'm so sorry, miss, but I ordered a side of coleslaw with this. I seem to have gotten these mashed peas instead. Not that I don't like peas, mind you, but I was so looking forward to that delicious slaw. No one else makes it the way you do."

Talia smiled at her. "I'm very sorry. Keep the mushy peas, and I'll bring you some slaw right away."

She knew Martha had messed up the order, but she certainly wouldn't fault her for it. Martha's heart was breaking for Lucas, as was Talia's.

Talia delivered a large helping of slaw to the woman's table and was rewarded with a grateful smile. By two thirty, the bulk of the lunch customers had trickled off. Martha sat down at the circular table that was tucked out of sight at the back of the kitchen.

"Aren't you going to eat?" Talia poured herself a cup of coffee, dumped in a dollop of half-and-half, and joined her.

Martha shook her head. "Can't. The thought of putting food in my mouth makes me want to vomit." Her fierce gaze met Talia's. "You have to do something, Talia. You have to figure out who did this to Lucas."

Talia's insides churned. "Me? I don't work for the police. How can I help?"

"Seriously? You solved two other murders for them, didn't you? I was only here for one of them, but everyone in town knows you were the star investigator."

Inwardly, Talia groaned. "Martha, you've got it all wrong. Both times it was just happenstance. Sheer serendipity."

"Yeah, right." Martha curled her lip. "I've heard you say it all before. Right place, right time. Or wrong place, wrong time . . . whatever."

"Yes—exactly!"

"Well, if you think I believe that for even a second, then you can kiss my a—"

"Martha."

"I was going to say 'my aunt Fanny.'" She gave Talia an indignant look.

"You know what's really sad?" Talia shot back. "All we've talked about is Lucas, but an elderly woman was murdered.

Right here, in this lovely, quiet little town, where I grew up feeling safe and secure. It's an outrage, all of it!"

Martha paused and then sat back and gave Talia a smug look. "You're quite right," she said, folding her arms over her chest. The challenge in her gray eyes was unmistakable. "So what are you going to do about it?"

Talia wagged a finger at her. "Oh, no, you don't. You're not going to trick me into investigating the murder." She thought about Detective Prescott's warning. "Besides, I've already been cautioned by my favorite detective against sticking my nose into other people's business. She said she'd better not hear about me asking any questions, or she'll have my butt thrown in the pokey."

Martha sat back and gave her an enigmatic smile. "So? Who says she has to hear about it?"

A little after three, Molly poked her head inside the door and glanced around. "Oh good, no one's here," she said, stepping inside.

Talia smiled from behind the counter, where she was tidying up the workstation. Martha had asked Talia if she could walk over to Saint Agatha's Church to say a few prayers for Lucas and maybe light a candle for him. Naturally, Talia had said yes. "Well, it's not actually *good* that I don't have customers," she joked, then turned serious. "You holding up okay?"

"I guess so." Molly gathered up her loose hair and tossed it behind her. It was the first time Talia had seen her without her pretty French braid. The young woman's eyes were puffy, and her face was pale, save for a few peeling remnants of sunburn on her nose. She went over to the blue speckled counter and leaned her elbows on it.

"Why don't you help yourself to a root beer?" Talia dipped her chin toward the cooler near the front of the eatery. "My treat today."

"Thanks. I think I'll take you up on that." With a solemn look, Molly went over and pulled a bottle of her favorite drink from the cooler. "I just came over to get away for a few minutes. Between Crystal and Mom, I was going a little cray-cray." She twisted off the top of her drink and took a long swig. "By the way, thanks for the meatballs. They really hit the spot earlier. I'm gonna miss this place once I'm back at school."

Talia smiled. Though it made her feel like a grade-schooler, she couldn't help being pumped when someone praised her food.

Molly's expression darkened, tears forming on her lashes. "I can't stop thinking about Lucas, Talia," she said in a shaky voice. "He's in that hospital bed because of me! If he hadn't gone out to his car to get me a sweater—"

"Molly," Talia said, in a gentle voice. "What happened to Lucas was not your fault. The person who hurt him is to blame, not you."

"In my head I know that, but . . ." Molly shook her head. "Oh God, I wish I could rewind the clock. I wish I could go back to that moment when we were sitting on the bleachers. I never would've let on that I was chilly." She sniffled. "Worst of all, I knew he had a crush on me. Even though I know he's too young for me, I was having fun flirting with him. I'm a terrible, terrible person, aren't I?"

"You are a kind and caring person, so stop beating yourself up." Talia heard the door open and glanced up.

"There you are," Audrey said, striding over to her daughter.

Molly rolled her eyes at Talia. "What did you think, I ran away?" she snapped at her mom.

"There's no need for attitude, young lady." Audrey twisted her hands. "I just wanted to be sure you were all right."

Molly slugged back another gulp of root beer. "Thank you for the drink, Talia. I'm going to head back to the shop to help Crystal."

She left without another word. Audrey closed her eyes for a moment and then looked at Talia, her expression a combination of bewilderment and sorrow.

"I'm sorry, Talia. You shouldn't have to listen to our family squabbles." She smiled, but tears perched on her lashes.

Talia went over and gave Audrey a long hug. "She's hurting, Audrey. She blames herself for what happened to Lucas." *And you're hurting,* she wanted to add. "What's really wrong, Audrey?"

Audrey swallowed. "I know how people talk, so I wanted to tell you something before you heard it from someone else."

Talia waited. She could see that Audrey was trying to work up the courage to reveal whatever it was she had to say.

"Is it okay if I sit for a minute?"

"Of course it is." Talia led her over to one of the tables, and they both sat.

Audrey folded her hands in her lap. "I knew Norma, you know. From way back."

"You did?"

Audrey nodded, her gaze unfocused. "She worked in the cafeteria when I was at Wrensdale High. You're about five years younger than me, so she might've been gone by the time you were in high school. Anyway, she was a horrible woman. All the kids hated her."

Talia frowned. "What was horrible about her?"

"Oh, she was always spreading gossip, pitting one kid against another. I think she wished she was a teenager herself, so she tried to act like one of them, you know?" Audrey swiped at her eyes. "She'd pass notes to kids over the cafeteria counter. Snitch on them. Stuff like that."

"What kind of snitching?"

Audrey's eyes took on a hard sheen. "Oh, you know, if she saw a girl flirting with someone other than the guy she was going steady with, she'd pass a note to the guy over his chili con carne and squeal on her."

Childish, Talia thought, *but not exactly earth-shattering.* "It sounds like pretty minor-league stuff," Talia said, "even though it was mean."

"It hurt a lot of the kids' feelings," Audrey said. "The more trouble she could cause, the better she liked it. It got so everyone hated her."

Talia was surprised at the revelation. Norma had given the impression of being afraid of her own shadow—a scared little mouse that shrank into the shrubbery to avoid being noticed. Still, she didn't see Audrey as the kind of person who exaggerated. She'd always been pretty straightforward.

"Audrey, did you notice Wesley Thurman's reaction when Norma stepped onto the stage? He looked . . . almost enraged. It was like he recognized her from somewhere."

Audrey flushed to the tips of her delicate ears. "No, I wasn't really paying much attention. The whole thing bored me, to tell the truth. I was only there to support Crystal, and you. Plus, Molly would've been ticked if I hadn't gone."

"So you don't know why Wesley would have reacted that way?"

"No." Audrey gave her a cross look. "Why would I know?"

"Sorry. I didn't mean to be pushy. I just think the police should be focusing their investigation on him, not on—" She broke off, remembering Prescott's warning not to discuss anything with anyone. "Not on the other people who finaled in the competition," she finished.

"I agree," Audrey said, "and I'm sorry I sniped at you."

"Audrey," Talia said gently, "I've been sensing that you're under a lot of pressure. I don't want to pry, but if there's anything I can do—"

"You don't want to pry?" Audrey barked out a laugh. "Please. From what I hear, you're quite a pro at it."

Ouch. That stung. Talia tried to think of a retort, but nothing would come out. Nothing polite, anyway.

"Oh God, Talia. I'm so sorry. You're the last person I should be taking out my frustrations on. You've been so wonderful to Crystal and me ever since we opened the cooking store."

Talia felt mildly pacified, but the remark still hurt. "Hey, look, don't worry about it. I can tell you've been under a lot of stress lately."

Audrey nodded. "Molly and I have been arguing a lot. Mostly about dumb things. She's going to be a senior in college this year. I can't help feeling that she's slipping away from me."

"My folks felt that way about me, too," Talia said. "It's a normal feeling."

"And look at you today." Audrey smiled, and her pale brown eyes glistened. "Thanks. I feel a little better. Guess I should head back to see if anyone needs me. Although, truth be told . . ." She shook her head.

"What is it?" Talia asked.

"We . . . haven't had a single customer today. Crystal

thinks it's because of her, that people think she might've killed Norma."

"For the prize money?"

Audrey shrugged. "I guess so. Or maybe they just think the shop is bad luck."

Talia remembered Martha's warning about the place being cursed.

For the first time, Talia wondered if she was right.

6

Martha returned shortly after Audrey left. With her drooping shoulders and mouth turned down in a frown, she looked more forlorn than ever.

Orders started to come in, and the tables began to fill. Ever since the July Fourth holiday had rolled around, Talia had noticed an uptick in customers. Summers in the Berkshires were lively with visitors. The area was famed for summer theater, as well as for the fabulous concerts—both classical and contemporary—held at Tanglewood in Lenox. It wasn't unusual to spy the face of a legendary music star—some of whom had homes in the Berkshires—prowling the shelves of a local gift shop or enjoying the daily special at the diner.

The Norman Rockwell Museum in Stockbridge also attracted scads of tourists every year and even held painting workshops for aspiring artists. The outlet shops, located a stone's throw from the turnpike, didn't hurt, either.

All of it translated to new business for Fry Me, which was why Talia forced herself to put on a happy face, no matter how sad the face inside her heart felt. As for Martha, no matter how hard she tried, she couldn't make herself smile at the customers. Talia tried to make up for it by pasting on fake grins for everyone, but she felt like a clown doing it.

At quarter to seven, Talia's phone buzzed with a text from Detective Prescott. She wanted to stop over around closing time to have a little confab with Talia.

See you then, Talia texted her back.

"Try to get a good night's rest," Talia said to Martha as they were closing up. It was a hollow statement, but she didn't know what else to say.

Martha shot her a doubtful look and then shuffled out the door. "See you tomorrow," she said dully.

Talia was wiping down the workstation when Prescott tapped at the door. "It's open," she called out, too depressed to even greet the detective at the door.

Detective Patti Prescott stepped inside. She looked more than exhausted—she looked half dead. Her lovely nutmeg-colored eyes were slightly bloodshot, and her coffee-colored skin wore a light sheen of perspiration.

"Glad your AC's working," she said. She grabbed a chair from one of the tables and sat down. "Anything I can do to help you clean up?"

Talia bit off a smile. "While you're on duty?"

"Who says I'm on duty?"

Prescott had the irritating habit of answering a question with another question. Most times Talia didn't mind, but every so often it drove her crazy. Especially at a time like this, when she really wanted information.

Talia wiped her hands on a towel, poured out two glasses of iced tea, and sat down opposite the detective.

"Ah, you read my mind. Thanks." Prescott took a long sip of the cool drink.

"So, what is it you wanted to talk to me about?" Talia asked with a sigh. "More bad news?"

Prescott curled her slender fingers around her glass. "I want you to listen to me, Talia. I have Sergeant O'Donnell's permission to reveal a few critical details to you. But I can't emphasize enough how confidential it is. You need to promise me first that you will not share this with a single soul, not even Martha. In fact, especially not Martha."

Talia felt her heart pound. "Okaaayy."

Prescott gave her a hard look. "Do I have your word?"

"I swear I will not tell a solitary soul." She crossed her heart with one finger, feeling more than a bit silly.

"Item one," Prescott said. "Right before Lucas was loaded into the ambulance, he said something we think might be important. So far, though, we haven't been able to make any sense of it."

"Wait a minute. He was still conscious when they found him?" Talia gasped.

Prescott nodded. "He was confused and disoriented, but he managed to mutter the word 'mercury.' Does that ring any bells with you?"

Mercury. Didn't it mean the obvious?

"It has to be someone's car that he saw," Talia said. "The killer must have been driving a Mercury!"

"Yeah, sounds nice and pat, doesn't it? Problem is, we've checked out every single participant in that cooking competition, and not a single one drives a Mercury."

"But the killer isn't necessarily one of the contest finalists,"

Talia said, feeling a bit miffed at being included in the suspect pool. "I'm not seeing the logic."

Prescott took another sip of her drink. "Maybe not, but it was a starting point. We're expanding the search to some of the other players in the competition, but so far nothing looks promising."

"Oh. Well, that's disappointing." Talia thought about the Ferringers, but then recalled that their car was an Avalon. Plus, they both seemed to have adored Norma. "Wait a minute. What about Norma's car? Maybe that's what Lucas saw!"

Prescott shook her head. "Norma drove a Chevy, an old Cavalier. It's been impounded, but so far it hasn't turned up anything useful."

Talia sighed, and then another idea struck her. "Did anyone in the . . . suspect pool drive a Lincoln? That's technically a Mercury, right?"

Prescott gave her a flat smile. "You've hit the nail, as they say. Turns out Wesley Thurman's rental—the one he picked up at Bradley when he flew in last week—is a brand-new Lincoln MKX. Prettiest shade of metallic gray I've ever seen on a car." Prescott looked almost envious.

Well, isn't that interesting? Talia thought. Wesley Thurman was looking better and better as a suspect. In fact, she'd put him at the top of the list!

"I hope you're homing in on him as your primary suspect," Talia said fiercely. "I'm telling you, Detective, he had the most hateful, awful look on his face when Norma first stepped onto that stage. There's got to be some past history there!"

Prescott nodded. "Mr. Thurman has been very cooperative. He has allowed us to search both his car and his room at the Wiltshire Inn. Discreetly, of course."

Oh, sure—of course he was being cooperative. He wanted

to put the authorities at ease to throw them off his trail. Talia sensed he was a smooth talker.

"How does he know Norma? Did he tell you?" Talia demanded.

Prescott leaned one arm over the back of her chair. "I'm surprised your friend Audrey hasn't already told you. Thurman spent his senior year in high school in Wrensdale. He graduated the same year she did."

Talia felt her stomach do a backflip. Now things were beginning to tumble into place. It wasn't only Norma who had a history with Thurman. Audrey did, too. She *must* have. Something tickled Talia's brain like a tiny, annoying feather, but she couldn't quite grab onto it.

"I assume, then, that you've already talked to Audrey?"

"Talia, the only reason I asked you about the word 'mercury' is to see if it jingled any chimes with you. I'm not here to discuss the investigation. Is there any other reason why that word could mean something? Something Lucas might have mentioned in the past?"

Talia thought for a moment, but then shook her head. "Well, at this time of year, people are always talking about tipping the mercury, temperature-wise. He might have said something like that when we suffered through that heat wave in July. But even if he did, I can't see how it would help."

Prescott furrowed her brow. "I can't, either." She sighed. "Well, it was a long shot, anyway."

"For what it's worth, Detective, it's not like Lucas to be cryptic . . . well, except when he was keeping the new big wheels on his skateboard a secret. But that's because he wanted to surprise us all."

Prescott smiled. "That came in handy, didn't it?" She reached over and gave Talia's wrist a gentle squeeze.

"Yes," Talia said in a strangled voice. She felt tears push at her eyelids. "Weren't there any surveillance cameras in the parking lot? I thought every place had them nowadays."

"Every public place *should* have them," Prescott said. "But this is a quiet little town, with almost no serious crime. Well, at least until . . ." She gave Talia a pointed look.

"Yeah, I get it. Until I showed up in town like a bad dream."

"I didn't mean it that way. Anyway, there've been a number of proposals to install cameras in that parking lot, but the Select Board turned them down every time. Funny thing about taxpayers—most of them don't want to spend money on things that don't affect them directly. Besides, other than the occasional beer brawl after a ball game, nothing bad ever really happened at the park."

Talia pressed her fingers to her forehead. Another bout of depression was beginning to sweep over her. "Can you at least tell me what the murder weapon was?"

"No, I can't." Prescott folded her long fingers in front of her. "Talia," she said quietly. "I have one more thing to tell you, but it's big. When I say big, I mean *huge*."

Talia's ears perked. "What is it?"

"First, you have to understand that if you were to reveal this to anyone, you would be risking the life of someone you care very deeply about, and possibly others, as well. You have to swear that you will *not*, under any circumstances, tell this to anyone. Not even your cat."

Talia held up her right hand, although she was fairly sure Bo would never murmur a meow. "I swear."

Prescott leaned forward and spoke quietly. "Talia, Lucas is not in critical condition. He's actually recovering pretty nicely, all things considered. He's still confused. He doesn't remember anything about what happened to him yesterday. The last thing he recalls is leaving the game to get a sweater for Molly, and even that's fuzzy."

Talia felt her heart nearly leap out of her chest. "Oh dear God, but he's okay? I mean, he's really going to be all right?"

"Looks that way, but we have to keep up the charade. We want the killer to be completely at ease with the knowledge that Lucas will never be able to identify him . . . or her."

Or her.

Why did Audrey suddenly flit through Talia's mind? She'd left without a word after the winner of the competition had been announced yesterday. She could have been anywhere when Norma was murdered.

Never mind that. Right now all that mattered was that Lucas was going to be okay.

"His dad's been staying in his room and refuses to leave. Kid's got a nice family, for sure. The mom's a sweetheart."

"If there's anything I can send them or do for them—"

"You can't. Just let us handle things our way and stay out of it."

"I will," Talia agreed. She was so relieved about Lucas she'd agree to anything right now. She'd run across the plaza at high noon in her undies. She'd paint her bungalow neon purple. She'd—

Wait a minute.

"Detective," Talia said, "did you ask him why he said 'mercury'?"

"Of course we did, but he has no memory of it. His mom told us he was never much of a car aficionado, so we think it must mean something else. Or the more likely scenario is that it means nothing."

Talia jiggled her fists. "Oh gosh, I'm so happy. I mean . . .

I know there's still a killer out there, but the thought that Lucas is okay—"

"Stop it," Prescott said sharply. "From this point on, you have to act and look and feel as if you know Lucas isn't going to make it. Do you hear me? One slip from you and this could all fall apart."

"I hear you, and I promise I will not utter a word."

Prescott let out a breath. "I'm already beginning to think I made a terrible mistake."

"Patti, you didn't. I swear by all that is dear to me. My lips are sealed with Gorilla Glue." Talia made a zipping motion over her mouth.

Prescott gave her an odd look. Talia suddenly realized that it was the first time she'd addressed the detective by her first name. How had she let that slip out? But honestly, why shouldn't she? She'd known the woman long enough. And they were *kinda sorta* friends, weren't they?

She focused on calming her heartbeat. "Detective," she said slowly, "I will not let you down. I will not breathe a word to anyone."

"Martha can't know, either, Talia."

Talia concentrated on keeping her expression blank. "No one will ever hear it from my lips, not even Martha. Now please go out there and find Norma's murderer."

7

"Morning, Martha." Talia was wiping down the tables with lime-scented cleaner when Martha shuffled through the front door. An old expression—*you look like something the cat dragged in*—came to mind. Talia instantly felt terrible for thinking it.

"Morning" was all Martha said. She plodded around the side of the speckled counter and headed for her locker. As part of the renovations that were done in the spring, Talia had installed four wood-front lockers discreetly out of sight. Each employee had their own. It was a vast improvement over the old system of tossing their things over the hooks that were attached to the kitchen's rear door.

Talia finished up the last table and went back to the kitchen. She put away the cleaning supplies and went over to Martha, who was pouring herself a cup of coffee. "Did you manage to get some sleep?" she asked.

"Some, but I kept waking up. I couldn't stop—" She sucked in a long sniffle. "Let's not talk about it, okay? Right now I need to keep my brain focused in one direction—food prep."

"Then let's get to it," Talia said. Sure, easy for her to sound chipper. She knew about Lucas and Martha didn't. Oh Lord, if only she could tell her.

The morning seemed to drag by. It was right before eleven when Talia heard a hesitant knock on the eatery's front door. She peeked out through one of the diamond-shaped windows and saw Molly standing there.

Talia opened the door. "Hey. What are you doing here so early?" She greeted Molly with a smile.

Molly lifted her arms and then dropped them to her sides. Today she wore a candy-cane-striped tee and cutoff denim shorts. "I'm going a little nutso over there. Crystal sent me over to see if you needed any help. Yesterday was totally dead—oops, sorry—I mean, we barely saw a customer. With Lucas on, um, temporary leave, she thought you might need an extra hand. 'Course, I don't know how to do anything, so you'd have to show me . . ."

Talia smiled at her. "We could definitely use a hand here, but I should warn you—it's mostly grunt work."

"No problem," Molly said. "It'll help keep my mind occupied. Plus, I love kitchen stuff. You don't even have to pay me."

"Of course I'll pay you. I'll pay you the same salary I—"

"Don't say it," Molly said soberly. "Things are still bad, aren't they?"

"Nothing's changed, as far as I know. Come on in and scrub your hands, and I'll give you an apron. Then Martha and I will give you a brief introduction to the world of deep-fry."

Martha nodded at Molly and mumbled a hello. She didn't seem to care if Molly lent them a hand or not.

Talia, however, was grateful to have the extra help—and a friendly face. She set Molly up with a mountain of spuds and a heavy-duty potato peeler. She looked adorable in the blue Fry Me a Sliver apron that could probably have been wrapped twice around her slender figure.

"When I was a kid," Molly said, "Mom always made me peel the potatoes for supper. My dad loved scalloped potatoes like you wouldn't believe. He could eat a whole casserole by himself! Mom wasn't much of a cook, but that was one thing she always made for him. Anyway, I used to set the peels aside and make them into different shapes. Sometimes I'd spell out 'I love you, Daddy' in peels and leave them on his napkin." Tears formed on her long lashes. "Sorry."

"Don't be sorry. I know you lost him when you were pretty young."

"I was twelve," Molly said.

"That must have been so hard. Something congenital, your mom said?"

"Heart disease, on his dad's side. I always wonder if I'll end up with the same fate, but Mom says I get my genes from her side, so I shouldn't worry." Molly flipped a peeled potato into a steel pot filled with cold water.

"Speaking of your mom, how is she today? She seemed out of sorts yesterday." Talia knew she was prying, but couldn't stop herself. Audrey had bailed on everyone Sunday without even a *good-bye*. Norma's body was found shortly thereafter. Talia couldn't imagine her as a killer, but then, weirder things had happened.

Molly shrugged. "Okay, I guess. Still acting a little cray-cray, if you ask me. She and Crystal barely speak now, and I don't know why." Molly's face collapsed. "Oh God, I can't stand it anymore, Talia. The tension over there is horrible."

Talia went over to Molly and slipped an arm over her shoulder. "I know things are bad right now, Mol, but it will get better. Give it some time, okay?"

Molly nodded. "I know. I'm acting like a baby, aren't I?"

"Not at all. Your feelings are perfectly normal." Talia smiled at her. "Hey, I'm glad you're here helping Martha and me. We all need a little moral support right now."

Martha, who'd been quiet until then, spoke kindly to Molly. "I'll show you how to batter and fry the fish once the orders start to come in. It'll take a while to get the hang of it, but you'll be a pro before you know it."

"Thanks, Martha." Molly blinked. "You guys are so great. I already love working here."

Martha turned away quickly. Talia knew she was thinking of Lucas, wondering if he would ever return. Oh, how she wanted to share what she knew! But unless she wanted to put Lucas in danger and be drawn and quartered on the cobblestone plaza by one Detective Patti Prescott, she'd have to keep her lips zipped and her mind on frying for the masses.

A few minutes after the eatery opened, a youngish man lugging a boxy, oversized briefcase strode in. Lanky with curly carrot-colored hair, he looked distinctly uncomfortable in his khaki blazer and green-and-white-striped shirt. Talia suspected he'd have preferred wearing cutoffs and a tee, but he looked the part of a salesman, which he was.

"Are you the owner?" he said to Talia as she came out from behind the counter.

Talia smiled at him, already feeling her impatience creep to the surface. Lunch orders would start coming in at any moment. The man's timing was terrible. "I am. I'm Talia Marby. What can I do for you?"

The man plunked his briefcase onto the nearest chair he could find and then stuck out his hand. "I'm Larry Jefferson, ma'am. Pleased to meet you."

Talia briefly shook his hand, hoping that whatever his spiel was, he would make it short and snappy. He dug a business card out of his jacket pocket and gave it to her.

"Ma'am, I know you're very busy," he said politely, "but I wonder if I could show you just a few things I think might interest you. I feel they're perfect for your charming restaurant." Talia started to ask if he could come back at a better time, but the man barreled on with his practiced pitch. "My company, Nifty Squeezables, has developed a line of vintage-style condiment containers that your customers will fall in love with. I guarantee it!" He lifted his case onto the table, snapped the latches, and opened the case wide.

Resigned to enduring his pitch, Talia moved in for a closer look. Lined up on one side of the briefcase—which was more like a suitcase—were red, yellow, and white condiment containers. Some had whimsical faces molded into the plastic. Others were textured and somewhat barrel-shaped, with snap-close caps designed to protect the contents. She had to admit, they *were* kind of nifty.

"Now, this is just a small sample of our entire line," Jefferson said cheerily. He whipped a glossy brochure out of a pocket on the other side of the case and unfolded it for her. "As you can see—"

"Mr. Jefferson, these really are quite nice," Talia interjected. "I'm just not sure they're right for us. We're a small eatery, and we've always gotten by with the standard ketchup bottles. I suspect these require more work than they're worth, what with filling and refilling, not to mention keeping them clean."

The man grinned. "Cleanup is so easy with these that you'll be amazed. Simply amazed! They are dishwasher safe and free of BPAs. And they squeeze with ease, as we like to say in the biz." Now he was getting animated, and Talia was beginning to fear she'd never get rid of him.

The door opened and a young couple walked in, chattering about what they were going to order.

"Okay, I know you're starting to get busy in here," the man said, in a slightly softer voice. "May I leave you with a sample pack? I feel confident that once you start using them, you'll be *hooked*." He winked at her as if he'd made a remarkably clever quip.

Talia couldn't help smiling at his enthusiasm. She'd once been in sales herself—commercial real estate sales—and knew how it felt to be dismissed. "Um, sure," Talia said. "They really are kind of cute."

Jefferson whipped a prepackaged array of condiment holders out of another pocket of his briefcase, grinning as he deposited it in her hands. "Will you call me once you've had the chance to sample them?"

The man looked so earnest Talia couldn't say no. She promised to give them a test and then breathed a sigh of relief as he made his way out the door.

By ten to twelve, lunch orders started flying in. The guys at the Wrensdale Fire Station called in a huge order. After a few mishaps with the fresh haddock, Molly really got into the swing. Martha handled the side goodies, and they managed to form a reasonably competent team.

"Hey." The voice came from Jay Ballard, one of the

young firefighters. Talia noticed him send an appreciative glance Molly's way.

"Your order's all set, Jay," Talia said. She plunked two brown shopping bags onto the counter and rang it up.

"Any news about our boy?" Jay said quietly.

"I'm afraid not." Averting her gaze, Talia shook her head. Lucas delivered orders to the fire station at least twice a week, and the firefighters all loved him.

"Well, um, if you should *happen* to stumble over the creep who did that to him"—he flushed and looked her in the eye—"you know, like you did the last time? Well, just give a quick call to the firehouse. A few of us would like to, um, *escort* him to the police station, if you catch my meaning." He winked at her.

Talia nodded, biting off a smile. They wanted some "alone time" with the person who'd hurt Lucas. They also seemed positive the assailant was a man, but Talia wasn't quite so sure.

After Jay left, the dining room got even busier. By the time the last customer trickled out the door, it was nearly three. Talia prepared a huge helping of Molly's favorite— deep-fried meatballs—while she and Martha settled for some slaw and a few hand-cut fries. At least Martha was eating, even if it was only a fraction of what she normally had. Molly played with her phone while she shoveled meatballs into her mouth at approximately the speed of light.

Meanwhile, a million thoughts were scrambling around in Talia's brain. The night before, buoyed by the knowledge that Lucas was going to recover, she'd tossed around some ideas.

There were two contestants from the competition she knew almost nothing about: Dylan McPhee and Harry Summers. In her mind, she'd dubbed them the wild cards. No doubt the police had already questioned them. But while she didn't doubt the interviewing skills of the authorities—been there, sweated through that—she understood how frightening it was to be treated like a suspect.

Dylan worked at the Wrensdale Diner, and Harry worked for his wife, Sandra, at Summers Realty. The realty company had a storefront office on the main drag in Wrensdale. Talia was thinking about paying each of them a visit. Since it was getting late, she'd try to plan a time tomorrow to drop in on both men.

"Hey, I took some pictures at the festival," Molly said suddenly. "I just realized I never showed them to anyone."

"Anything interesting?" Talia peeked over Molly's arm at the high-tech smartphone.

"Not really." She flipped through them slowly. In one photo Molly had captured the Wrensdale Arcade table, with everyone chattering and enjoying their food. Ryan looked adorable helping his dad tuck a napkin into his shirt. Talia sighed, realizing how much she missed him. Ryan had left early Monday morning for a software conference in Dallas he couldn't get out of. He hated leaving her with things the way they were. They'd been texting each other every chance they got, but it wasn't the same as being together.

"Oh, look, Tal. Here's you heading up to the stage when Mr. Thurman was introducing the contestants. From the look on your face, someone would think you were going to a hanging."

Talia chuckled. "I was pretty nervous. I didn't realize I looked that scared, though."

"Ugh, how did I get Bruce Ferringer in one of my pictures?" Molly said. "Look at him, glad-handing the fire chief. He's such a sleaze. How could anyone think of voting for him? *Delete*," Molly said acidly, tapping her finger on the display.

"I don't get the attraction, either, but he seems to have quite a following," Talia pointed out.

Molly moved on to the other pics, some of which were rather fun. There was a good one of Rachel and Derek having batting practice with the local kids. Derek looked handsome in his softball jersey, his arms firm and muscular. Rachel looked fabulous, as usual, her dark ponytail dangling through the back of her ball cap. "Can you send me that one, Molly? Rachel will love it."

"Sure," Molly said. "Do you think I should post some of these on the website?"

"You mean *our* website?" Which hadn't been updated in weeks, Talia thought guiltily.

"No, the festival's website. Haven't you seen it? The town puts it up every year. They invite people to post their own pics. Most of them are sorta lame, but some are pretty funny."

"I'd like to check it out later. What's the link?"

"I'll flick it to you," Molly said, tapping at her phone. "When you get to the site, just click on the—" She stopped abruptly and grabbed Talia's forearm. "Did you hear that?"

Talia sat up in her chair. Her ears picked up the sound of a high-pitched wail coming from outside on the plaza.

Talia and Molly leaped to their feet at the same time. Molly raced out the front door with Talia at her heels. A small crowd had collected in front of the Fork and Dish, the door to which was wide-open. A young uniformed officer was doing his best to keep the gawkers at bay, but heads were bobbing every which way in an attempt to see around him. "Move back, folks. There's nothing to see," he told them. "Move along, now."

Molly made an end run around the gathering onlookers. Talia followed close behind her. Even from thirty or so feet away, Talia could make out the imposing form of State

Police Sergeant Liam O'Donnell. And the less imposing but equally intimidating outline of Detective Patti Prescott.

Molly clapped her hands to her face. "Oh God, Talia, look—the cops've got Crystal in handcuffs!"

Talia felt her insides do a somersault. She stared in horror at the sight of Crystal being tugged out onto the plaza by the two officers. Prescott caught Talia's eye, gave her an odd look, and then shook her head and turned away.

Behind Crystal, framed in the doorway with a stricken expression, Audrey stood with her hands folded around her arms.

"You can't take me to jail!" Crystal was shrieking. "I didn't do anything!"

Ignoring the uniform trying to hold her back, Molly raced around him and went over to where Crystal was being led out onto the plaza. Talia tried to follow, but the officer blocked her path. "Ma'am, you cannot go in there!"

"I'm not trying to go in," Talia said. She resisted stomping her foot on the sun-warmed cobblestone. "Crystal is my friend and I want to know what's happening."

The uniform, a fresh-faced young man with a smattering of acne, stuck his hands on his hips. "Ma'am, I said you *cannot* go in there. *Capisce?*"

Talia bristled at his rudeness. *"Io capisco,"* she said, grateful for the tidbits of proper Italian her nana had taught her. Then, in one swift move, she darted to the side and went over to where Molly was gesturing wildly at the police.

"Are you people crazy?" Molly shrieked at O'Donnell. "Why are you taking her away?"

"Move aside, young lady," O'Donnell barked at her. "Or you'll be riding along with her in the van."

Molly's face fell like a collapsed soufflé. Clutching each

other, she and Talia watched as Crystal was led to a waiting state police van parked in front of the plaza on Main Street. When the door slid shut, Talia cringed.

"This is terrible," Talia said in a choked voice. "How could they—"

"Talia."

Talia spun on her heel and saw Patti Prescott staring at her with an unreadable expression. "What's happening, Detective? Where are they taking Crystal?"

"We're taking her in for questioning. Some evidence was found in the Dumpster behind her shop that ties her to the murder."

For a moment Talia was speechless. She swallowed back a lump of fear. "What . . . what kind of evidence?"

"Fingerprint evidence," Prescott went on. "We found what we believe is the murder weapon. Galardi's prints are on it."

"That's . . . that's just impossible," Talia sputtered.

Prescott fixed her with a granite gaze, her nutmeg-colored eyes blazing. "Are you saying the fingerprint evidence is wrong?"

"I didn't say that. I—" Talia suddenly halted. "Murder weapon? You have the actual murder weapon?"

"The lab is doing more tests, but we believe we have. It has traces of Norma's blood and hair."

"May I ask what it is?"

"You may, but I don't have to tell you."

Talia let out an inward groan. Why hadn't she learned to phrase her questions better with Prescott? "*Will* you tell me, then?"

"At this time, no." Prescott turned and shot a glance back at the police van, which was pulling out into the stream of traffic on Main Street.

Talia blew out a breath. "Okay, but I have one more thing to say. Why would Crystal murder someone and then toss the weapon in her own Dumpster? With her prints on it?"

"You're asking the wrong question, Talia. What you should be asking is why Crystal's prints are all over the murder weapon."

Talia felt the cartilage in her knees turn suddenly into mush. "I—"

"You should also be asking," Prescott added quietly, "if anyone else's blood was found on the weapon."

And with that, Talia knew. Whoever murdered Norma had used the same weapon to attack Lucas. "Lucas," she said in a near whisper. "His blood was on the weapon, too, wasn't it?"

Prescott nodded. "Now, stay out of this, Talia. I warned you once, and I'm warning you again. It's one thing to be supportive of a friend, but it's another to go digging around in people's affairs."

"Don't worry," Talia said stiffly. "I have no interest in doing the jailhouse rock from behind bars. *Threat* received, loud and clear."

"It's not a threat, Talia. It's a promise." Prescott's face softened. "We will bring the killer to justice. I give you my word. Just let us do our jobs, okay?"

Talia nodded. She wanted to believe Prescott. But how could she when the wrong person was being taken into custody? Crystal was innocent. Talia felt that down to her very bones. Yet the evidence seemed to be aimed straight in her direction. There had to be an explanation.

The Dumpster. The one behind the Fork and Dish. Who else had access to it?

"Detective," she called out as Prescott was striding away. "Couldn't someone else have thrown trash into that Dumpster?

If it's like the one behind my restaurant, there's nothing to prevent a stranger from using it, right?"

Prescott turned and narrowed her gaze at Talia. "Why would someone else use it to throw away a . . . weapon with Crystal's prints on it? Wouldn't the killer be more likely to throw away a weapon with his—or her—own prints on it?"

Talia tried to make sense of that, but the words turned into one big jumble clogging her head.

A loud cry erupted from the cooking shop, and then the door slammed shut. "Sorry, ma'am," the young officer was muttering to Audrey. "Shop's closed for the day. We'll notify you when you can reopen."

"What's that about?" Talia asked Prescott.

"We have a warrant to search the cooking store. We're closing it until further notice."

Talia felt her shoulders sag. "This . . . this can't be happening."

Audrey hurried over to where Molly was standing. They threw their arms around each other. The two looked helplessly at Talia.

Talia went over to them, her legs feeling like rubber. "The cops have a warrant," she told them calmly. "They're searching for more of their so-called evidence"—she sent a withering glare in Prescott's direction—"so they can railroad Crystal into confessing."

Prescott rolled her eyes, waved a quick good-bye, and then hustled off toward her own unmarked car parked in front of the arcade.

"Come on, let's go over to Fry Me," Talia said. She slipped one arm through Audrey's and the other through Molly's, and together the trio headed back to the eatery.

8

After two glasses of fresh iced coffee, Audrey's color was looking a bit better. Martha's, unfortunately, had morphed into a sickly shade of gray. Her angst over Lucas was taking its toll. Talia was worried about her friend, even more so because there was so little she could do to relieve her mind.

Unless—

No. She'd given her promise to Prescott that she would not utter a single word. As desperately as she wanted to divulge her secret to Martha about Lucas's condition, she knew even the tiniest slip—by anyone—could put his life at risk.

Customers were streaming in for the supper hour earlier than usual. The hullaballoo on the plaza over Crystal's arrest had attracted a number of looky-loos, many of whom realized that fresh, delectable fried food was only a few steps away across the cobblestone.

Molly dove right into frying mode, handling everything Martha had taught her with incredible ease. She was a quick learner, and Talia was grateful to have her as a temporary employee. Martha went about her usual tasks, but the grim expression never left her face.

Audrey, meanwhile, sat huddled at the small table tucked out of sight at the back of the kitchen. The misery in her eyes was palpable. She'd spoken very little, except to offer the occasional compliment to Molly for being such a help in the kitchen.

"Getting hungry yet?" Talia said quietly to Audrey. "It's after six. You must feel like eating something." She gave her an encouraging smile.

"Maybe just a scoop of coleslaw?" Audrey finally agreed.

It wasn't much, but it was better than an empty stomach, Talia thought. She gave Audrey a large helping, hoping she would finish it all.

"I'm sure you'll hear from the police soon." Talia tried to sound soothing as she slid onto the chair adjacent to Audrey's. "I bet you'll be able to open up shop tomorrow."

Audrey shook her head and shrugged. "Even if we can, we've barely had a customer in two days. I feel for Crystal. I really do. But if she hadn't entered that stupid contest, none of this would've happened. We wouldn't be in this horrible mess!"

She was still blaming Crystal for her troubles, but Talia felt sure that wasn't the origin of her anguish. Something had been eating away at Audrey for a while now. Even before the contest, she'd been jittery and irritable. Talia thought back to Sunday, to the way Wes Thurman's gaze had homed in on Audrey after the contest was over. When Audrey had caught him staring, she'd dashed off. No one had seen her after that. She'd blown off the softball game without a word to anyone.

"Audrey, I know I'm prying here—yes, this time I freely admit it—but what was it that really bugged you about that contest? Did it have anything to do with Wes Thurman?"

Audrey's pale face flamed. "Of course not. Why would you think that?"

Methinks thou doth protest . . .

"I don't think it, not really." She crossed her fingers under the table. "Did you know Wes before he came to town for the contest?"

For a long moment Audrey remained silent. Then she looked at a spot on the wall, her gaze distant. "He was in my high school class, senior year," she finally said in the tiniest of voices.

Talia sat back. "So . . . you did know him."

"You really are nosy—you know that?" Audrey shoved aside her coleslaw and rose abruptly from her chair. "Come on, Molly, we're going home," she called to her daughter.

Spatula in hand, Molly turned and stared at her mother, her mouth hanging halfway to her collarbone.

Audrey fixed her gaze on Talia. "Listen, I know you want to find the person who hurt Lucas, but if you'll pardon the cliché, you're barking up the wrong tree. I appreciate your hospitality, but it's time we went home. Molly, did you hear me?" she said sharply.

Molly looked stricken, as if she didn't know which way to turn.

"It's okay, Molly," Talia said. She went over and gave the girl a firm hug. "Things are pretty quiet right now, and you've already helped out so much. Why don't you head home with your mom?"

"Okay," Molly said glumly. "But I'll be back tomorrow, okay?"

"Of course. Martha and I will be happy to have your help."

Molly scowled at her mother and stormed out the front door. Audrey followed without another word.

"Wow. That was strange," Talia said. She glanced at her watch—it was already twenty to seven. She began putting away the perishables and wiping down the work space in the kitchen.

"Something's up with Audrey for sure," Martha said. "I just can't put my finger on it." She heaved a sigh. "Guess my brain's getting old along with my body. Either that or I'm plain worn-out."

"Of course you are," Talia said. "Worrying about Lucas has us both a little *cray-cray*." She grinned at Martha, hoping to elicit even a ghost of a smile.

"I know you're trying to make me laugh, but I can't. Not with things the way they are." Martha pulled her blue apron over her head and tossed it in the bin for the laundry service.

Talia bit her lip. She so badly wanted to tell Martha that Lucas was out of danger. If only—

No, she had to keep her promise. She'd told Prescott she wouldn't utter a word, and she had to remain true to it. With her fingers she made a twisting motion over her lips, as if locking them closed.

"What are you doing?" Martha said, frowning at her.

"Oh, um, nothing. I was just thinking about how secretive Audrey's been behaving."

"Yeah, well, you nailed that one. She didn't like it one bit when you asked her how well she knew Thurman." Martha pointed a finger at her. "There's bad blood there, Talia. Mark my words."

Talia rubbed her fingers over her eyes. "I think you're right. But unless it has something to do with the murder, it really is none of our business."

"At this stage," Martha said darkly, "let's not rule out anything. In my book they're both suspects—Audrey *and* Wes Thurman. Crystal wouldn't kill a fly if it was doing the tango on her nose."

Talia opened the commercial fridge and shoved the container of coleslaw onto a shelf. "Someone tossed that . . . whatever the weapon was in the Dumpster behind the cooking store. The killer must've known the police would search there."

"And while the cops are putting all their eggs in a basket named Crystal," Martha said, "the real killer is out there celebrating."

A sharp ache was beginning to work its way up Talia's spine and into the nape of her neck. She couldn't go on this way. She had to find time tomorrow to talk to Dylan McPhee and Harry Summers. If she could dream up a valid reason to visit each of them, it wouldn't really be poking her nose into other people's affairs.

She hadn't had much of a chance to do any food shopping lately. Why not eat breakfast at the diner? If Dylan was there, which he should be, she'd ask to have a little chat with him.

As for Harry, he'd rescued her from a bad fall on Sunday. She'd never really thanked him properly, had she? No, she had not. A gift certificate to Fry Me might be the perfect way to do that.

"Talia, if you don't mind, I wanna get going a few minutes

early. Father Francese is holding a special Mass for Lucas at seven fifteen tonight."

"Oh, Martha, that is so sweet of him. I didn't even know about it."

Every Friday at noon, like clockwork, Lucas delivered a fish-and-chips meal to the elderly priest at Saint Agatha's. Talia had come to think of the pastor as one of her best customers.

"It was kind of a last-minute thing," Martha explained. "Anyway, I want to get there early if I can. Have a few minutes alone with the Big Guy. Or Gal." With a wry smirk, she pointed skyward.

Talia hugged Martha good-bye, thankful for a few minutes to herself. Today had been the equivalent of an emotional nightmare. No one had heard from Crystal, so it wasn't clear if the police were holding her or not. Talia planned to text Detective Prescott as soon as she got home to see what she could find out.

Talia glanced at the wall clock in the dining area—a pottery octopus with a deep-fried goody clutched in each of its eight tentacles—and saw that it was four minutes to seven. She went to her locker, grabbed her purse, and slung it over her shoulder. After ensuring that the back door was double-locked, she headed for the front entrance. She was just turning the doorknob when someone pushed the door open forcefully. Talia took a startled jump backward.

"Oh my," Bruce Ferringer blustered. "I'm sorry if we frightened you. Is it closing time already?" His smile was like a barracuda's—all teeth and about as warm as the deep blue sea.

"Um, well, actually it is. We close at seven, I'm afraid."

Next to Ferringer stood a diminutive thirtysomething

woman wearing a white blouse and a pale yellow pencil skirt. Her shiny brown hair was stick straight and hung just above her thin shoulders. The woman pasted on a smile far more genuine than Ferringer's and stuck out her hand. "Hi. I'm Stacey Russell. So glad to finally meet you. If you haven't already guessed, I'm Bruce's campaign manager."

Talia accepted her handshake but then quickly recovered. "I'm sorry. Did . . . did we have an appointment?" She knew they didn't, or at least she hoped they didn't, but at this point she just wanted to get rid of them.

Ferringer, dressed casually in Dockers and a short-sleeved garnet-colored polo shirt, moved deftly around his companion and stepped inside the dining room. He looked all around, sizing up the place. "The AC works nicely in here, Stace. This will be absolutely perfect."

A blade of anger poked through Talia's polite demeanor. "I'm sorry, Mr. Ferringer, but we really are closed. May I ask why you're here?"

"Talia, you really must start calling me Bruce," he said smoothly. "And we're the ones who should be sorry." He looked sternly at his companion. "I thought you were going to call first."

The woman, Stacey, flushed. "I was, but then you told me not to." She clenched her small perfect teeth into a fake smile.

"Oh, glory yes, you're right. I do remember that now." Ferringer stroked his square chin and then winked at Talia. "Every man needs an efficient woman to keep him on the straight and narrow, doesn't he, Talia?"

Talia resisted rolling her eyes at the textured ceiling.

"Anyway," Ferringer plowed on, "you remember at the festival on Sunday you said we could chat later in the week?"

Drat. She *had* said that. But that was before Norma's body was found and before—

Talia swallowed. "I do recall that, um, Bruce," she said, trying to maintain her cool. "But that was before my employee, Lucas Bartolini, was viciously attacked and left for dead in the parking lot at the ball field. As you can well imagine, I've thought of little else since then."

Ferringer closed his eyes in a pained expression. He splayed his large manicured hand over his heart. "Oh my, yes. And you're right. I should have thought of that. How is the young man doing, by the way? Have you heard anything?"

"Nothing has changed," Talia said. "According to the authorities, he's in critical condition. Father Francese is even holding a special Mass for him this evening."

Stacey clasped her hands over her lips. "So it *is* that bad?" she said hoarsely. "I'm so sorry." To her credit, she looked as if she meant it.

"And now I really do have to dash," Talia said, inching toward the door.

"To the hospital?" Ferringer asked.

"No. No one is allowed to visit Lucas. Honestly, I'm afraid I'm going to have to lock up now. I have a number of things to do at home, not to mention a hungry cat to feed."

"We won't keep you, then," Stacey said. At least she had the decency to look embarrassed at the way they'd barged in at closing time.

Ferringer, meanwhile, had strolled over to the counter and was perusing one of the paper take-home menus. "This will be perfect for our luncheon," he said, going back over to his campaign manager. He gave Stacey the menu and then looked directly at Talia. "Have you thought any more about our having it on a Sunday?"

Talia was ready to blow hot steam out of her ears. "No, I haven't, Mr. Ferringer, because, as I already mentioned, Sunday is out of the question."

Ferringer's eyes hardened. "I see. You do realize, Talia, that hosting our luncheon would be very good for your future? One of my primary supporters is a semiprofessional golfer whose name, I assure you, is quite recognizable. Think of the business he could send your way. And that's only the tip of the iceberg."

Talia plopped her handbag onto the nearest table. "Mr. Ferringer, I'm really going to have to ask you both to leave now. It is past closing time and I need to lock up." She gave Stacey an apologetic smile. The woman seemed decent enough, even if she did associate herself with a sleaze like Ferringer.

"We'll be in touch," Stacey said quietly. "I'm sorry we disturbed you at a difficult time." She slid the paper menu into her beige and blue designer handbag. The bag would have been pretty sans the GO FAR WITH FERRINGER! button attached to its leather strap.

Ferringer nodded at Talia and whipped open the door. "Thank you for your time, Talia. I will be praying for your young employee." He snapped his fingers at his campaign manager. "Speaking of praying, we should try to catch that Mass. And make sure we get a seat up front so everyone sees us coming in."

His last words trailed behind him as he and Stacey stepped outside onto the plaza. Relieved to be rid of them, Talia locked the door securely behind the pair. She wanted to be sure they were long gone before she went outside herself.

Something occurred to her, though. Ferringer must have

wondered why Talia herself wasn't attending the Mass. It would be a logical thing to do, if Lucas were really in bad shape.

Had she given herself away?

Actually, what was she thinking? She *should* be attending the Mass.

With a weary sigh, Talia stepped out onto the cobblestone plaza and locked the door behind her. Her furry calico angel would have to wait a big longer for her supper.

9

Exhausted as she felt, Talia couldn't help beaming at her beloved Bo.

"There's my little sweetie," Talia cooed to the cat. "I'm late tonight, aren't I?"

The cat was perched on the arm of the tattered tweed chair that Talia's grandpop had always loved, and that Bo had claimed for her own the day she walked into Talia's life. The chair now sat closer to the front door, where the cat waited patiently—or maybe not so patiently—for Talia to walk in every evening.

Meoowwww. Bo's plaintive cry was drawn out into several beats—the sure sign of a cat who was perishing from hunger.

Talia dropped her purse onto the chair and scooped up the cat. She nuzzled Bo's whiskers and headed for the kitchen. "Let's see what we can find in the cabinets, shall we? Maybe some savory baked salmon or some lamb kabobs?"

All of which came from the fancy cat food cans Talia had bought at the specialty pet supplies store. For sure, the stuff was pricey. But with only one cat to feed, Talia didn't mind the splurge. The dry kibble she left out for daytime snacking was also top quality, but Bo definitely preferred the moist food.

After Bo had been fed, Talia returned to the living room. She turned on the tower fan that blew in gentle waves toward the sofa. On most summer days, the bungalow managed to stay comfortable. After spending all day at the eatery with conditioned air blowing out of the vents, Talia was happy to have only a few fans to cool down the small house.

The church where Lucas's Mass had been held had been dreadfully warm. A few of the older folks had looked ready to faint. Many of them had fanned themselves with paper programs left over from the past Sunday's events. Luckily, Father Francese had wrapped things up more quickly than usual. No doubt the elderly pastor sensed that most of the attendants were there only to say a few prayers for Lucas. He might also have been on the verge of passing out himself and saw the wisdom of cutting the Mass short.

Talia had spotted Martha sitting in the front row, her head bowed. She could only see her from the back, though. She'd thought about joining her, but had the feeling Martha needed the time alone. The poor woman was suffering mightily over Lucas. If only—

No, no, no. Stop thinking that way. You can't tell. You can't utter a word.

Shaking away those thoughts, Talia grabbed her phone from her purse and plopped onto the sofa. The breeze from the tall fan caressed her face.

The bungalow had been her grandparents' home for most of Talia's formative years. Her grandpop had passed on well over a decade ago, but Nana had remained in the tiny house until she died last year. Talia still thought about her every day. She missed her nana's comforting presence. Every so often, she'd swear Nana was standing beside her, soothing her with kind, unspoken words. On more than one occasion, the faint scent of her grandmother's dusting powder had tickled her senses. She knew it was only her imagination working overtime, but it was soothing nonetheless.

Talia kicked off her Keds and wiggled her toes. She leaned her head back on the brocade pillow she'd picked up at one of the outlet shops. She loved having the outlet mall so close to where she lived. She wasn't a big shopper, but when she needed something, it was practically at her fingertips.

She tried reaching Ryan on his cell, but it went directly to voice mail. She opted instead for texting him, omitting any mention of Lucas's condition.

Almost immediately, Ryan texted her back. Sorry. Stuck in a dinner meeting. Miss you terribly. XO. Maybe chat later?

She knew the *XO* was supposed to mean "hug and kisses." But with her and Ryan, the subtle message was there: *I love you.* The word "maybe" threw her a little. It wasn't like Ryan to sound vague. But she knew the Dallas meeting was a biggie for his company, so he must have felt the pressure.

Talia felt a smile widen her lips. She texted back: You got it. Call me when you're free, no matter how late. XOXO

When he didn't text back within the next few minutes, Talia set her phone down on the sofa. A tiny mewling sound vibrated in Talia's ear. She glanced down and saw Bo gazing up at her, the kitty's breath reeking of fish. In the next instant, the little calico leaped onto Talia's chest. She curled up and settled there, closing her eyes and purring in a display of sheer bliss.

Talia grinned at her little darling. She was so glad Bo

had found a home with her. In fact, Bo had been with her now for nearly a year.

She'd spotted the skittish little cat prowling the neighborhood after she'd first moved into her nana's bungalow. Later, she'd learned from one of her neighbors that the kitty had been tossed out like unwanted trash after its elderly owner had died. The woman's son, apparently, had no use for cats. He'd abandoned the little creature on a cold autumn night, leaving her to fend for herself. Talia had named the kitty Bojangles after her nana's favorite song, even knowing that a calico cat was almost certainly a female.

Talia picked up her cell phone again. She flipped through her e-mails until she found the link Molly had sent her—the one to the town's website where pictures from the festival were posted. She was glad now that she'd opted for the larger-screened phone. It was so much easier to read.

She touched the link, and almost instantly myriad photos popped onto the screen. Colorful pix of the vendor booths filled the page.

Talia grinned at the photo of an eager little girl biting into a hunk of sugar-dusted fried dough. Others showed the softball field, where Rachel and Derek had given batting lessons to the kids. Those had been taken from a higher vantage point—maybe from the raised scoreboard behind center field? The scoreboard was accessed by a set of stairs, so the photographer would have been twenty or so feet above the ground, assuming that was where these were shot from.

Scads of other photos were posted, most of them taken from too far a distance to discern much of anything. She flipped through the remaining ones more quickly. Most had little content—only a jumble of random faces and scenes, as if they'd all been hired as "extras" in a movie.

One photo caught Talia's attention. The photographer had homed in on Bruce and Jodie Ferringer standing behind their gaudily decorated table. Bruce's expression had been captured midsnarl—he'd apparently been in the midst of a contentious convo with his wife. *Not surprising,* Talia thought. The only time Ferringer truly smiled—and even then it was phony—was when he was chatting up potential constituents.

She flipped her way through the remainder of the still shots. Nothing of interest caught her eye. Then she spotted another link—this one to a video. She tapped the link and saw that it was four minutes long. It began with a slow scan of the empty bleachers, then moved to the section of the park where the booths and tents had been set up. If she squinted, she could just make out the table at the back where she'd been seated with Ryan, Arthur, and the "Arcade Brigade." The videographer moved slowly, and with a remarkably steady hand, capturing the happy faces of kids and adults alike.

Then the video shifted focus. The area where the temporary staging had been set up came into view. The camera panned to the right, toward the entrance to the park. Adjacent to that were the cooking stations, and beyond that was the judges' tent.

A sudden swatch of magenta caught Talia's eye. Jodie Ferringer, wearing her enormous floppy hat, was meandering away from the Ferringer table in the direction of the parking lot. Her huge blue cooler was draped over her arm. Talia noted the time on the video—2:11.

Hmmm, that was odd. At 2:11, the six contestants, including Talia, were hunkered in their respective stations, preparing their entries for the judges. But Jodie had stayed until after the grand prize was awarded to Norma, so she couldn't have been leaving.

Then Talia remembered. Jodie had used the cooler to transport those obnoxious brochures. She'd forced them on anyone with a pulse, whether they wanted one or not, so she'd probably run out. No doubt she'd been heading to her car to fetch another batch.

The video was nearing the end. None of it had been very revealing. And then, all at once, Talia spotted something that made her body jerk involuntarily. Bo's eyes shot open, and the cat gave her a worried look.

Talia stroked the cat's head soothingly, her gaze drawn back to the video. The videographer had turned around and was strolling back toward the heart of the festivities. The next frame lasted only a few seconds, but the dark red hair, drawn into a French braid, made Talia gasp.

There stood Audrey Feldon, a frightened look on her face. In her hands she clutched a slip of paper. Pale green, just like the one Talia had—

Oh dear God—the note. The one she'd scooped up off the grass right before the softball game was going to start. The one written on a Steeltop Foods sticky note, its bold message reading:

WE NEED TO TALK.

She'd tucked it into the pocket of her linen slacks and forgotten all about it. Now she realized she should have given it to the police. It might have meant nothing, but then . . . it might have meant everything.

Talia thought back to when she'd last done wash. It was Saturday, she remembered. The linen slacks she'd worn on Sunday should still be in her hamper.

With gentle hands she moved Bo aside, set her phone down, and hopped off the sofa. Within seconds she located the wrinkled linen slacks stuffed at the bottom of her laundry hamper.

She shoved her hand into the right-hand pocket. A sigh of sheer relief escaped her lips. She clamped her fingers around the note and carefully withdrew it. Though a bit rumpled, it was still intact. With Norma dead and Lucas injured, the message WE NEED TO TALK sounded more ominous than ever.

Next dilemma: should she call Prescott or text her? Considering everything the detective had on her plate, she opted for a text.

First, the note. She padded into the kitchen, found a clean plastic sandwich bag, and sealed the note securely inside. She attached it to the fridge with a Fry Me a Sliver magnet, then went back to the living room to grab her phone.

She located the detective's contact info and texted. Have physical info that might be important. Call me when you can. Any more news on L? So glad he's going to be okay. Any chance Crystal's been released?

Almost instantly, she got a return message. L still critical and unresponsive. I'll stop by early AM.

Talia choked out a cry. Lucas was critical? Unresponsive?

A wave of nausea gripped her. She clapped a hand over her mouth. Poor Lucas—he must have taken a turn for the worse. If only she could see him, talk to his folks . . .

Wait a minute. Prescott's text said *still* critical and unresponsive. What did that mean?

Talia shook her head. Pretty soon her brain cells were going to explode through her ears. Had she only imagined that Prescott had told her Lucas was recovering? Or had it been some wacky dream spawned by her own anxiety?

Her thoughts drifted to poor Crystal. Had the police held her? Was she languishing in a jail cell for a crime she hadn't committed? How did everything turn so bad, so fast?

She located the remote and flicked on the television. Maybe she could find a mindless sitcom to drag her thoughts away from Lucas. She clicked her way through the lineup, groaning at nearly every program she landed on. Eventually she settled for an old movie—a comedy with John Candy.

But even John Candy, funny as he was, failed to quell the negative thoughts racing around in her mind. Shortly after eleven, she turned off the television. Ryan still hadn't called, which was definitely not like him. He'd never promised to call and then not followed through. And he always texted her a row of pink hearts before he shut off his light at night. But so far, nothing.

She'd eaten little since earlier in the afternoon, but even now she didn't feel hungry. Too tired to wash her hair, she showered quickly and headed for bed. Bo curled up next to her pillow, her purring muted. The cat always knew when Talia was troubled.

She needed a good night's rest if she was going to accomplish anything tomorrow. It was time to step up the action, in spite of Detective Prescott's warning. She'd already come up with a game plan.

Now all she had to do was put her plan into play.

10

The persistent ringing of the doorbell woke Talia out of a sound sleep.

"What on God's green earth . . . ?" she muttered, forcing her eyes open to throw a baleful look at her bedside clock.

5:42 a.m. Could that be right?

The doorbell rang again, followed by a forceful knocking.

"I'm coming. I'm coming," she snapped at whoever it was. She slipped her arm out from under Bo's furry one, slung on her summer robe, and stuck her feet into flip-flops.

"Open the door, Talia," a voice commanded from the front porch.

Talia made a face. She recognized the voice. Those dulcet tones came from none other than Detective Patti Prescott.

Talia tied her robe and turned the lock. Almost instantly the door flew open.

"Uh . . . yeah, come on in," she mumbled, closing the door.

Prescott, wearing a pale blue cotton shirt and lightweight navy trousers, plunked her hands on her slender hips. Her nutmeg-colored eyes blazed with fury as they searched the room. "Is anyone else here?"

Talia frowned. "Only my cat. Why?"

"What part of 'don't utter a word' do you not understand?"

Talia scrubbed her eyes open with her fingers. "Wha— what are you talking about?"

Prescott whipped her cell out of her pocket. "Does this sound familiar: 'Any more news on L? So glad he's going to be okay'?"

Talia gawked at her. "*That's* what you're mad about? I only sent the text to you. It was completely private!"

"Nothing is completely private, Talia. What if one of my nosy coworkers, or even my mother, had been looking over my shoulder when I read it? Do you realize you could have cost me my job? Or Lucas his life?"

"I—"

"Even worse, what if your boyfriend, or Martha, or anyone picked up your phone and read your texts?"

Talia ran a hand through her hair, which by now had to be standing on end. "Look, Detective. My *boyfriend*, as you call him, is out of town on business. And no one I know would read my texts," she added meekly.

Prescott moved toward her. "Oh, they wouldn't? How do you know that? Are you one hundred percent—"

"Okay, okay! I messed up. I'm sorry. I honestly didn't think—"

"That's just it," Prescott said soberly. "You didn't think. That sad part is, I trusted you. I'll never make that mistake again."

Talia felt her shoulders slump. She really *had* screwed up. But if Prescott had warned her in the first place about not texting, she never would have done it. "So . . . Lucas is okay, then?" Her voice came out in a mousy squeak.

Prescott replied with a stiff nod. "What is it you have to show me?"

Relieved about Lucas, Talia beckoned the detective to follow her into the kitchen. "Want some coffee? I can make a pot in no time."

Prescott shook her head. "Just show me this so-called physical info you supposedly have. Or was that just an excuse to text me?"

Talia glared at her. The detective was seriously beginning to tick her off.

"It's right here." Talia pulled the plastic bag off the fridge and handed it to her. She gave Prescott the background story, including the fact that it might be the same note Audrey had picked up off the ground on Sunday.

"I suppose your prints are all over it," Prescott said. This time a slight twinkle shone in her eyes.

"I suppose they are, since I didn't think it meant anything when I first picked it up."

Prescott examined the note. "For future reference," she said, "this should have been put into a paper bag, preferably a glassine bag. Although I wouldn't expect you to have one of those on hand."

Talia risked a tiny smile. "Who knew?" she said, with a lift of her shoulders.

"I did," Prescott said. "That's why I'm the one wearing the badge." She turned, and with a few strides was in the living room. Her face softened when she saw the little calico gazing up at her with wary gold eyes. She bent and spoke soothingly to the cat, offering her fingers for Bo to sniff. "Sorry if I scared you, little one. You're a good girl, aren't you?"

Bo purred and pushed her head into the detective's hand. Talia couldn't help smiling at the scene. It really was pretty adorable. She followed Prescott to the door with tiny, flip-floppy steps. "Um, any word on Crystal?"

Prescott's expression was unreadable. She dipped her chin at the television. "I suggest you turn on the six o'clock news."

Talia watched in mute horror as the perky reporter, every blond hair sprayed into place, chirped into a mic. She was standing in front of the Wrensdale Police Station, her exquisitely made-up face looking appropriately somber.

"According to Sergeant Liam O'Donnell of the Massachusetts State Police," the reporter said, "Crystal Galardi, the forty-four-year-old co-owner of the Fork and Dish, was arrested yesterday afternoon at her store in the Wrensdale Arcade. After an exhaustive search, the murder weapon—a wooden rolling pin—was found in the Dumpster behind the shop. Galardi denies knowing anything about the weapon, or the murder, despite the fact that preliminary lab tests turned up her prints on the handle. Galardi is also being charged with the attack on twenty-year-old Lucas Bartolini, who remains in the hospital in grave condition."

Stunned, Talia shook her head. No way was Crystal the killer. It just wasn't possible. And never in a zillion years would she have harmed Lucas.

What made far more sense was that the rolling pin had been purchased at Crystal's shop. Naturally her prints would have been on it—she'd probably handled it when she stocked the shelves, or when she sold it to the buyer. She hoped the police were checking into that.

Talia shuddered as the reporter droned on. Crystal was scheduled to appear in court in approximately three hours. What a nightmare for the poor woman, and for her elderly mom. Talia prayed Crystal had a good attorney.

"That stupid contest is to blame," Talia mumbled to Bo, who was making yowly protests about her breakfast not having been served yet. "Now I wish neither of us had entered."

Bo looked up at her and licked her whiskers in response.

"I know," Talia said, unable to resist a smile. "You can't think on an empty stomach, can you? Come on, let's go into the kitchen and get you some turkey and giblets. As for me, I'm going to enjoy a hearty breakfast at the Wrensdale Diner."

Talia slid onto a stool at the counter, inhaling the enticing aroma of fried eggs, pancakes, and cinnamon muffins. Breakfast was one of her favorite meals, despite the fact that she rarely had time to indulge in a leisurely one. Most of the time she gulped down cereal on the run, anxious to get to the eatery to start cooking for the day.

A fresh-faced girl with teal-streaked hair and eyes to match set a cream-colored mug down in front of her. "Coffee?" the girl said, holding the steaming pot aloft.

"You bet," Talia said, with the brightest smile she could muster.

The girl filled the mug with the fragrant java. Talia reached for the ceramic bowl that held a pile of nondairy creamer packets. "What's good today?"

The girl grinned at her. "Well, everything here is, like,

delicious. But this morning the cook made some cinnamon chip muffins that are to *die* for."

Talia suppressed a shiver at the word *die*. "Ah, that must be Dylan, right? I've heard so much about his luscious baked goods."

"Yeah, he's a legend around here. At least in his own mind." She winked at Talia. "He entered a baking contest this past weekend, but he didn't win. I don't think it set too well with him. He thought he was a shoo-in. Like nobody else in the world can bake except him, ya know? Just because he invented a few good recipes, he thinks planet Earth revolves around him." She made a rotating motion with one finger and then leaned in closer to Talia. "I mean, the guy lives with his mother, right? He's not exactly a catch, if you see where I'm going." She grinned, pleased with her revelation of this delectable tidbit of gossip.

Ignoring the barb about Dylan, Talia snapped her fingers as if she'd just recalled the contest herself. "Hey, that's right. Wasn't he one of the finalists in the Steeltop Foods contest?"

The girl nodded. "Yup. That's the one. Then some poor old lady got offed after it was over. In fact, it was the *winner* who got murdered." She gave an exaggerated shiver. "So awful, right? But you prob'ly saw that on the news."

Talia nodded sagely. "Were you there, at the festival?"

"Nah. That type of thing bores me to tears. I went to a friend's barbecue on Onota Lake that day. Her folks have a lakefront cottage there. They had some cool fireworks! The kind you're not supposed to have, ya know?" She gave Talia an exaggerated wink.

Yes, the kind that blows off fingers.

Talia smiled, and after a momentary pause said, "Did

Dylan know her, by any chance? I mean, did he know the murdered woman?"

Still gripping the coffeepot, the girl gazed at the wall with a thoughtful expression. "I don't think so. At least he said he didn't. Truthfully, I don't totally trust him, though. He's not exactly Mr. Congeniality."

"I know the type," Talia said, nodding again.

The girl glanced toward the other end of the counter. A portly, balding fellow in a stained apron was giving her the evil eye.

"Hey, maybe you better order," the server whispered. "My boss is giving me that look, you know?" She crossed her eyes playfully.

Talia grinned. "Oh, sure. I'll have a cinnamon chip muffin with two scrambled eggs. And, um, is Dylan in the kitchen, by any chance?"

The girl scribbled Talia's order on a lined pad. "Yeah, sure. He's back there. You want to see him?"

"Actually, I do. I have something to ask him. If he has a free minute, that is. It's about his muffins," she added quickly. No point in arousing any unnecessary suspicions. Besides, she had a twinkling of an idea she wanted to pursue, and muffins were definitely involved.

The girl winked at her again and then scurried off through the swinging metal door almost directly behind her.

A few minutes later, Dylan McPhee, his curly mud brown hair tucked into a matching hairnet, pushed through the same door. He glanced around, and then his gaze landed on Talia. Scowling, he looked around briefly before walking over to her. "You the chick that wanted to see me?"

Friendly fellow. "Yes, I'm Talia Marby. And I am the person who wanted to see you."

"I know you," he said. His thin lip curled. "You were one of the other losers."

"Yeah, well . . . that's true, but it's not why I'm here." Boy, what a surly dude. "Do you have a few minutes to talk? Privately, that is."

He shook his head. "If it's about the murder, I don't have anything more to say. I told the cops everything I know."

"I'm sure you did, but—"

Talia's server chose that moment to return with her eggs and muffin. The girl set them down in front of her and then went off to wait on two men in army green work clothes who'd just seated themselves at the counter.

Dylan's thin chest puffed slightly. "You ordered one of the muffins, I see. It's a new recipe I'm experimenting with."

"It smells heavenly," Talia said, taking in a long breath. "I can't wait to taste it. Anyway, I'd still like to have a brief chat with you, if you have a free minute or two. I promise, I'm not trying to pry. I only want to clarify a few things. I also have a culinary question to run by you."

Her last statement, she hoped, would be an enticement.

Dylan studied her for a moment. "Meet me in the parking lot out back at seven thirty. That's when I take a cigarette break. And don't worry," he added brusquely. "It's an electronic cigarette. You won't smell anything."

With that, he slammed through the swinging door back into the kitchen.

Talia resisted the urge to pump her first. She cut the muffin in half and slathered it with butter. Combined with the fluffy, perfectly cooked eggs, it was the best breakfast she'd had in ages.

After she gobbled it all down, paid the bill, and left her server a hefty tip, she grabbed her purse and headed in the direction of the rear entrance. She'd parked her Fiat in the back lot anyway, so it was a good place to meet up with Dylan.

Outside, grayish clouds had begun to gather. A thunderstorm was headed for the Berkshires, according to the morning newscast. So far the summer had been a dry one. A good, soaking rain would be a welcome change.

Dylan, sans hairnet, was already waiting for her. Leaning against a boxy-looking blue car that looked old enough to be a classic, he puffed on a black cylindrical device. The object looked more like a fountain pen than a cigarette. Talia couldn't help staring when he blew out a puff of something that looked like steam but had an odd, nondescript scent.

He looked amused at her confusion. "It's called vaping," he said, an edge to his voice. "No obnoxious smell to bother the whiny nonsmokers."

Talia suppressed a snarky retort. It was whiny not to want cigarette smoke blown in your face?

"Oh, well, then," she offered tactfully. "I learned something new today. By the way, your muffin was fabulous." She gave him a generous smile. "You must have a secret ingredient."

"Matter of fact I do," he said, a hint of pride in his voice. "Since you're a cook yourself, you probably figured out what it is."

"Uh-uh. I'm more of a fry cook than a baker. Speaking of which, I wondered what your opinion was of deep-frying muffins. Mini ones, that is. Not the regular size."

Dylan nodded. For the first time, his dark eyes looked animated. "I've seen it done. For starters, you need a good funnel cake recipe to make the batter." He pointed the fingers holding the e-cigarette at her. "Don't refrigerate it, though.

Changes the whole texture. Plus, your batter'll thicken too much. You want it thin enough to coat the muffin. 'Course, you deep-fry all the time, so you probably know all that stuff."

"Thanks, Dylan. That actually helps me. I've been hesitant to try it, but now I think I'll give it a whirl!"

"Another thing. I'd dust them with powdered sugar before serving them. They'll look pretty and it'll add a touch of sweetness."

His passion for his chosen profession was admirable. Talia wondered if he'd learned it on the job or if he'd attended a culinary school. The powdered sugar would have been a no-brainer for her, but she didn't want to sound ungrateful. "Another excellent idea. Thanks. Mind if I ask you something else? About Sunday?"

Dylan's face went stone still, his dark eyes opaque. "Figured that's why you wanted to talk to me. You're the nosy girl I heard people talking about."

Other people called her a nosy girl? Well, wasn't that a kick in the can?

"Look," Dylan said, "I told the cops everything I know, which is *nada*. That possession charge goes back three years. It was my first and only offense. I got a fine and community service. Big frickin' deal. I smoked a little pot. Doesn't make me a killer, does it?"

"Of course it doesn't," Talia agreed. "And your . . . possession charge is really none of my business."

That was the first she'd heard of Dylan having a criminal record. She was also fairly sure that on the application for the Steeltop Foods competition, each contestant had had to swear under oath that they'd never been found guilty of a criminal offense. Had Dylan flat-out lied on his form?

"Got that right," he snapped. "Look, my break's almost over. Are you—"

"I'm sorry. I know I'm using up your break time. I only wanted to ask if you heard anything that day. When we were all in our separate cooking stations?"

He eyed her warily. "What would I have heard that you didn't?"

"I'm not sure, but your cooking station was adjacent to Norma's. Mine was on the other side, closest to the generator."

The generator, Talia remembered, had been powered by the cables snaking from the appliance store's truck. The sound it gave off was a low drone, but after a while it melded into the background, like white noise. Loud white noise.

Dylan blew out another puff of vapor. All at once he froze, his brow furrowed in concentration. "There was one weird thing," he said. "But it has nothing to do with the murder. At one point I heard a radio—or maybe it was a CD player—come on from Norma's side. I guess she brought it along with her and decided to turn it on. Nothing strange about that, except that she was listening to Led Zepp." He shrugged. "No skin off my nose if the old bat liked to play heavy metal. When she first turned it on, it sort of blasted, but she lowered it right away. After a few minutes she turned it off. Guess she thought it might be disturbing the other contestants."

Talia never heard any music from her own cooking station. "Did you hear any voices?" she asked him.

"Voices?" Dylan frowned. "No, nothing like that. But I had a fan on. Between that and the generator, any voices would've gotten drowned out. Why are you asking all this stuff?" He began edging toward the back door to the diner. Talia followed him.

"Crystal was arrested yesterday. The police think she murdered Norma. I know she didn't do it, Dylan. I'm just trying to make sense of what happened that day."

He stopped and looked at her, his face draining of color. "Arrested, huh? Geezum, I didn't hear that. Crystal seemed like a real nice lady. Why do the cops think she did it?"

He apparently hadn't heard the news this morning.

"The police found the murder weapon in the Dumpster behind her cooking store. It was a rolling pin, with Norma's blood on it."

"Huh." He shook his head slowly. "I never would've pegged her for something like that. Just proves that anyone can snap. Hey, I gotta go before I get canned." He turned and headed toward the building.

Talia couldn't let him escape that easily. "You didn't like Norma, did you, Dylan?" she said quietly to his retreating form.

Dylan stopped in his tracks. He turned slowly and faced her, his mouth pinched in anger. "What the *frick* are you talking about? I didn't even know Norma Ferguson."

Talia shook her head. "Well, you sure couldn't prove it by me," she said. "I saw the way you glared at her the day of the contest, when she stepped onto that stage. Poor Norma. She looked quite frightened at your expression. 'There's bad blood there,' I told myself. Bad blood." She knew she was fishing—and being a drama queen. But if she didn't toss her line into the water, what chance did she have of catching anything?

Dylan's jaw dropped. "I—"

"Come on, Dylan. You wear your feelings on your face. An actor, you are not." Lord, where was she getting this stuff? "It was painfully obvious to anyone who saw you that you had some sort of beef with Norma." Talia shrugged and held out her palms, as if it were no business of hers. Which, technically, it wasn't—if you didn't count the fact that she wanted to find Norma's killer. "Well, anyway, whatever it was, I hope you told the police about it. They don't seem to like it when they have to find out these things from other sources. Trust me, I speak from experience."

Dylan swallowed. Talia would have sworn she saw beads of sweat populating his forehead. He took a sudden step forward, and a tiny squeak escaped her. She hated it when that happened. Made her look like a scaredy-cat.

"What's the matter with you? I was only going to show you something."

Now it was her turn to blush. "I know. I just . . . well . . ."

He swept past her, circling around to the rear of the old car he'd been leaning against. It was an odd-looking car, with a half window at the back that angled toward the trunk. In spite of the vehicle's obvious age, it appeared to be in great condition.

Dylan crooked a finger at her. "Come here," he said tightly. "Let me show you something."

Talia hesitated. Dylan wasn't very big, but he was wiry. And young. How easy would it be for him to open his trunk and shove her inside? Her folks would never see her again. Ryan would wonder why she'd never said good-bye. Bo would have to find a new home—

"Are you coming or not?" Dylan snapped at her. "I haven't got all day, you know. I have to get back to work."

Talia floated her gaze over the parking lot. Not a soul was in sight. On legs of clay, she hustled over to where Dylan was pointing at something on the back of the car.

"Look at this," he said crossly.

From where Talia stood, which was six or seven feet away, she couldn't see much of anything. "I'm not sure what I'm supposed to be seeing," she said, feeling a nerve jump in her neck.

"Yeah, no kidding. You'd need a telescope to see it from there." With a flick of his wrist, he signaled to her to move closer.

She inched closer to the car's rear bumper and her heart almost seized up.

"See that?" Dylan was saying, his finger aimed at a minuscule mark on the car's trunk. "Norma did it with her shoe in the parking lot that day. She was trying to shake out some dirt. I caught her slamming the heel of her sandal repeatedly against my car. It made this mark. Look!" he screeched.

Talia nodded robotically. If there was a mark made by Norma's sandal, it was smaller than a gnat because she definitely couldn't see it. What she could see, however, was the silver tag displaying the model of the car.

MERKUR.

"Just because it's an old car doesn't mean people can treat it like garbage," Dylan ranted on. He smoothed his hand lovingly over the rear bumper. "I have plans for this car. It needs to stay in pristine condition."

Talia nodded mechanically. "I . . . see your point," she managed to sputter. "That was thoughtless of Norma, wasn't it?" She moved slowly backward, pretending to get a better angle from which to view the scratch. She was actually trying to calculate how far it was to her Fiat in case she had to make a run for it.

All at once, Dylan slumped. He looked like a sad little boy whose favorite toy had gotten stomped to pieces. Talia was tempted to feel sorry for him, but she knew better than to let her guard down.

Somewhere during his tirade Dylan had dropped his e-cig. He glanced around, spotted it on the pavement behind the car, and then bent and scooped it up. "Okay, so the old bag ticked me off," he admitted. "You think I'd kill over something so stupid?"

"Of course not," Talia said, thinking that people had killed for less.

"So I've got a temper, okay? It's the way I've always been. If you grew up in my household, you'd have a temper, too."

Talia didn't really want to go there—not unless it was connected to the murder.

Dylan's gaze scraped the ground. "And don't think I don't know I'm the butt of jokes because I still live with my mother." He pointed a finger at Talia. "Let me tell you something. My mother would be living on the street if she didn't have me. All she's got left is me and my brother, and he's about as useful as a pimple on my backside." His voice grew hoarse. "If it wasn't for me, my mom's house would've been foreclosed on. I'm not living with her by choice. I'm living with her by necessity."

Oh, wow. Now Talia felt terrible. Dylan had some heavy-duty issues going on in his life.

Which led her to another thought—was Dylan feeling the pinch financially? If he was pitching in to help pay his mother's mortgage, it was no doubt putting a strain on his wallet. After all, how much could his job at the diner pay? Not a whole lot, Talia guessed. She paid her own employees as much as she could afford and gave out bonuses if they'd had a particularly good month. But she knew that most restaurateurs paid minimum wage, or only slightly more. Definitely not enough to live on, at least for most people. A lot of restaurant workers took second jobs just to keep their heads above water.

Her thoughts circled back to the prize money from the Steeltop Foods contest. After Crystal, Dylan was next in line for the award. What if, by some horrible twist of fate, Crystal was found guilty of murdering Norma? Would Dylan succeed to the prize and collect the twenty-five thousand dollars? Could that have motivated him to kill Norma and then sabotage Crystal? It seemed way too far-fetched to be an actual plan. Too many things would have to fall into place. She couldn't see it happening.

Unless Dylan was desperate.

"You look like you're in outer space," Dylan said testily.

Talia shook away her thoughts. "Sorry. I was thinking about all the things I have on my agenda today." She plastered on a smile, but Dylan wasn't fooled.

"Let me tell you something, lady." He pointed his e-cig at her. "You'd better not be accusing me of murder. Because if you are, you're gonna have a big problem. Get it?"

Dylan was clearly the one who didn't get it. Didn't he realize that he'd just issued the equivalent of a threat?

"I'm not accusing you of anything," Talia insisted, pulling her Fiat keys out of her purse. She gripped them tightly in one hand and took a tiny step backward. "And I'm sorry if it came out that way. I'm just so frustrated with all of this."

"Why do you even care?" he said with obvious disgust.

"I care," Talia said softly, "because an innocent woman is being accused of murder. And because my friend Lucas is still fighting for his life in the hospital." Technically true, because the killer was no doubt monitoring his progress.

"Yeah, I heard about that," Dylan said gruffly. "Tough

break for the kid. Still, it's got nothing to do with me." He shook his head. "Now I know why everyone calls you the nosy girl. Good-bye. I've said everything I have to say." He fled into the diner, the old wooden door slamming hard behind him.

Talia hurried toward her car, leaped into the driver's seat, and pulled the door shut. She locked it immediately, then dug her cell out of her purse.

Dylan drove a Merkur. It was a Ford, not a Mercury, but the names were too similar to ignore.

If only Talia could think of how to alert Detective Prescott about the car without looking like she'd been investigating.

Yeah, right. She'd never fool a sharpie like Patti Prescott. Maybe she ought to simply tell the truth and deal with the consequences. Just come out with it and take her lumps— whatever those were.

Although . . . the more she thought about it, there was more than one way to tell the truth. She wasn't under oath, right? She didn't have to tell the *whole* truth and nothing but the truth, did she? A partial truth, as long as it got the point across, would serve just as nicely.

She found Prescott's number and shot off a text.

Happened to see Dylan M taking a break in the diner prkg lot this morning when I stopped off for quick brkfst. Did you know he drives a MERKUR?

There. Not one single word was a lie. She hit Send before she could change her mind.

Oh, glory, who was she trying to fool? Prescott would know she'd been nosing around. But really, what could she do? That business about arresting her for interfering with an investigation was all a bluff.

She hoped.

That name, Merkur, kept racing through her head. It circled relentlessly, slamming to a stop only when it reached the obvious conclusion. Lucas must have seen Dylan's car that day, right before he was found in the parking lot with that gash on his head. Had he tried to identify his attacker? Was that why he'd muttered the word "mercury"? Had he really been trying to say "Merkur"?

Talia knew the police would probably call it circumstantial. And unless they had real evidence to tie Dylan to the crime—to both crimes—it would probably be dismissed as such.

Talia started her car and whipped out of the lot. She'd have to think about it later. Right now she had a business to run, hungry customers to feed.

The day was only just starting.

12

By ten o'clock Talia had done an entire morning's worth of work. Molly arrived early, eager to start peeling potatoes. She was such a joy to work with, Talia thought. Or she would be, if she didn't have guilt weighting her mind like an anvil.

"I wish we'd get some positive news on Lucas," Molly said, tossing a skinned potato into the vat of cold water. "I don't suppose you heard anything new?"

Talia shook her head. "No, nothing new." She cringed at the deception. Understanding the need for it was one thing. Pulling it off was another, especially when Lucas's friends and loved ones were suffering over what they thought was his grave condition.

"I went to the Mass for him last night." Molly sniffled. "Can you believe that blowhard Bruce Ferringer was there? He actually had the b—*gall* to glad-hand people as he was looking for a seat down front."

"Not surprising," Talia said wryly. "The man's about as self-centered as they get. I was there, too. I got there a little late, so I sat in the back."

"It's wonderful how everyone's pulling for Lucas," Molly went on, "but I'm just so terrified he'll stay in that coma."

Talia slid a tray of meatballs out of the oven and set them on the work counter to cool. "Call me an optimist, but something tells me Lucas is going to be okay. We just have to keep praying for him, Mol, and have faith in the medical profession."

"I know. It's just so hard." Molly gathered up the pile of potato peels she'd been collecting for the trash compactor. "Look at these peels. Wasted, every day. Did you ever think of making the French fries with the potato skins on?"

Talia smiled. "You trying to get out of peeling potatoes?"

"No, honestly! Look." She waved a slender hand over Mount Potato Peels. "A lot of restaurants serve fries with the skins on. They're delish!"

"I hear you, Molly. But Bea always did it the traditional way. I'm afraid our customers wouldn't like it if we changed. People get very set in their ways, you know."

Mired in the trauma of the past few days, Talia hadn't given Bea and Howie Lambert so much as a momentary thought. Now she remembered how much she missed them. They'd always brought such joy into her life—especially Bea, who had been like a second mom to her.

After operating the restaurant as a fish-and-chips shop for more than twenty years, the Lamberts had sold it to Talia last December. In January they'd bought a condo in Myrtle Beach and moved there shortly thereafter. From some of the e-mails she'd gotten from Bea, Talia sensed the sixtysomething woman was missing the Berkshires in the worst way. As was her hubby.

"What if we tried it for a week?" Molly suggested. She was still gawping at the pile of peels she'd set aside to wrap up for the trash.

"What . . . ? Oh, you mean, offer skinned or nonskinned fries? I don't know, Molly . . ."

Molly gave her a pleading puppy-dog look. "Pleeease. Let's just try it. Instead of a week, we'll pick one day. We'll announce it ahead of time, like we're having a contest." She snapped her vinyl-clad fingers. "Yesss! I can set up a ballot box, and people can vote for their preference."

One look at Molly's imploring expression, and Talia couldn't say no. "All right," she said with a sigh, "but you're in charge of setting it up *and* counting the ballots."

Molly grinned. "Thanks, Tal. This will be fun. And I promise to count ballots the fair way, not the Ferringer way. Hey, that sounded like poetry, didn't it?"

"Well, I wouldn't exactly call it 'Poe,' but it does have a certain appeal."

Molly rolled her eyes at the bad pun, then went over and gave Talia a quick hug. "I love working with you. I wish Mom could be as laid-back as you are."

"Don't judge her, Molly. She seems to have a lot on her mind these days. Plus, with Crystal being charged for Norma's murder, this has to be really tough on her."

Molly's face fell, as if she'd suddenly remembered Crystal's arrest. "I wonder if the police will let Mom open the shop today. They tore the place apart yesterday looking for evidence." She glanced over in the direction of the plaza. A solitary tear perched on her left eyelid.

"We need to give your mom all the moral support we can," Talia said softly. She plucked a massive pickle from the fridge and set it down on the cutting board.

"I know," Molly choked out. "But you need help, too, and I can't be in both places at once."

"You don't have to be. You've helped me so much already. If your mom needs you, you have to put her first."

Molly nodded and sniffled. "I know Crystal didn't do it. How could the cops be so blind? Why would she toss evidence into her own Dumpster?" She stamped her sandaled foot on the tile floor.

"I agree, Mol. You obviously heard the news about the rolling pin they found."

"Yeah, I heard it this morning. Mom turned ghostly white when she saw the newscast." Molly tossed another peeled spud into the pot. "I know the police are only doing their job. But sometimes it seems like they latch onto the first suspect they think they can pin the evidence on. Meanwhile, the real killer is laughing at them behind their clueless backs!"

Talia had thought the same thing on occasion. She had great respect for the police. For the most part they performed their jobs admirably. But she also knew that pressure from higher-ups made them want to solve cases quickly. How many times, lately, had she heard of people being released from prison after serving decades for a crime they hadn't committed? She knew of one case in particular that had hit too close to home.

She would not let that happen to Crystal.

Talia went back to making the homemade tartar sauce the eatery was known for. The recipe was one that Bea had toyed with and improved over the years. A careful dose of hot pepper sauce lent the condiment its tangy taste, and it was definitely a customer fave. She grabbed a sharp knife from the utensil drawer. With sure, quick movements, she began chopping the pickle into minuscule pieces.

Talia and Molly both looked up when the front door opened. Martha trudged into the dining area. Talia would have sworn her face was even grayer than it had been yesterday. As if to match her mood, she'd dressed in a short-sleeved charcoal gray tee and black capris.

"Hi, Martha," Talia said, a lump blossoming in her throat. "Why don't I get you a cup of coffee?"

"You don't have to wait on me. I'm not an invalid." Martha navigated through the opening next to the speckled blue counter and tossed her handbag in her locker. With her puffy red eyes, she looked one step away from bursting into a waterfall. She grabbed a blue apron from the shelf and slung it around her neck. "I'm sorry. I shouldn't have spoken to you that way."

Molly dropped her peeler and rushed over to Martha. She squeezed her in a fierce hug.

"Martha, we all understand," Talia said. She didn't mention that she'd seen her in church the prior evening. "But things are going to be okay. I feel it in my bones." *My lying bones*, she thought to herself.

It was killing her not to let Martha in on the secret. If only there were a way . . .

Talia breathed a sigh of relief when she turned the CLOSED sign to OPEN. Things got busy quickly, and before long they were frying up meals as fast as they could plunk them into the hot oil.

By two thirty, the lunch crunch had whittled down to only the occasional diner. Maybe this was a good time to spring a surprise visit on Handsome Harry.

Molly was sitting at the tiny table at the back of the kitchen, her thumbs moving over her cell phone at the speed of sound. In between gulps of root beer, she seemed to be searching frantically for something on one of her apps.

Martha was wiping down work spaces in the kitchen, her movements slow and robotic. She'd never been the bubbly type—it simply wasn't her personality. But she'd always been pleasant and quick with a humorous retort. It tore at Talia's heart to see her this way. She was a phantom of her former wonderful self.

Talia removed her apron and hung it in her locker. "Hey, guys, do you mind if I scoot out for a bit? There's someone in town I want to talk to. About . . . Sunday," she said, lowering her voice. "I shouldn't be gone long."

Martha turned, and her eyes flared. "If it's about the murder, you take as long as you want."

Molly waved a hand. "Yeah, sure, whatever. Go ahead. We can handle things." She peered at her phone. "When you get back, I want to show you something. Something I found on my Facebook page."

Talia nodded and scooted toward the door. "See you both in a bit."

Talia headed for the building on the main drag that housed Summers Realty. The sky was overcast. A light breeze blew from the west, cooling Talia's skin. After the unusually hot summer they'd been having, it was a welcome change.

Anxious to see if she would find Harry in the office, she quickened her pace as she approached Summers Realty. The realty company occupied a storefront space in an older brick building that housed a local dentist, along with a few other miscellaneous businesses.

Talia peeked through the glass door. She spied Harry Summers seated at a desk along the right-hand wall, his fingers tapping away at an old-fashioned keyboard. She'd just started to tug open the door when a reflection in the glass suddenly caught her attention. Across the street, in front of LaFleur Jewelers, a familiar figure emerged from the shop.

Jodie Ferringer.

Talia turned around to snag a peek at her. Wearing a stunning pair of hot pink capris and a gorgeous flowered halter, Jodie had a fancy gold bag with the jewelry store's logo dangling from her bejeweled wrist. She stopped briefly, dug into her designer purse, and whipped out her sunglasses. For one single moment, Talia was sure Jodie had spotted her staring across the street. Only to be polite, she waved at the stylishly dressed woman.

For a nanosecond, Jodie froze. Then she quickly looked away and strode off. Was she giving Talia the cold shoulder?

Duh. Of course she was. No doubt her husband had told her about his visit to Fry Me the evening before. He most certainly hadn't been happy when he'd left with his manager. Talia's refusal to host a campaign luncheon for him on a Sunday had definitely kicked his grits.

Talia opened the glass door and stepped inside the realty office. A bell over the door jangled.

Harry jerked his head up. His face brightened when he saw Talia. "Hey, this is a pleasant surprise. Come on in." He stood and ushered her over to the chair that rested adjacent to his desk. "I was just going over some of our listings to see if I can spice up the language a bit. When a property's been on the market too long, the ads start to sound stale, you know? It's a sure sign that no one's interested. So, I go over the listings periodically and play with the wording a bit." He flushed. "Sorry. I'm babbling. Can I get you something? A lemonade? We have some bottles in the back."

"Oh, no, thanks, Harry." She sat down in the proffered chair, her gaze drawn to his long-lashed green eyes and fabulous cheekbones. For sure he had killer looks. But that didn't mean he *was* a killer. Like Dylan, he was a wild card—a suspect, for lack of a better term, about whom she knew next to nothing.

"Then what can I do for you?" he asked. "I don't suppose you're looking for a condo? We have a lovely one that just came onto the market, in the new complex in Lenox. Oak flooring, Sub-Zero appliances, cathedral ceilings. And the owner is offering to pay the first three months' condo fees. Sandra is out showing a house right now, but she could take you there when she returns."

His sales pitch had devolved into a stream of babble. He was so eager to push the condo on her, Talia found herself feeling sorry for him. The real estate market had taken a fierce hit from the troubled economy. No doubt Summers Realty was feeling the pain.

"Actually," she explained, "I live in the bungalow that used to be my nana's. Right now it's perfect for me. And my cat," she added with a polite smile.

Harry sighed. "You're lucky. I love cats. I wish my wife did."

The more Talia talked to Harry, the more she liked him. For such a great-looking guy, he seemed so down-to-earth and unassuming.

"Harry, I really came by to thank you for rescuing my

clumsy butt, and my pies, at the festival on Sunday. I would have been *mortified* if they'd splattered all over the ground. Can you imagine how that would've made me look? People would think I was the biggest klutz ever!" She cringed inwardly at her grand exaggeration, hoping Harry wouldn't see straight through her.

He stared at her for a long moment, then sat back in his chair. "Well, I'm glad I was there to help," he said quietly.

After an awkward pause, Talia opened her purse. "Anyway," she said, "here's a little something for you. It's a gift certificate to Fry Me a Sliver. It doesn't expire, so you can use it anytime."

He stared at it for a moment and then shook his head. "Talia, there's really no need to do that."

"Honestly, I insist," she said, and pushed it toward his mouse pad.

"Thank you. That's very sweet of you." He took the envelope and tucked it under his keyboard. His face clouded. "Talia, I heard about what happened to the young man who works for you. I'm so sorry."

Talia fidgeted in her chair. "Thank you," she said. "We're all praying for him. He's always been a strong kid. I'm confident he's going to pull through this."

Kid. How could she call Lucas a kid? He'd turned twenty in the spring. She and Martha had presented him with a birthday cake from Peggy's Bakery—his favorite cherry cheesecake. The memory made a soft lump rise in her throat.

"My heart sank when I heard he was in critical condition," Harry went on. "Has . . . there been any word on his condition? Any improvement?"

Talia struggled to keep a passive look on her face. "I haven't heard anything new."

Harry nodded distractedly. He looked torn, as if he wanted to get something off his chest but wasn't sure if Talia was the right sounding board. "Well, um, that's too bad," he finally said. "Um, Talia, if you don't mind my changing the subject, can I share something with you?"

"Certainly," she said. *Share away!*

"My wife was furious with me when I entered that contest. And now, looking back, I wish I'd never done it. Imagine that poor old woman getting bashed on the head like that! Even the thought of it makes me shiver." He shuddered slightly, and Talia sensed that it wasn't just an act.

"Did you know Norma?" Talia asked him. Time to get down to the nitty-gritty.

Harry sat back in his chair. "No. I'd never met her before that day. Although I must say, she wasn't terribly friendly. After Thurman instructed us all to go to our respective cooking stations, I wished her good luck. She opened her mouth and looked at me as if I'd sprouted antlers." He let out a tiny laugh.

"Huh. That's strange."

"Another weird thing." He turned in his chair and leaned forward, his hands resting on his knees. "Remember how the six finalists were told to have their cooking supplies in their assigned stations *before* the start of the contest?"

Talia nodded. "That's right. The contest instructions were quite specific about that." She recalled stashing her things in her assigned station when she first arrived at the ball field. "I guess they wanted to be sure there wouldn't be any delays."

"Probably," Harry said. "Anyway, Norma apparently didn't get the memo, because she had to go out to her car to fetch her cooking supplies when the contest was about to start. The rest of us were heading toward our stations when we all heard kind of a dull clang come from behind. I turned and there was Norma, staring at the ground in dismay. She'd dropped her box, and her utensils and a casserole dish had fallen out. She looked so forlorn, standing there. Honestly, I felt so sorry for her."

Poor Norma, Talia mused. She'd seemed totally out of her comfort zone during the entire debacle. She couldn't even get her act together enough to put her things in her cooking station on time.

"A couple of us helped her repack her box," Harry said. "She didn't even bother to thank us. And when I offered to carry the box for her, she just gave me a nasty look and shook her head."

"I didn't know that," Talia said. "I must have already been in my own cooking station."

He nodded. "I think you were—you'd walked ahead of us. Anyway, it struck me then that Norma didn't seem very likable, poor soul." He shook his head sadly. "I guess she was one heckuva cook, though. Of course none of us got to sample the winning recipe. The whole contest was strange, in my opinion. It didn't seem very well planned. Not to me, anyway."

Talia bit her lip. "I tend to agree with that. But I suppose you have to cut them some slack. It was the first time they'd held the competition. They were probably testing the waters." She hesitated for a moment. If she was going to do a bit of prying, he'd given her the perfect segue. "Harry, why did your wife object to your entering?"

He blinked, and his handsome features went slack. "She says it's an embarrassment to her, having a husband who only cares about cooking. I can't help it—it's the single thing that gives my life joy. I love creating new recipes. She tells me all the time that I don't live up to my looks. I'm not *macho* enough for her. I'm not . . . forceful enough." His face reddened. "In her opinion, real men don't cook. It would be different if I owned a high-end restaurant, but I'm just a lowly slob who loves to play around in the kitchen." He saw Talia start to object and said, "In *her* lofty opinion, that is. When I pointed out that one of the other contestants was a man, she said Dylan was just a druggie and didn't count."

Sandra Summers was sounding more and more like a very disagreeable woman. But Talia was only hearing Harry's side of it, so she didn't want to be too quick to judge.

"Harry, I'm sorry to hear that," Talia said. "That really is so unfair." While his admission made her squirm with discomfort, she knew she had to press him for more.

"Over the years she's called me some horrible names," Harry continued. "Names that weren't very nice or appropriate."

Talia could only imagine. "Harry, you and I both know that some of the best chefs in the world are men."

He laughed, but his eyes darkened. "Tell that to a woman who subsists mostly on salads. One extra calorie a day and she bloats up like risen dough, so she doesn't bother eating food that has actual flavor." He picked at a corner of his desk calendar. "But . . . well, that wasn't the only reason she didn't want me to enter the contest."

"Oh?" Talia sat up straighter.

He glanced toward the door, then leaned closer to Talia. "The real reason was that she desperately wanted to work behind the scenes with Wesley Thurman. She volunteered to help him coordinate the contest. Told him she could be his 'local liaison.'" He rolled his eyes at the dropped ceiling.

"Really. So she'd met Wesley before?"

His eyes popped open wide. "Oh, she'd met him, all right. In high school he was her heartthrob. Even back then, she told me, he was a *real* man. The implication being that I'm not." Harry shook his head. "Sandra never got over him. She's still in love with him. I guess she always will be."

Talia's heart broke for the man. "Are you sure, Harry? Did she tell you that?"

His sad smile was the picture of heartbreak. "No, but she doesn't have to. Over the years she's told me in a thousand different ways."

Now Talia felt her own cheeks redden. She suddenly remembered seeing Sandra standing next to Wesley at the festival on Sunday, her hand on his arm. "So, did Wes Thurman accept her offer of help?"

"Not hardly," he said, a slight gleam in his eye. "When he heard that her husband—me—was a contestant, he quickly gave her a thumbs-down. Truthfully, I don't think he wanted her help. She'd sent him, like, a thousand e-mails and he ignored every single one."

Talia was willing to bet that Sandra blamed Harry for the fact that Wesley had rejected her offer of help.

Harry glanced toward the door again, then sat up in his chair. "Hey, Talia, can I show you something?" he said, a mischievous glint in his eye.

"Of course!"

His slender fingers tapped expertly over the keyboard. The site he was looking for came up within seconds. He turned the monitor so that Talia could see it. "So what do you think?" he said. His eyes practically danced.

On Harry's screen was a photo of a nicely maintained older home flanked by neatly trimmed shrubs. The two-story house was white, with trim and shutters painted a darling shade of lilac. A flower-lined walkway led to the front porch. On the lawn was a wooden sign that read HAINSLEY HOUSE.

Talia had seen it before. She just couldn't remember where. "This looks so familiar, Harry," Talia said. "But right now I can't place it."

He turned the monitor back so that it faced him, then hit a few more keys. "It's a restaurant on Elm Street in Pittsfield," he said. "The owner's been struggling to keep it going. His health is failing, and quite frankly, so is his menu. But look." He flipped the monitor so she could see it again. "Aren't these rooms to die for?"

Talia couldn't help smiling as Harry clicked through the photos. The dining rooms were small but cozy, with a hearth in each one. The floors were gleaming hardwood, and the walls had been papered with scenes that looked straight out of the French countryside.

"Fantabulous, isn't it?" he said.

Talia grinned. "It's beautiful, Harry. The decor is so warm and inviting. Are you . . . thinking of buying it?"

He nodded eagerly. "I want so desperately to have it, Talia. Oh, I have so many wonderful menu ideas. I'd like to offer a combo of new age concoctions and old American favorites. You know, a dish to please every palate? I've been talking to the owner, and he's keen on my taking it over. Poor fellow, he's losing business every day. At this point he just wants to unload it."

Talia wondered if Harry had too many stars in his eyes. Taking over a thriving restaurant was one thing, and even that didn't ensure success. But investing in an eatery that was floundering was, at best, a risky venture.

Oh, who was she to talk? When she took over Lambert's

Fish & Chips, she'd had no idea what she was doing. There were so many times, especially in the beginning, when she'd wondered if she'd made the right decision. But each time she doubted herself, she would think of Bea and Howie and their blind faith in her. She was determined to make the eatery work. Or die trying.

Talia couldn't help thinking that if Harry had won the contest, the award money would have been most timely. He desperately wanted to buy the failing restaurant. A twenty-five-thousand-dollar cash prize would have given him a tidy boost toward a down payment. Was that why he'd entered the competition?

"Now, it does need an electrical upgrade," Harry admitted, "but otherwise it's not in bad shape. And there's a huge parking lot in the back, which is a definite plus." His shoulders slumped. "The problem, of course, is the money." He waved a hand at the realty office's colorless walls. "These days we're not exactly rolling in it."

Talia couldn't help wondering if Harry had shared his vision with his overly critical wife. "Let's say the money weren't an issue, Harry," she said quietly. "Would Sandra be on board with it?"

"Oh, heavens, I wouldn't dream of telling any of this to Sandra. Not until it was a done deal."

Out front, a car door slammed. Talia craned her neck and peered through the storefront window. An older-model Grand Marquis, similar to the one her dad used to drive, had parked directly in front.

"Oh God, that's her." Harry wrung his hands in his lap. "Please don't tell her what we talked about, okay? She'd slice my head off and serve it up for brunch on a bed of parsley."

Talia gave him what she hoped was a reassuring smile. "No worries, Harry. My lips are sealed." How many times had she said *that* lately?

"And thanks for letting me vent, Talia. I don't normally have anyone to talk to, and—"

The glass door flew open, dispensing a whoosh of warm air. Sandra Summers sashayed into the office, her blond hair gelled into a helmet of soft curls. The style might have been attractive on her if it hadn't been so obviously glued to her head. She rubbed a hand over the back of her neck and then stopped short.

When she saw Talia, she pursed her lips into a lemon-sucking frown. And then, apparently rethinking her bad manners, she pasted on a smile so fake it looked as if she'd popped it out of one of those new 3-D printers.

"Well, I see we have a visitor," she said, shooting a dark look at Harry. "Not surprising, of course. Handsome Harry here always attracts the pretty ones." She tossed her purse onto an adjacent desk—her own, apparently—then plunked down into her swivel chair and kicked off her stylish pink espadrilles. "Of course, it's even better if the pretty one is looking to buy a house. I don't suppose you are?" she said.

Talia forced a pretend smile. Her intense dislike of the woman was growing by leaps and bounds, as her dad would say. "Sorry. I'm not looking to buy. Not right now, anyway."

All at once, a flash of recognition crossed Sandra's features. Her phony smile morphed into a scowl. "I just realized who you are. You're a friend of Audrey's, aren't you?"

"Guilty as charged," Talia said, rising from her chair. "And I'm afraid I have to leave. I only stopped by to thank Harry for picking me up off the ground on Sunday after I tripped." She didn't mention the gift certificate. The way he'd slipped it under his keyboard made her think he was hiding it from his wife.

Sandra's gaze flitted to her husband. "I see. Well, as I always tell people, Handsome Harry is nothing if not helpful. Why, you're the proverbial knight in shining armor, aren't you, dollface?"

His lips pressed tight, Harry shot a furious look at his wife. "Enough, Sandra."

"Too bad he saves all his amorous moves for the kitchen," Sandra went on, taunting him. "Did you ever know a man who was in love with his food processor?" She leaned toward Talia and in a rude stage whisper said, "I swear he uses it for everything, even—"

"Stop it!" Harry's face turned ketchup red. "Talia didn't come here to listen to your diatribes. For God's sake, Sandra, can't you leave our squabbles at home?"

Sandra's jaw dropped like an anchor thrown overboard. Talia would swear the woman blanched beneath the rosy glow of her makeup. Was that the first time Harry had ever spoken up to her?

Recovering quickly, Sandra drawled, "Well, well, well, it seems my little prince has developed a temper. That's *so* not you, Harry. You really need to find a new act."

It was Harry's turn to blanch. "And how would you know the real me?" he said softly. "You've never taken the time to care."

Sandra stared at him, openmouthed. Talia was more convinced than ever that he'd never spoken to his wife so bluntly. Until now.

"You might want to rethink your attitude, Harry," Sandra said in a low hiss. "I can easily run this place without you."

Well, isn't this charming? Talia thought. She'd managed

to wedge herself into a marital spat that was shaping up to be a doozy.

Harry shrank back into his chair as if he'd been slapped. Talia took that as her cue to make like a roadrunner and dash off.

"Listen, it was great seeing you both again," she half lied, inching toward the door. "I really do have to get back to the restaurant."

She waved a hurried good-bye to the pair and practically ran for the door. Even from outside she could hear their raised voices. She scurried along the sidewalk, back to the eatery.

If Sandra hadn't arrived when she had, Talia might have pried a little more information from Harry. It was clear that he craved a sympathetic ear. He'd been lugging around a lot of hurt for a very long time.

What the man had ever seen in a woman like Sandra, Talia couldn't begin to imagine.

As for Talia, if she never saw Sandra Summers again, it would be about fifty years too soon.

13

Talia glanced at her watch. She'd been gone about thirty-five minutes. She hated the idea of leaving Martha and Molly alone to run the eatery for much longer. Even though they were perfectly capable of handling customers on their own, if a slew of phone orders suddenly came in, the two would be swamped.

But while she had the chance, she wanted to pop into LaFleur Jewelers and chat with someone there. She wasn't sure why, but something told her she should check out the politician's wife. Judging from the way Jodie Ferringer outfitted herself, Talia had the feeling that she might be a regular at the pricey shop.

And besides, hadn't it seemed as if the well-heeled Jodie had been Norma's sole friend and supporter? Jodie was young, pretty, and fashionable. Norma was elderly, unsociable, and not terribly stylish. What did the two have in common? Could Jodie be Norma's long-lost love child?

Talia instantly scolded herself for such uncharitable thoughts. She hadn't really known Norma, had she? For all she knew, the woman could have been a kind, unselfish humanitarian with a heart of pure gold.

She looked both ways and then jogged across the street, narrowly missing getting clipped by a sedan that was in far too much of a hurry. Talia waved an apology at the driver—she *had* been jaywalking—but he'd been going too fast in downtown traffic. Talia could never understand drivers who treated a busy main thoroughfare as if it were their own personal drag strip.

Ignoring the driver's rude gesture, she opened the glass-front door to the jewelry store. A blast of cool air caressed her face, while a tiny bell jingled a tune to announce her arrival. Inside the shop, the soothing notes of a classical piece drifted from an invisible speaker. A delicate scent—lilacs?—perfumed the air.

On either side of the shop, the walls boasted gorgeous displays of figurines—behind locked, glass-front cases, of course. One entire section was dedicated to bridal accessories. The ambience was clearly designed to encourage browsing. At the rear of the store, a middle-aged woman with a raven black updo smiled brightly at Talia from behind a glass counter. Talia pasted on a smile of her own and strode up to the woman.

"And what may I help you with on this fine summer day?" the woman chirped, and folded her slender, manicured hands atop the sparkling glass display case.

Oh boy, Talia thought. Maybe she should have planned out what she was going to say before she'd barreled through the door! Adopting what she hoped was a wide-eyed look, she bounced her gaze all around, as if the sight of so many glimmering treasures was making her light-headed. "I . . . Oh my, you have such beautiful things in here," she gushed.

The woman's welcoming smile never faltered. "Yes, we surely do, don't we? Are you looking for something special? Perhaps I can offer some suggestions."

Talia pretended to think. She actually *was* thinking, but not about what to buy. Her gaze drifted to the collection of diamond rings in the case. One in particular had an antique setting that Talia thought was stunning. She couldn't help wondering if Ryan would present her with a diamond one day. Would he choose it himself, or would he suggest they choose it together? Would he—

"Miss?"

Talia looked up to find the woman staring at her. "I'm so sorry. My mind was lollygagging."

"That's perfectly okay. Easy to do in here." The woman grinned and stuck out a manicured hand. "I'm Kasey," she said, "with a 'K.'"

Talia smiled and accepted the woman's handshake but omitted giving her own name. "Nice to meet you, Kasey. I'm actually looking for, um, something for my mom. Her birthday is coming up." It was four months away, but Kasey with a K didn't need to know that.

"Well, then, you've come to the right place," Kasey said. "Did you have anything particular in mind?"

"You know, this is going to sound crazy, but . . . well, I saw Jodie Ferringer coming out of your store a short while ago. I knew she must have bought something, because she was carrying a pretty bag. I couldn't help wondering what she'd picked out. She has such exquisite taste, doesn't she?"

Talia tried to look awed by Jodie's fashion sense, hoping she didn't overplay it and sound like a ditz.

Kasey nodded, her smile shrinking only slightly. "Mrs. Ferringer has very specific, and extremely fine, tastes. Fortunately she has a husband who indulges her in her . . . little luxuries."

Little luxuries? That was a strange way to put it. Was it Talia's imagination, or was there a tiny hitch in the woman's tone?

"Oh, wow, she *is* lucky, isn't she?" Talia sighed as if she couldn't possibly imagine having such a generous husband. She put on what she imagined was a girlish grin. "I wonder if I'll ever be that lucky someday."

"Oh, I'm sure you will!" Back in full sales mode, Kasey beamed. "Now, about your mom's birthday. We just got in a new line of white gold earrings set with birthstones that are simply classic. What's her birth date? Is it this month?"

Talia felt two blotches of red staining her cheeks. "Oh, um . . . you know what?" She waved a hand at the woman. "My mom actually hates all that birthstone stuff." Okay, she was definitely headed to a hot place in the afterlife.

"I see," the woman said, her smile fading again. "What *does* she like, then?"

Talia crossed the fingers of her left hand against her thigh, then leaned over the counter and spoke in a conspiratorial tone. "Um, can you tell me what Jodie Ferringer bought? My mom *adores* everything that woman wears! Maybe if I got her something similar . . ." She let the thought drift off and ride the wave of fibbery.

Kasey looked down and smoothed her fingers over the glass. For one horrible moment, Talia was sure the woman was going to accuse her of being an outright phony . . . or a spy. She didn't know which would be worse.

"The item Mrs. Ferringer picked up," Kasey said quietly, "was a . . . special order. I can tell you that it contained rubies and was set in eighteen-karat gold."

"A special order?" Talia prompted, hoping Kasey might take the bait.

Kasey's eyes lit up. "Actually, it was a pendant, meant to be worn on chain." Kasey held up her hands, as if trying to describe it. "You had to see it, I guess, but it was a meat cleaver, about two inches long."

A meat cleaver? "Well, isn't that different?" Talia mused aloud. "Why a meat cleaver? I wonder."

"Oh, the woman loves to cook!" In a cryptic tone Kasey added, "Other than spending, it's her favorite hobby, if you know what I mean. That cleaver isn't just eighteen-karat gold. Each rivet on the handle is a ruby of the highest quality. Quite a spectacular piece, actually. We had it made especially for her."

Talia winced. "Sounds expensive."

Kasey nodded. "As you can imagine, it's not *in*expensive to create a custom-made piece. And it seems we've gotten off track," she said sharply. "Your mother's birthday . . . ?"

At that point Talia was trapped. After telling the poor woman all those whoppers, she'd feel terrible walking away empty-handed. And her mother's birthday would be coming up . . . eventually.

"You know, I was thinking," Talia said. "My mom has a little cairn terrier that she just adores. Do you have any charms like that?"

A smile reclaimed Kasey's expression. "My dear, you are in luck. We have a new supplier that specializes in charms of every dog breed imaginable. I'm almost certain we have the terrier you're looking for. Let me go out back and check our inventory." She turned and pulled a sales book from the counter behind her and plopped it on the glass display. "I'll be right back," she promised, with a cheery wink.

Talia heaved out a sigh of relief. If nothing else, she wouldn't have to agonize over her mom's birthday gift this year.

But she'd also gleaned a few tidbits about Jodie Ferringer. Her two "hobbies," as Kasey called them, were cooking and spending. Did that mean anything? Talia wasn't sure. The cooking part might explain why Jodie had bonded with Norma Ferguson. Maybe Norma had volunteered to work on Ferringer's campaign, met Jodie, and discovered their mutual love of all things culinary.

Talia peeked around the doorway through which Kasey had disappeared. She heard the sound of a key turning, then footsteps, but still no sign of Kasey.

Getting antsy now, Talia looked over at the sales pad Kasey had dumped on the counter. When she saw the name "J Ferringer" scribbled at the top, her heart sped up a beat. It was apparently the carbon copy of the original receipt. Reading upside down—something she'd never been good at—she could just barely make out the word *custom* followed by a bunch of other stuff, and the price of $149.00 plus tax.

Wait a minute. Was she seeing that right? Keeping one eye peeled for Kasey, she swiveled the sales pad around so that she could read it better.

Yup. The order was for a "custom cleaver with three 1.05-carat oval-cut rubies." The price was exactly as she'd first read it.

Something didn't add up. Only $149.00? For three rubies set in eighteen-karat gold? And custom-made, at that?

Talia had just started to turn the sales pad back to the way Kasey had left it when the woman suddenly reappeared from the back room.

"What are you doing?" Kasey said, her tone now laced with suspicion. She set the box she was holding onto the glass display case and snatched up the sales pad.

"Oh, gosh, I'm so sorry," Talia sputtered. "I . . . I couldn't help peeking when I saw the name 'Ferringer' on the sales slip. That custom-made piece sounded so gorgeous the way you described it that, um—"

"That you couldn't resist checking out the price?" Kasey's lips pressed themselves into a furious line.

Talia sagged. "Guilty as charged." *Again.* "I guess that's why people call me nosy." She smiled and offered up an apologetic shrug.

Kasey sucked in a breath of what must have been poisoned air, because the look she gave Talia was positively toxic. "Listen, miss," she said softly, "I don't know what your game is, but I have already said far too much about Mrs. Ferringer."

Talia instantly felt terrible for taking advantage of the woman. The last thing she wanted to do was get her in trouble. "Listen, I'm awfully sorry for prying," Talia said, picturing a horned demon setting the thermostat in her room on *roast.* "When I saw her name on the sales pad, I guess I couldn't resist a look-see."

"She is one of our best customers," Kasey went on, "and what she does with her money is her own affair."

"I totally agree," Talia said, trying to sound chastised.

Kasey gave her a crisp nod. "Okay, then. If you still want the terrier—"

"Oh, I do!"

She paid for the charm, which was really quite adorable, and chose a white gold chain from which to hang it. She was fairly sure her mom would love it, and it was one more future errand she could cross off her list.

After thanking Kasey profusely, she slunk out the door. She really needed to get back to Fry Me. Pausing on the sidewalk, she texted Martha and Molly, although she knew Martha would never read hers. On my way! Had a slight delay.

No prob! All good! Molly texted back.

Talia smiled and stuck her phone in her purse. She was going to miss Molly after she was back in school. Audrey was lucky to have such a terrific daughter, even if they did clash on occasion.

She hustled back to Fry Me, her thoughts bubbling. So many things had been clamoring for her attention that she'd pushed something else out of her mind. Ryan hadn't texted her this morning.

Nor had he called.

During the months they'd been seeing each other, he'd never failed to send her a text each morning. Usually it was along the lines of a Hey, Sunshine, have a great day! followed by XOXO and a row of pink hearts. Sometimes he added a little fish symbol. That always made her smile. And last night she hadn't gotten the row of pink hearts he always texted her before going to sleep. She'd checked her phone several times, but there'd been nothing.

A sick feeling gripped her. Something was up with Ryan. He'd never not kept in touch with her for this long a period. Even when he'd gotten a bad flu bug this past winter, he'd managed to send his daily text. His spelling had been off, but that was because he'd been horribly sick.

Talia couldn't help wondering if her propensity for stumbling onto murder victims had finally sent him over the edge. Even though she hadn't been the one to find poor Norma, she'd participated in the contest that had triggered the terrible events, including the attack on Lucas.

Maybe it was all too much for him. Maybe instead of three times being the charm, this time it was the ax.

Or maybe—

Or maybe Ryan had met someone else. Surely he met all sorts of people when he took his business trips for his company. Maybe he'd met a career-woman type, like Talia used to be. Maybe she was savvy, sophisticated, and suave, with a laugh that sounded like the tinkle of chimes.

Talia smacked herself lightly on the cheek. She was letting her imagination run crazy wild. This wasn't a soap opera—this was real life. She'd never doubted Ryan before, and she didn't intend to start now.

In a way, it was like that old song—whatever will be will be.

She didn't remember all the words, but she hummed the tune all the way back to Fry Me.

14

The eatery was quiet when Talia returned. Someone, probably Martha, had turned down the AC a smidge. Instead of the icy blast that normally blew from the vents, the air was pleasantly cool, like an early-autumn day.

Molly was wiping down the tables in the dining room. When she saw Talia, she scooped up her cleaning sponge, grabbed Talia's hand, and dragged her into the kitchen. "There's something I have to show you," she said urgently.

Her tone sent a jolt of dread through Talia. "Why? Is something wrong?"

"No. It's just—"

The eatery door burst open and Vivian Lavoie trotted in, a white straw bag slung over one plump shoulder.

"Lordy, but it's a nice day! I love it when it turns cool like this in the summer." She plopped her handbag onto a table and then dropped onto a chair behind it.

Molly had just nabbed her iPhone off the tiny table at the back of the kitchen when she saw Vivian come in. Her face fell with disappointment.

"Don't worry. We'll talk later," Talia whispered to Molly.

Molly pouted and tossed her phone back on the table, while Talia went out to greet the elderly woman.

When Talia had first met Vivian last year, she'd found her to be a terrible gossip. But over the last several months Vivian had become a regular customer, as well as a friend, and Talia had learned to cull the truth from the "almost" truth. Mostly Vivian was lonely and wanted a friendly ear.

"How are you doing, Viv? Can I get you a drink?" Talia asked her.

"Some of that luscious iced tea of yours would be delightful. And since I've sampled every fried treat on your menu, I think I'll go for the traditional fish and chips today." Her round face beamed as she glanced around. Clearly she was pleased by the absence of competing customers.

"I like it when it's quiet in here," Vivian said. "You and I get a chance to chat." She winked at Talia.

Talia poured an iced tea for Vivian and then sat down and made small talk with her while Molly whipped up her meal. Minutes later, Molly set the lined, cone-shaped serving dish down in front of Vivian. Talia couldn't help smiling at Molly's presentation. She'd nestled two pieces of crisp golden haddock atop a bed of "chips" that were fried to perfection. Next to that she set down a ramekin of coleslaw, a small container of tartar sauce, and a bottle of malt vinegar.

"Thank you, dear. That looks wonderful!" Vivian instantly grabbed the vinegar and sprinkled a hefty dose over her fish and her fries.

Talia sensed the woman wanted to sprinkle a few tidbits

of gossip, as well. She had that look in her eye that said, *Let's dish, shall we?* Molly, meanwhile, was giving Talia the high sign that she needed to talk to her.

"Excuse me, Vivian. I'll be right back."

Talia trailed Molly into the kitchen. "What did you want to show me?"

"I can't do it now, not until we're alone. In the meantime, do you mind if I run over to Queenie's Variety? I need to get a few, um, feminine supplies." Her cheeks flushed pink.

"Say no more. And take your time," Talia told her.

Molly looked relieved. "Thanks. Oh, and if you're wondering where Martha is, she walked down to the church to light a candle for Lucas."

Her throat tight, Talia nodded.

After Molly left, Talia noticed Vivian staring after her. The woman furrowed her gray eyebrows, as if trying to remember something.

Talia went back to Vivian's table. She knew it was bad form to plunk herself down with a customer while they ate. She also knew that this particular customer welcomed it. At home, Vivian probably ate most of her meals alone. She seemed to light up whenever Talia was able to join her.

"That's the Feldon girl, isn't it?" Vivian said, after swallowing a mouthful of fish.

Talia grinned. "Yes, that's Molly. She's helping out while Lucas is . . ." She stopped herself, unsure how to finish the sentence.

Vivian patted her hand. "I heard about your young helper. I'm so sorry, Talia. He seemed like such a dear boy to me."

Talia didn't like her referring to Lucas in the past tense. "He *is*, Vivian. He's a fine young man. We're all praying for his recovery."

"Oh yes, of course." She munched another mouthful, dabbed her napkin to her lips and then pressed it back into her lap. "You should have seen that girl's mother in high school. Pretty as can be, she was. But a quiet girl, not one of those flirty, floozy types that throw themselves at the boys."

"Wait," Talia said. "You knew Molly's mom when she was in high school?"

"Oh, of course I did. I worked in the cafeteria there for a number of years."

Talia pulled her chair a tad closer to the table. "Did you know Wes Thurman, too?"

Vivian nodded, her mouth full of coleslaw. She washed it down with a slug of iced tea. "He was one of the semi-popular boys. Didn't play football, but he starred on the track field."

Talia mulled this over. "So Wes was from here originally." She knew he was, but she wanted Vivian's take on it.

"Well, now, I wouldn't say he was *from* here originally. He and his folks—and a sister, I believe—originally came from somewhere in the Midwest, if my memory serves. The father got transferred up this way, and they ended up settling here in Wrensdale. In fact, if I recall correctly, Wesley didn't enter Wrensdale High until his senior year." Her face sagged. "He didn't seem to remember me, though. I guess I've aged a lot since I worked at the school."

"Are his folks living?"

Vivian shrugged. "Who knows? I really don't keep track of that sort of thing."

Talia bit off a smile. Vivian kept track of far more things than she admitted.

"I'll tell you, though"—Vivian's blue eyes flared—"that

other one was always after Wesley. A conniving piece of work, she was." She stabbed her fork a bit too forcefully into her last bite of haddock.

"Other one?" Talia prodded. She had a feeling she knew who it was.

Vivian gave a crisp little nod. "I'm talking about that Bosley girl—Sandra. If they handed out a prize for loosey-goosey morals, that woman would win, hands down."

"I'm guessing you mean Sandra Summers."

"That's the one. You should have seen the way she pursued Wes Thurman back then. Like a hound after a fox." She shook her head with disgust. "Of course, Norma made matters worse, always plotting against Audrey. I think she and Sandra were in cahoots to push Audrey out of the picture."

Out of the picture? Talia's pulse spiked. Vivian really was a font of information. The question was, how much of it was truth?

"Viv, are you saying that Audrey was after Wes, too?"

"It was more like Wesley was after her. Oh, you should have seen her back then! Pretty as an angel, that girl was. Sandra tried to pretend she wasn't jealous, but you could see it in those mean eyes of hers—how much she hated Audrey. She never gave up trying to sink her claws into Wesley."

She was still trying, Talia thought, if what Harry told her had any truth to it.

Still, it all sounded like a lot of teenage drama to Talia. She'd seen plenty of it back in her high school days, even had an unrequited crush or two of her own. What amazed her was how fresh everything was in Vivian's mind. The woman truly had the heart and soul of a premier gossip.

"Wesley didn't care a fig about that Sandra girl, though. At least, not in the beginning." Vivian spat the words as if Sandra had been a troll who lived under a bridge. "Back then, he only had eyes for Audrey. Sandra tried to pretend she wasn't jealous, but she wore her envy like a shawl."

"So Wesley wanted Audrey," Talia mused, almost to herself.

Vivian nodded. "Did he ever! Around the middle of that school year, I started seeing the two of them in the cafeteria line, chatting and giggling with each other. Pretty soon she was wearing his ring on a chain—you know the way the girls do."

Talia had never worn anyone's high school ring on a chain, but she knew plenty of girls who had. "It's symbolic, I guess. Like saying, 'He's mine, so don't even think about stealing him.'"

Vivian laughed. "I suppose you're right. It's like staking a claim on someone, isn't it?"

Talia nodded distractedly.

"But then, right around prom time—late May, as I recall— Wes dumped poor Audrey for Sandra. Oh, it was the talk of the school! Sandra strutted around like a cat who'd swallowed a bucket of cream, while poor Audrey looked absolutely devastated." Vivian shook her headful of gray curls.

Okay, this was getting interesting. Now things were beginning to make a modicum of sense. Audrey's resistance to attending the festival. Her anger at Crystal over entering the contest. The thought of seeing Wesley Thurman again must have triggered some horribly painful memories.

Vivian went on. "It was after Wesley dumped Audrey that she started seeing the Feldon boy. Such a nice, shy boy he was. Very smart, too. They had a whirlwind courtship and eloped the night of the prom. Their folks didn't even find out about it until after graduation. It wasn't even nine months later that Audrey and Brad had little Molly. Wesley, meanwhile, had gone off to college out west somewhere, and never came back."

Until now, Talia thought. And even though he'd never hooked up with Sandra, it was obvious from her recent behavior that she was still interested in him. Sandra's husband as much as said so, poor man.

Talia took a deep breath and then slowly let it out. Trying to process everything Vivian was saying made her head buzz like an electric saw. What gnawed at her like a flesh-eating virus was the fact that five of the players in the Steeltop Foods debacle—Wes, Norma, Sandra, Audrey, and Vivian—had all been at the high school, in one capacity or another, around the same time.

Way too coincidental for her liking. She leaned in toward Vivian. "I just want to be clear, Vivian. Did you and Norma work in the school cafeteria at the same time?"

Vivian balled up her used napkin. "We sure did, for a couple of years anyway. After a few years I had my fill of it and left. Norma stayed on longer. She's a tad younger than me. Mostly she washed dishes, but she also did some minor food prep." Vivian jerked her forefinger at the ceiling, as if she'd just remembered an important point. "Oh, and back then she was Norma Taylor. Her first husband was still living. After he died, Norma married Freddy Ferguson. He's long gone, too—rest his poor soul."

So back when Wes knew Norma, she was Norma Taylor. So when she entered the contest as Norma Ferguson, her name wouldn't have jingled any bells with him. He had no way of knowing she'd been widowed and remarried.

No wonder he'd looked so taken aback when she'd stepped onto that stage and faced him.

"I have to tell you, Talia," Vivian said, lowering her voice, "I couldn't have been more shocked when I heard Norma entered that contest. Back when I worked with her, she couldn't cook to save her life."

"What do you mean, she couldn't cook? She won the contest!"

Vivian nodded. "I know. She surely did. All I can think of is that she must have enrolled in some cooking classes after she quit working at the school. Probably got tired of everyone teasing her about the salt incident." She dropped this little tidbit with a sly smile.

"Salt incident? Okay, Viv—spill it. Tell me everything."

Vivian fluttered like a bird. *"Well,"* she said, "about two weeks after she started on the job, there was this one day when they put her in charge of the macaroni and cheese. Now, keep in mind, we prepared food in large batches. I'm sure you've seen those huge stainless-steel pans we used." She spread her hands almost a yard apart to indicate the size.

Talia nodded. She could easily picture the large rectangular pans filled with standard school fare such as lasagna, shepherd's pie, or macaroni and cheese. Most kids complained about the food, but Talia actually liked most of the stuff they served. She'd never admitted that, of course.

"I remember," Talia said. "Go on."

"Well, this one day she was making the cheese sauce for the macaroni, and someone reminded her to salt it. So Norma—get this—dumped an entire *cup* of salt into the mixture. A whole cup! Needless to say, the entire batch had to be tossed. The school had to pay for a huge order of pizza to be delivered that day. Norma took a lot of ribbing for that one."

"I can imagine," Talia said thoughtfully. Not that it made one iota of sense. How did a woman go from having zero cooking skills to winning the Steeltop Foods contest? "But she must've learned to cook in the meantime for her to win that contest, right?"

"I suppose she must have," Vivian agreed. "The school offers some excellent adult education courses, and I'm sure cooking is one of them. Norma probably enrolled and then realized she really enjoyed it. I mean, what else did the woman have in her life?"

What else, indeed? Unless her volunteer work for Bruce Ferringer's campaign kept her wildly fulfilled. Hard to imagine, but . . . to each her own.

"Did she ever have kids?" Talia asked her.

Vivian chewed her lip. "Yes, a son. I don't think he lives in town, though." She speared the last fry in her serving cone and held it aloft. "In a way I felt sorry for Norma. She never seemed to fit in, you know? No one liked her very much. I guess that's why she tried to bond with some of the kids." She popped the fry into her mouth.

Talia's brain was on overload. She needed to write all of this down so she could try to connect the dots. Norma's killer was in the mix somewhere—she felt sure of it.

"Vivian, did you tell any of this to the police?" Talia said.

"Why, yes. Well, most of it, at least, but that O'Donnell fellow just looked at me as if I was boring him with ancient history." She looked troubled. "It bothered me when they arrested poor Crystal. I really can't imagine that nice woman killing Norma. Can you?"

"She didn't kill Norma, Vivian. That's what worries

me—that they've stopped searching for the real killer. Whoever it is, he or she is still out there, and—"

A sudden thought stabbed her. If the police believed they now had the killer in custody, what was going to happen to Lucas?

"Is something wrong, Talia? You look like you've seen a ghost." Vivian's mouth hung open in a look of concern.

Talia scraped back her chair and rose. "I'm not sure, Vivian. But I really appreciate everything you've told me. It helps more than you know."

"Always glad to help," Vivian said. She hoisted her straw handbag off the table and dug out a hand-crocheted, zippered purse. After paying for her meal and leaving a small tip, she gave Talia an impulsive hug. "Take care, okay? Let me know if I can help with anything else."

"I will, Vivian. Thanks."

After Vivian left, Talia raced into the kitchen and dug her cell phone out of her locker. She called Detective Prescott's private number. "We have to talk," she said urgently. "Now."

15

Martha and Molly returned almost at the same time, one looking glummer than the other. Weariness had etched deep lines in Martha's face. Molly's normally neat French braid looked scraggly, as if she'd braided it days ago and slept on it for several nights.

It seemed to Talia that both employees had been gone for quite a while. Normally, she'd speak to them about their lateness. But Molly was only helping out as a temp, and Martha wore such a look of gloom that she didn't have the heart to even mention it.

In their absence, Talia had handled two take-out orders and served the lone customer—an elderly gent with long white braids and an iPod stuck in his extraordinarily large ear—sitting at the single table near the restroom. The man had chosen the deep-fried veggie sampler, a combo of green beans, cauliflower, and eggplant rounds coated in batter and deep-fried to a crisp golden brown. At the man's request, Talia had served the meal with salsa dip and a scoop of coleslaw.

"You make good food," the man complimented her.

Talia thanked him. She watched as he dug a wallet out of his pocket. Made from worn leather cobbled together with strands of red gimp, it looked as if he'd made it at summer camp when he was twelve. He pulled out a wrinkled twenty, smoothed it, and handed it to her.

She'd been behind the counter ringing up his tab when her two employees had returned. The man approached the counter, took his change, and whispered in a loud voice, "I left your tip on the table. Don't let someone snitch it, okay?"

"Thank you, sir. I won't." Talia smiled at him. "Please visit us again soon."

The man winked at Talia, his gaze lingering on Martha for a moment before he strolled toward the door.

"What's his problem?" Martha said in a sharp tone.

Talia stifled a giggle. "Isn't it entirely possible, Martha, that the man might have been flirting with you?"

Martha snorted. "Flirting, my—"

"Martha."

Molly grinned. "Talia's afraid you'll forget one of these days and say it in front of customers. Aren't you, Talia?"

"I'm *afraid*," Talia said carefully, "that once the horse is out of the barn, Martha's delightful turns of phrase might devolve into something a bit too spicy for some of our patrons."

"And she'll start cursing like a longshoreman!" Molly roared.

"None of that makes an ounce of sense," Martha said. She snatched her apron from her locker and looped it over her head. Molly darted over and tied it for her in the back.

"Martha, I'm sorry. We shouldn't be teasing you," Talia said. "Stop it, Molly."

Molly giggled.

Martha gave them both a grudging smirk. "Yeah, I know. I'm just a big ole pill these days, aren't I?"

Molly instantly sobered. "It's because of Lucas," she offered quietly. "None of us can stop thinking about him."

A horrible wave of guilt washed over Talia. She had the power to ease their pain, and yet she was sworn to keep her lips zipped. Any leak could put Lucas at risk, plus Detective Patti Prescott would kill her.

Neither prospect was very attractive.

While the two were gone, Talia had taken a few minutes to scribble out her thoughts on a chart she'd been working on. The chart reminded her of that silly flavor wheel—or whatever it was called—that she'd received from Steeltop Foods. On a sheet of paper she'd sketched a circle, with Norma's name in the center. She hadn't gotten very far with it, but tonight, after she got home, she planned to give it some serious attention.

"What's that?" Molly asked, noting Talia slip the sheet of paper into her locker.

"Nothing, really. Just some thoughts I was writing out."

Molly chewed her lip. "I still need to show you something." She glanced over at Martha, who was wiping down the already spotless worktable. "You know what? There's no reason I can't show Martha, too. I trust both of you."

Martha looked up. Talia signaled her toward the table at the back of the kitchen. "Have a seat. Molly has something to show us."

Her face pale, Molly fetched her iPad from her locker. "I brought in my iPad so you can see it better. It's harder to view it on my cell. Anyway, I don't know what to make of this, but it seriously creeps me out." After a few quick swipes of her nimble fingers, Molly brought up her Facebook page.

Talia glanced over at it. Molly's profile picture was a shot of Molly sporting a huge grin, her sunglasses propped atop her head. "Cute pic," Talia said.

"Thanks. Now look at this." She frowned at the iPad. "Like, seven months ago, this old dude tries to friend me. I thought, 'What a perv,' and deleted the request."

Talia peeked over her shoulder and gave a start. "Molly, that's Wesley Thurman."

"Yeah, it is," Molly said darkly.

Talia poked Molly's arm playfully. "Just for the record, he's only about five years older than I am."

Molly blushed. "Yeah, sorry. I didn't mean it that way."

"What does 'friend me' mean?" Martha asked. "I don't do Facebook."

"It just means that someone wants to be added to your list of"—Molly made air quotes with her fingers—"'friends' on your page. Some people think it's a big deal to have hundreds of friends, but I think it's just silly. I want my Facebook friends to be my real friends, too."

"I'm with you, Molly," Talia said. Her own Facebook page was still in its infancy. So far she had about five friends, and one of them was her dad. Plus, she hadn't taken the time to post very much, mostly because she didn't have much free time to spare.

"Plus, like I said," Molly continued, "I definitely don't want some weirdo I don't even know friending me. The world is scary enough without having strange men trying to be Facebook friends."

Things were getting curiouser, Talia thought. Why had

Thurman tried to friend Molly long before he set up the Steeltop Foods contest in Wrensdale? It wouldn't have been so strange if he'd tried to friend Audrey, but why Molly?

"So get this," Molly went on. "About three weeks ago, I got another friend request from him. His profile shows him as COO of Steeltop Foods, so I knew he had a connection to the contest Crystal was entering."

"Persistent, isn't he?" Martha said, her eyes hard with suspicion.

Molly swallowed. "I didn't want to tell Mom. I was afraid she'd think some lech was after me. But I did show it to Crystal." Her voice grew soft. "It's . . . so much easier to talk to her." Her fingers flitted over the iPad, and for a long moment she was silent.

"So what did Crystal think?" Talia finally asked her.

Molly heaved a sigh. "She's never had kids, so I don't think she has the same protective sensibilities a mom has. I'm not knocking her. Don't get me wrong. I just think she sees it from a different perspective, you know? She didn't think there was anything wrong with my friending him."

Talia chewed this over in her head. She had the feeling Molly didn't know that her mom and Wesley had been an "item" in high school. Even now, she wondered how much Audrey had told her daughter about Wes.

"So, Molly, did you friend him?" she asked her. The suspense was making her skin itch.

Molly slowly shook her head. "I just couldn't. Some little voice in my head told me to stay clear of the guy. I can't explain it—it was just something I felt. He gives me the willies." She gave a slight shudder.

"Always go with your gut," Martha said firmly. "Look, Molly, I'm not a mom, either, but I wouldn't have given you the advice Crystal did. My antennae would have been zinging in every direction if I knew he tried to friend you right before the contest." She clenched her fists in front of her on the table. "I wouldn't be shocked to find out that he killed Norma, or that he hurt Lucas. My advice is to stay away from him—on Facebook or otherwise."

Talia looked over at Martha and saw pain radiating from her eyes. Martha might never have been a mom, but before she'd moved to the Berkshires she'd had a foster child—a teenager named Dakota, whom she adored. After Martha lost her corporate job for speaking her mind, she gave up fostering. The child went to live with a family who could better care for her—in Martha's opinion anyway. Talia knew that a big part of Martha still mourned the loss.

Molly looked relieved. "Thanks. I'm glad I talked to you guys about it. But don't tell my mom, okay? She'll get all—"

"Cray-cray," Martha finished, giving them all a chuckle.

Talia glanced at the clock. It was already 3:52. Detective Prescott had agreed to meet her outside on the plaza at four o'clock on the dot.

"I have a quick errand to do," Talia informed them. "But first I have to whip up an order of deep-fried hot dogs to go."

"I'll do it!" Molly offered.

Talia smiled. "Great. That'll give me a few minutes to run to the restroom."

"Some mysterious meeting?" Molly said, a grin spreading over her face.

Talia coughed. Had Molly guessed something? "No, nothing too mysterious. Just a little information gathering, I guess you could call it."

Molly widened her eyes and gave Talia an exaggerated wink. "Gotcha."

Seven minutes later, Talia was sitting on one of the new stone benches outside on the plaza, her brown take-out bag resting beside her.

Thirteen past the hour. Prescott still hadn't arrived.

Talia had wanted to surprise the detective with her favorite take-out snack, but it now looked as if Prescott would be forced to eat the meal cold. If she ate it at all.

So much for good deeds.

The temp was in the high seventies today, but the graying clouds hinted at the wetter weather that was predicted to roll toward the Berkshires. By tomorrow they'd be getting a good soaking, along with some high winds.

In truth, Talia didn't mind taking a short breather outside on the cobblestone plaza. The Wrensdale Arcade had been designed to resemble a scene out of sixteenth-century England. The storefronts were Tudor in style, boasting herringbone brickwork painted white, its upper sections graced with cross timberwork. It really did resemble something out of Dickens, Talia thought. She'd never been to the UK herself, but from the photos she'd seen of the tiny villages that dotted the countryside, she could easily believe she was there right at this very moment.

She sighed. Thinking of England reminded her of how much she missed Bea and Howie Lambert, the couple from whom she'd bought the eatery. The Lamberts had emigrated from the UK when they were both in their thirties, and during the 1990s they'd opened the fish-and-chips shop on the plaza.

When Talia was in high school, Bea had been like a second mom to her. Talia's folks had been going through a rough patch back then, and her home life had turned topsy-turvy. She couldn't imagine how she would have coped if Bea and Howie hadn't given her the after-school job at the eatery. She'd loved the job and quickly caught on to the various tasks—and perils—associated with frying food. *Ah, luv, you've got vegetable oil flowing through your veins,* Bea used to tease her.

Last year, when Talia had met her landlord for the first time, she'd asked him why he'd never set out some benches on the plaza, where shoppers could rest their feet or meet up with friends. He'd taken her suggestion to heart. One day early in the summer, four curved granite benches mysteriously arrived, along with a landscaping truck. Three men jumped off the truck and immediately went to work. By the end of the day, the benches formed a square of sorts around a central area in which clusters of colorful petunias had been planted. The town even agreed to place a covered trash bin nearby, and it was emptied on a regular schedule.

Talia turned slightly on the bench she was occupying. She gazed at the gorgeous petunias that had spread out over the summer in a lush wave. Pinks and purples with a touch of white graced the area that would soon be replaced, she surmised, by an explosion of mums. For now she was happy to cling to the last shreds of summer.

When she swung back around, she saw Detective Patti Prescott jogging toward her.

"Hey," Prescott said, blowing out a breath. "Sorry to be late. Got stuck behind a minor accident over on Oriole Road."

"Not a problem," Talia said. She held up the brown bag, as if she were teasing a dog with a bone. "Except that your deep-fried mini-dogs are now cold."

"Whoa. Didn't expect that." Prescott relieved her of the take-out bag. "Never fear. I'll zap these bad boys as soon as I get home. It'll be the best supper I've had all week." She opened the bag and peeked inside. "So, what's the big yank? Why did you need to see me so urgently? And by the way, I got your text. We need to talk about that, too."

Talia glanced around to be sure no one could hear them. Deeming the coast clear, she patted the bench next to her. "Sit, so we can talk. I started thinking about Crystal's arrest, and then I started thinking of *you-know-who* in the hospital."

"You're not supposed to talk about that," Prescott said tightly. "Do you even listen—"

"I listen, and I heard you," Talia said, trying to keep her cool. "But now that you have someone in custody for the murder—the wrong person, I might add—what are you going to do about that . . . *other* person?"

Prescott stared at her for a moment, those nutmeg-colored eyes homing in on her like twin high beams. Then she spoke in a low, quiet voice. "So far, status quo. But it's not easy to maintain this kind of deception, Talia. The hospital wants to release him as soon as they can. He's well enough to—"

"You can't let them do that, Patti! The real killer is still out there. If Lucas gets sent home, he won't be safe."

Prescott cast a swift glance around their immediate surroundings, then met Talia's gaze with her own. "Listen to me. I agree that the evidence against Crystal is extremely shaky. But at least one of her prints, plus a partial, is on that rolling pin, and she can't explain why. The DA is willing to run with what we've got. There's a lot of pressure on him right now to get this case solved quickly. Elections are coming up, and, like most politicians, the man has delusions of grandeur. Plus, think about it, Talia—three murders in one year, in the same little town? It's not sitting well with a lot of people." She paused to let that sink in.

Talia looked off into the distance, her brain trawling for an answer. "What about Dylan's car?" she said pointedly. "Don't you think it's the least bit weird?"

Prescott had the decency to look mildly embarrassed. "We missed that," she said, with a sheepish look. "That's what I get for trusting the task to the wrong officer. The guy's a patrolman, but he wants to get promoted to detective in the worst way. Passed the written test by the skin of his teeth." She shook her head. "As far as I'm concerned, he'll make detective after I'm elected pope."

"So what you're saying is, the cop you assigned to the job of finding out who drove what messed up."

Prescott nodded. "Big-time. All he gave me were the manufacturers, not the models. It didn't even occur to me that Lucas might have seen a Merkur. Who even drives one of those clunkers anymore? That model goes back to the late 1980s. It was one of Ford's biggest flops. I'm amazed there's one still on the road."

"Well, this one is not only on the road," Talia said, "but it's in very fine condition. Dylan obviously takes good care of it."

Prescott narrowed her gaze at Talia. "Seems you caught more than a glimpse of it," she said. "You want to tell me what really went down? Why were you at the diner in the first place?"

Averting her eyes from Prescott's piercing stare, Talia brushed an imaginary speck off the stone bench. "I stopped there, if you must know, to have breakfast. I don't get much of a chance to buy groceries these days, and my cupboard was pretty bare."

"Yes, Mother Hubbard, I'll just bet it was."

"Anyway, after I sampled one of Dylan's delicious cinnamon chip muffins, I decided it might be a good time to have a chat with him."

Prescott's expression went taut. "Go on."

Feeling a blush creep up her neck, Talia told the detective everything, from the radio blasting in Norma's cooking station, to the nearly invisible mark on Dylan's trunk that had sent him into such a snit.

For one long, scary moment Prescott was silent. She looked toward the main drag, then back at Talia. "First off," she said in a frighteningly soft voice, "you did exactly what I warned you not to do."

"I know," Talia said, feeling the skin on her neck itch. Prescott's tone reminded her of her own mom's the time she tried to get oil paint—which she'd been forbidden to use without supervision—out of her clothes by adding a cup of pure bleach to an entire load of laundry. Needless to say, Talia wasn't allowed to do laundry again for quite a long time. Or to do any painting without a terry-cloth smock.

"That said, I understand why you did it." Prescott smiled, and her features softened. Did Talia detect a hint of camaraderie in those nutmeg-colored eyes?

Talia swallowed back a batch of tears that threatened to erupt. "Thank you for understanding," she said. "For what it's worth, Dylan also said he has plans for the car. What he meant by that, I have no idea."

Prescott tapped her fingers on the stone bench. Talia could almost see the conflicting thoughts chasing one another around in her head.

"This is all making me hungry," Prescott said. She unraveled the paper bag Talia had given her and stuck her hand inside. A moment later, her mouth was filled with a miniature relish-coated, deep-fried hot dog in a cold toasted bun.

"How can you eat that cold?" Talia said, with a slight laugh.

Prescott chewed for a minute and then swallowed. "In my job, I eat cold food all the time. I'm used to it. I'll take it over starving anytime."

Talia let her finish her mini-dog and then got serious. "Patti, this isn't just about Lucas. Someone killed that poor old woman, and he—or she—can't be allowed to get away with it!"

The detective wiped crumbs from her fingers with the napkin Talia had provided. "He, or she, will not get away with it, Talia. But it's none of your business, and it's not your case to solve."

"But you've got the wrong person in custody!"

Prescott blew out a breath. "It seems we're at an impasse, aren't we? The old 'rock meets a hard place.'"

"Which one are you?" Talia said tartly. Then something popped to the surface of her brain. "Detective, did you check to see if Crystal could've sold the rolling pin to Norma? I know she sells them in the shop. I've seen them."

"Gee willikers! I never thought of that. But then, I've been so busy lately, what with spending my days eating bonbons and watching old episodes of *Cagney and Lacey* . . ."

"All right, all right. You don't have to go all sarcastic on me." Talia glared at her.

"To answer your question, of course we checked into it," Prescott said. "Norma's rolling pin was an old wooden thing, practically an antique. There was no way it came from the Fork and Dish. But there was something else. I didn't mention this before, but a pot holder that belonged to Norma was in the Dumpster, too—one of those woven types kids make on a loom."

"How do you know it was Norma's?" Talia asked.

"We know because we did our job, Talia." The edge to Prescott's tone was growing sharper. "We spoke to one of her neighbors, a woman she played Bingo with on occasion. The neighbor recognized the pot holder immediately, because her little grandkid sold it to Norma for some fund-raiser at the school."

Talia felt tears of frustration pushing at her eyelids. There was no way Crystal committed that awful murder, or hurt Lucas. There had to be another explanation—if only she could figure out what it was.

"I hear what you're saying, Detective, but what about Lucas? He's going to be in danger if you let the hospital release him."

Prescott shook her head. "Maybe I can stall them. The new info on McPhee's car will be helpful. Maybe we can delay Lucas's release for at least another day. But you need to cease and desist—do you hear me?"

"I hear you perfectly well," Talia said. She heard the ire filtering into her tone, but she didn't care anymore. "I just want to say one more thing. This murder is far from being solved. If Crystal is brought to trial, it will be a travesty. Because the real killer will still be out there, only he'll be doing the dance of joy."

"He?"

Talia fidgeted. Was she so sure the killer was a man? "I'm using the word in a generic sense, but yes, the killer could well be a 'he.'" Especially if it was Wesley Thurman. "Have you looked any more into Wesley Thurman's background?" Talia asked her. "I mean, showing up in town after being away for a couple of decades? Are you telling me he couldn't have had that ridiculous contest anyplace else?"

"You mean the ridiculous contest you entered?"

"Yes, I mean that one." Not for the first time, Talia wished she had a time machine that would let her roll back the clock. She would have told Crystal, "Thanks, but no, thanks," when she asked her to enter the contest. "I'm sorry now that I ever got involved in it."

"Too late for that."

Yeah, no kidding. "So what are you doing about Thurman?" Talia prodded her.

Patti snatched up her take-out bag and rose from the granite bench. "This conversation is over. Thanks for the goodies, Talia. And remember, I'll be watching you."

16

Not long after Talia's contentious conversation with Prescott, a thin, elderly woman with limp gray hair and a world-weary expression toddled in to Fry Me. In her hands she clutched a white plastic purse, the type that snapped open at the top. For several moments she stood stock-still. Her gaze roamed around the dining area, as if she didn't quite know where she was.

Noticing her hesitation, Talia grabbed a menu from the counter and went over to greet her. "Hello. Welcome to Fry Me a Sliver. Would you care to be seated?"

"Um . . . yes, I think I would," the woman said. She brightened a little when she saw the wall clock. "I like that octopus. It's quite the ticket, isn't it?"

Talia smiled. "Thank you. It's a unique piece. Our local potter made it for us."

Something about the woman's face was familiar, but

Talia couldn't quite think why. She was pretty sure she'd never met her before.

Talia escorted her over to one of the smaller tables. Upon closer inspection, she saw that the woman's skinny legs were clad in worn-looking cotton slacks. A ring of grime lined the collar of her short-sleeved pink blouse. The entire ensemble was in desperate need of an iron. A faint odor of sweat emanated from the woman. Not necessarily unpleasant, just . . . stale.

"I simply love fish and chips," the woman said, plunking her purse onto an adjacent chair. She barely glanced at the menu before pushing it aside. "By the way, I'm Ethel Anderson. I'm Norma Ferguson's sister."

Talia stifled a gasp. This was Norma's sister? No wonder she looked familiar.

All at once, Talia felt two sets of probing eyes from the kitchen turn and gawk at her.

"Oh my," Talia said softly. She touched the woman lightly on the shoulder. "Ms. Anderson, I'm Talia Marby. I was one of the contestants that day. I am so very sorry for your loss. I knew Norma only briefly, but—"

But what? Talia felt suddenly tongue-tied. She really hadn't known Norma at all. Plus, with the exception of Jodie Ferringer, she couldn't recall anyone having said a kind word about her.

"Actually, it's *Mrs.* Anderson," Ethel said, saving Talia from having to conjure up a polite response. "Not that it matters. I've been widowed for a very long time."

Talia nodded at the chair next to Ethel's. "May I join you for a moment?"

"Of course, dear. Although I wouldn't mind if you'd ask one of your cooks"—she peeked over the counter at Martha and Molly—"to make an order of fish and chips for me. And bring me a glass of lemonade."

Talia grinned. When it came to hunger, the woman was not shy.

Molly signaled that she would get started right away. Martha scooted over to the table with a tall glass of pink lemonade.

"Thank you." Ethel leaned in for a long sip. "My, that's good. The police called me yesterday," she went on. "They've released Norma's body for burial. I drove down from Maine to make the funeral arrangements. And to clean out her apartment. The landlord who owns her building wants to lease the space as quickly as possible. Affordable apartments are very much in demand, I understand."

The seed of an idea burrowed itself in Talia's mind. "So . . . the police said it was okay to clean out her apartment?" She tried to sound casual, but her nerves were jumping over one another.

"Oh, yes. They said they'd already gone through everything and wouldn't need to get in there again."

"Did they find anything, um, helpful?" Talia prodded. "I mean, anything that might help solve their case?"

Ethel scratched at a red welt on her forearm. It looked like a mosquito bite. "No. In fact they said they pretty much found nothing. Norma didn't even own a computer."

Talia tried to put on a blank face. "Have you been to Norma's apartment yet?"

Ethel took another, smaller sip from her straw. "I've been there since this morning, packing boxes," she said. "I managed to get all of her personal effects boxed up and loaded into my van. The landlord is going to take most of her clothes to the Salvation Army for me, bless him. I certainly have no use for them. I only took a break when I realized how hungry

I was. Norma didn't have much to eat in her kitchen except for frozen things, so I decided to drive into town and find something hot and fresh. I'm so glad I stopped in here."

"I am, too," Talia said. "I'm sure it was hard to, you know, have to go through your sister's things."

Ethel nodded. "Oh, it was. And whew, was it ever hot in there! All closed up like that for days." She waved a hand in front of her face, as if the apartment heat had followed her. "I turned on the air-conditioning unit, but it took a long time for it to kick in. Thank heaven her apartment is on the basement level. I don't know as I could have climbed stairs in that stuffy building." She shook her head. "My poor old legs. I'm afraid I've already worn them out, what with packing all those boxes. And I still have to pack up the kitchen."

Talia heard Martha clear her throat. Loudly.

"Mrs. Anderson—"

"Please. Call me Ethel," she insisted. She swung her attention toward Molly, who was approaching the table with Ethel's meal. "Oh my, doesn't that look delicious?"

Molly set the serving cone on the table, along with flatware, napkins, and condiments. She gave Ethel a tiny salute and then hurried back into the kitchen.

"I'll let you enjoy your lunch in peace," Talia said, rising. "But after you're through, why don't I follow you over to Norma's apartment? I can help you pack up the kitchen. Between the two of us, I'll bet we can get it done a lot faster."

Ethel stabbed a fork into a chunk of steaming fried haddock. Holding it aloft, she said, "You would do that for me?"

"Of course," Talia said, smiling. "It's really too much for one person to handle. Besides, I'm reasonably strong for my size."

Talia could almost hear Martha's cackle.

Tears welled in Ethel's eyes. "What a kind soul you are. I will accept your offer."

I'm also sneaky, Talia thought, feeling a smidge guilty. But she wasn't going to pass up this one opportunity to have a look around Norma's apartment.

While Ethel ate, Talia snagged a few peeks at her from the kitchen. The woman was devouring her fish and chips as if she hadn't eaten in days, poor lady. She must have been ravenous from having to pack up Norma's belongings.

Talia was itching to get into Norma's apartment, but she worked patiently in the kitchen, preparing a fresh batch of the eatery's tangy tartar sauce. She didn't want Ethel to feel rushed.

"Are you sure you're going to be okay if I leave again?" Talia whispered to Martha and Molly. "It's going to start getting busy."

"Yes!" they hissed at her in unison.

"You'll never get another chance like this," Martha added in a hushed tone. "Go. Do your thing over there. Play detective."

Exactly what Prescott had ordered her not to do.

But really, she told herself, how could she let this poor elderly woman pack up the kitchen by herself? Norma had to be an excellent cook to have won that contest. Which meant that her kitchen cabinets and drawers were probably jam-packed with stuff. It would be callous of Talia not to offer Ethel some help packing it all up, wouldn't it? And if Patti Prescott didn't like it? Well, then, she could just stuff it into a suitcase and toss it off a cliff.

For about the hundredth time, Talia glanced over at Ethel. This time the serving cone looked empty, and Ethel was wiping her fingers with a napkin. She waved at Talia, signaling that she was going to use the restroom.

Talia removed her apron and stuffed it into her locker. "Wish me luck," she murmured to her coworkers. "But don't get your hopes up. Remember—Ethel said the police didn't find much of anything."

"Yeah, but you're a lot nosier than the police, remember?" Martha pointed out. "They're doing a job to get a paycheck. You're fighting for justice."

"Martha!"

She shrugged. "I speak the truth. What can I say?"

Talia knew Martha meant it as an upside-down compliment. But she had to wonder—were people really calling her the nosy girl, like Dylan said?

Ethel walked over to the counter, white plastic purse clasped in her hands. She unsnapped it and pulled out her wallet.

"No, Ethel, your meal is on me," Talia said. "After everything you've been through, it's the least I can do."

"But—" Ethel's eyes grew misty again. She closed her purse. "Thank you," she murmured. "It'll help cover the cost of gas back to Maine. I guess we should go, then. I parked in that lot down the block. Parking is terrible in this town, isn't it?"

"It's not easy," Talia said, smiling at her. "Luckily, I'm parked in the same lot. I'll follow you in my car."

Talia followed Ethel's Nissan SUV into the parking lot of 379 Elm. The building itself was a three-story brick affair, its dreary front yard unadorned with flowers or shrubs of any sort. *Bare-bones,* Talia thought. Couldn't someone have planted a few bushes, or some impatiens? Maybe snipped the weeds that were curling around the cracks in the front walk?

Ethel pulled her SUV into a handicapped space near the

back entrance. Talia swung her Fiat into a slot farther back, then hopped out and followed Ethel into the building.

"Technically, I'm not supposed to be in the handicap spot," Ethel explained. "But the landlord said I could use it while I load up Norma's things."

They made their way down three stairs to the basement level and then along a dimly lit hallway. Ethel stopped about halfway to the end, scrounged through her purse, and pulled out Norma's key. She shot an apologetic look in Talia's direction and then opened the door.

The fusty odor was the first thing to assault Talia's senses. Rank humidity ran a close second. They stepped into a narrow vestibule that led to the galley-style kitchen. Ethel flipped up the light switch on the inside wall. A weak overhead light in the kitchen snapped on.

Talia tried not to wince as she skimmed her gaze around the kitchen. The cabinets were faux mahogany, with handles hanging loose every which way. A couple of screws and a screwdriver could have fixed them, but apparently no one had cared enough to bother.

The fridge and electric oven were avocado green, a color that had come into vogue during the 1970s. She couldn't imagine how Norma had ever prepared her delicious concoctions with such outdated appliances. A coffee-splattered microwave sat on the counter next to the tiny stainless-steel sink.

"Sorry it's so warm in here," Ethel said. "I had the AC unit running all morning and decided to give it a rest. Now I'm sorry I did."

"Don't worry about it, Ethel. With the two of us working together, we can probably finish up in no time."

Next to the kitchen was a combination dining/living area.

The worn sculptured carpet was—no surprise—a faded avocado green. The table where Norma had eaten her meals looked more like a patio table scrounged from a yard sale than a real dining table. Two dented metal chairs sat askew in front of it. The rest of the furnishings could have been a snapshot from a 1950s sitcom, well . . . except for the wide-screen television that rested against one wall. Talia wondered if Norma had had to save up all her pennies to buy such a pricey item.

"I left some more boxes in the bedroom," Ethel said, and pattered off to fetch them.

Talia quickly reached up and opened the cabinets above the sink. She wanted to do a bit of snooping before Ethel returned.

A few odd drinking glasses and some chipped mugs rested on the shelves. In the taller cabinets over the counter, a variety of store-brand soup cans and cereal boxes rested among jars of pears and peaches. Not much else was there, except for a box of powdered milk.

The next cabinet yielded a horde of snacks. Salty crackers, pretzels, and bags of hard candy filled the shelves to the brim.

Talia looked around to see if Norma had any canisters. She spotted only one—a dented metal thing that said SUGAR on the front. Wouldn't Norma have needed flour to make her flaky-top chicken stew?

Talia peeked around to see if Ethel was anywhere in sight, then clicked open the door to the microwave. The inside was splattered with stains. She quietly closed the door.

Ethel was still in the bedroom. Talia could hear her fussing with boxes and muttering to herself. She took the opportunity to investigate the fridge.

If Patti Prescott thought Mother Hubbard's cupboards were bare, she should take a gander inside Norma's refrigerator. With the exception of a plastic pitcher filled with what looked to be iced tea, there was almost nothing in there. A bag of white rice was tucked away on the top shelf. There wasn't even a single egg or a container of milk. How did she bake or cook? Or had she run out of eggs the day of the contest and hadn't gotten the chance to buy more? The vegetable bin had a few limp carrots and a package of bologna, half gone.

The mother lode was in the freezer. Stacks of frozen dinners were piled inside. Meat loaf with gravy looked to be the favorite, with mac and cheese the first runner-up.

Talia closed the fridge just as Ethel returned, dragging four empty liquor boxes. "I got these at the package store down the street. Not very large, but they're clean."

"Why don't I start with the lower cabinets?" Talia suggested.

"You're so sweet for doing this," Ethel said. She plucked two mismatched glasses from the cabinet over the sink. "I'll pour us each a glass of iced tea. That's one thing Norma always kept plenty of."

The iced tea came from the plastic pitcher in the fridge. Ethel took a sip from her own glass and smacked her lips. "Awfully sweet," she said. "That's how Norma liked it, I guess. I hope you like yours without milk. Norma's milk had gone sour and I had to throw it out."

Talia never used milk in hot tea, let alone iced tea. She sipped from her glass gingerly, and her lips instantly puckered. She had to resist the urge to spit the stuff into the sink. Norma must have dumped a pound of sugar into the pitcher! She remembered Vivian's story about the salt. Apparently Norma seasoned her concoctions with a heavy hand.

"It's fine, Ethel." Talia set her glass down on the counter and went to work.

The contents of the lower cabinets proved equally puzzling. *Scant* didn't begin to describe the state of Norma's cookware. It didn't take long for Talia to pack up the two scratched saucepans, an ancient Dutch oven, and a couple of casserole dishes. Talia set aside the first box, then knelt and tugged open the drawer beneath the oven. A large frying pan and its smaller mate nested in there, along with an old-fashioned egg beater. She stuck them in box number two and closed the drawer.

"Ethel, did the police remove any of Norma's cookware from the apartment?" Talia asked. "It doesn't seem as if there's very much left here."

Ethel swiped her brow. "Why, no. Not that I'm aware of. As I said, they told me they pretty much found nothing."

Pretty much found nothing.

That was exactly the way Talia would have described it.

"Did the police say they'd removed anything else? You know, for evidence?"

Ethel slowly shook her head. "No. At least they didn't mention it. Quite honestly, I'm not sure I'd know if they *did* take anything. I hadn't visited my sister in years."

Ethel finished emptying the utensil drawers, a task that took only about five minutes. A thin sheen of sweat coated her forehead. She swiped it away with the back of her hand. "Do you mind if we sit for a few, Talia? I'm getting a bit light-headed from the heat."

Talia instantly went over and took Ethel's arm. She led her to one of the metal chairs in the dining/living room. "Be right back," she said, and returned with Ethel's half-filled iced tea glass.

Talia sat down next to the woman. Ethel had to be at least eighty. Didn't she have anyone who could have driven here with her? Helped her with the unpleasant task of packing up her sister's things? She reached over and squeezed Ethel's hand. "This is really hard for you, isn't it? I wish there was more I could do."

"Oh my, you've already done so much. Why, even Norma's own son didn't want to help me! Said his mother never owned anything decent and that I shouldn't waste my time. His advice was to call a junk collector and pay them to haul everything out of here." Ethel wrapped her bony fingers around her glass. "You must be wondering why my sister lived like this, Talia. Without even a decent piece of furniture."

"Ethel, it doesn't matter if someone doesn't have a lot of nice things," Talia said. "If she was happy here, that's all that counts."

For a long moment Ethel was silent. Then, very quietly, she said, "I don't think my sister was ever happy. If she had been, she wouldn't have tried to make everyone else's lives so miserable."

Ethel's defeated tone tore at Talia's heart. She felt so bad for this woman. Again she wondered why someone, maybe another family member or a friend, hadn't offered to pitch in and help her remove her sister's belongings from this dreary apartment. Why did an elderly woman have to do this alone?

"Ethel, you mentioned that Norma had a son?" Talia asked her.

Ethel nodded and took a sip from her glass. "Yes, my nephew, Bill Taylor. He works at one of the gas stations on the turnpike. For now, at least." She pursed her lips. "Never keeps any job for very long. We'll see how long this one lasts."

"Bill Taylor. So his dad would've been Norma's first husband?"

"That's right. His father was such a nice man. Nothing to look at, but he had a generous heart. I think Norma married him just to say she had a husband. She treated him like something you'd step in on the sidewalk, if you know what I mean."

Talia shook her head. "That's a shame," she said. "Did he die fairly young?"

"Late forties," Ethel said. "Poor man was killed by a snowplow. He trekked out in a horrible storm one night to get Norma some ice cream, and the plow driver didn't see him. Killed him instantly."

"Oh, wow," Talia said softly. "That's so sad. Norma must have been devastated."

Ethel shrugged. "Not so's you'd notice. Norma took care of Norma, I'm afraid. That's just the way she was. It was only seven months later she hooked up with Freddy Ferguson. Freddy owned a machine shop in Housatonic. I suspect Norma thought he had a bit of money, but she got fooled. He was in debt up to his eyeballs. He died a pauper and left Norma with nothing."

Talia pressed her fingers to her forehead. Even with the wall unit in the living room chugging out cool air, the room felt stifling. "So she pretty much subsisted on Social Security?"

"That's right," Ethel confirmed.

"What about her son, Bill? Did he get along with his mom? I mean, were they close?"

Ethel pushed her glass aside and stared off into the distance. "No, they weren't. Norma never paid much attention to him when he was growing up. I guess he just returned the favor."

"I'm so sorry, Ethel. It all sounds very sad."

Ethel scratched at the mosquito bite on her arm. "I don't like talking about my sister this way, Talia. Especially now that she's gone. But the fact is, she was a bitter, unhappy woman. She was so jealous of anyone who might have a better life than she did that she always looked for ways to cause trouble."

It sounded to Talia as if Norma could have had a better life if she'd wanted to. She'd apparently enjoyed being contrary. In the end, what had she gained?

A cosh on the head, that's what. It was a word Talia had read once in an Agatha Christie book. She thought it fit the manner of Norma's death perfectly.

Talia now understood why no one had cheered for Norma at the festival. The woman probably had zero friends. Well, except for Jodie Ferringer. And that was a strange friendship, too, Talia mused. She couldn't imagine what the two had in common. With the exception of the obvious—their goal of getting Bruce Ferringer elected—why had a fashion maven like Jodie bonded with her?

"Talia," Ethel said, "I understand it was the young man who worked for you who was attacked the day Norma was killed. I am so very sorry."

Talia felt her stomach roll. Even though she knew Lucas was recovering, the thought that he could easily have died still stuck with her, like the gluey aftermath of a nightmare. "Thank you," she said. "We're all praying for him."

"I will, too," Ethel said, crossing herself. She looked around the apartment with a weary expression. "I think we should get out of here now. Why don't we start packing up my car? I've kept you here long enough, and you have a lovely restaurant to run."

"I was happy to do it," Talia said, relieved that Ethel suggested leaving. Martha and Molly had been alone for more than an hour, and it was the time of day when things started getting super busy at Fry Me. "Ethel, can I ask you one last question?" They headed into the kitchen.

"Of course you can."

"Did Norma get involved much in political issues? It seemed she was very keen on helping Bruce Ferringer get elected."

Ethel smiled and shook her head. "Funny that you ask. Not once have I ever known Norma to care about what was going on in the world—except to herself." Her smile faded to a puzzled frown. "Lately, when I talked to her, though, I had the impression she was feeling remorse about some of the things she'd done. Like the way she'd ignored her own son when he needed her most. Things like that."

"Did you chat with her often?" Talia lifted one of the boxes and set it on the scarred counter.

"No, and only when I called her. Except—" Ethel stared off at a spot on the wall. "Well, she did call me one day, about three weeks ago. That was odd in itself, her calling me. I chalked it up to her feeling lonely in her old age. Anyway, I was so glad she reached out to me. We chatted for quite a while, much longer than usual. And it might've been my imagination, but I sensed that something had her very worried."

"Did she say what it was?" Whatever had been troubling Norma could have been the reason someone wanted to get rid of her!

"No, she didn't." Ethel tapped a finger to her lips. "I didn't press her. I figured she'd tell me eventually, if she wanted to. And then . . ." Ethel's eyes grew damp again.

"I know," Talia said gently.

Talia looked around one last time. She couldn't wrap her

brain around the sparseness of Norma's kitchen. "Ethel, what are you doing about the furniture? That TV looks pretty new."

"The landlord is taking care of that for me. I told him he could do what he liked with it. I certainly have no use for it, and I don't need another television."

"Well, then," Talia said, "I guess we're done packing."

They loaded two of the boxes into Ethel's SUV and then returned for the others. That's as when Talia saw something she hadn't noticed before. On the side of Norma's fridge, a glossy brochure had been tacked there beneath a GO FAR WITH FERRINGER magnet.

"Before I get on the road, I want to use the bathroom one more time," Ethel said. She trudged off in that direction.

Talia slipped the brochure out from under the magnet. She briefly read it over, shaking her head at the clichéd rhetoric Ferringer was famous for spouting. How anyone could think of voting for him boggled her mind.

She flipped over the brochure. The word *volunteer* jumped out at her in huge black letters. Beneath that, someone had scribbled a phone number. Only seven numbers, so she assumed it was the local area code of the Berkshires.

"There, that's better," Ethel said, stepping back into the kitchen. She smoothed her pink blouse over her waist.

Talia held up the brochure. "Ethel, do you mind if I take this? It was stuck on the side of Norma's fridge."

Ethel squinted hard at it, then waved a wrinkled hand. "Of course, dear. I certainly have no use for it."

The last trip to Ethel's SUV completed, Talia bade her good-bye. "If there's anything else you need, please give me a call at the eatery," she told the elder woman. "It's my home away from home."

Ethel's faded eyes watered. "You've been so kind, dear. I haven't set a date yet for Norma's memorial service, but I do hope you'll attend."

"Of course I will," Talia said. "Once you know the details, give me a ring."

Talia watched Ethel start her SUV and back slowly out of the parking spot. With a final wave at Talia, Ethel drove out of the lot.

Talia couldn't help feeling bad for the woman, who now had to drive her sister's belongings all the way to Maine. She wondered if Ethel was going to keep Norma's meager possessions, or if she'd donate most of them to charity.

She hopped inside her Fiat. Before starting her engine, she wanted to call the contact number someone had scribbled on the Ferringer brochure.

Talia fished her cell out of her purse and punched in the numbers. After four rings, it sounded as if someone had answered. The person on the other end remained silent, but Talia was almost positive that he—or she—was listening. "Hello? Is someone there?" she said.

Nothing. Whoever answered had disconnected.

Exasperated, Talia blew a stray lock of hair out of her eye. She tried the number again. Her heart jumped when a voice said sharply, "Jodie here."

Jodie. It was Jodie Ferringer! The only time Talia had really talked to her was in the parking lot after Norma's murder. At the time Jodie had been blubbering so much that it was tough to tell what her regular voice actually sounded like. But, Talia reasoned, this had to be her personal cell number. And it was handwritten on the brochure.

Think fast, Talia told herself, *before she hangs up again.*

"Oh, I am, like, *really* sorry," Talia said, injecting a slight giggle into her tone. "I thought this was the . . . gas station."

Once again, Jodie cut off the call.

Talia shoved her phone back into her purse and started her engine, her head whirling with questions. Why did Norma have Jodie Ferringer's private cell number? Did Jodie hand it out willy-nilly to anyone who expressed an interest in volunteering?

Maybe.

But the way Jodie had cheered for Norma at the competition on Sunday had been way over-the-top. Something strange had been going on between those two. If only Talia could dredge up an excuse to have a little chat with Jodie Ferringer.

Of course she could always feign an interest in volunteering to work on her husband's campaign. Jodie would leap at a chance to talk to her then.

Ugh. There was no way. Talia wouldn't have been able to fake any enthusiasm for that. Especially after the kerfuffle she'd had with the big phony over having a campaign strategy meeting at the eatery on a Sunday.

Talia breathed out a sigh and checked her texts. There was nothing from Molly, which she took as a good sign. If anything had been wrong, Molly would have let her know right away.

She headed back toward Fry Me, aware that something else was bugging her. Something she'd shoved to the back of her mind but that now crawled to the surface.

Ryan hadn't called or texted her since early last evening. And she still hadn't gotten the anticipated row of pink hearts that he texted every night, without fail, before shutting off his light. She knew he was on an important business trip—a trip he'd been dreading—but it wasn't like him to be incommunicado.

An invisible weight pressed on her chest, making her insides ache. She tried to push it out of her mind, but it was useless.

By now Martha and Molly were probably elbow-deep in food orders and cursing her for being absent.

Pink hearts or no pink hearts, she had to get back to work.

17

By the time Talia turned onto the main drag, the image of the pink hearts was still marching in her head. Distracted, she almost failed to see the portly woman who was crossing the street against the light. By the time the woman entered Talia's line of vision, she was barely ten feet away. Talia braked hard, her heart pounding, and simultaneously flicked a glance at her rearview mirror. Fortunately, the car behind her was pretty far back, so she'd avoided what might have been a nasty fender bender.

The other side of the street was a different story. The woman, who looked quite elderly, had dropped one of her bags. Two oranges rolled toward the centerline. A blue package of a familiar brand of chocolate-chip cookies rested on the pavement. The poor woman was valiantly trying to stuff everything back inside the plastic grocery bag.

Talia checked her mirror again, then zipped her little car

over to the side of the road. Luckily, she spied a space just big enough for her Fiat—which was probably why it was unoccupied. She parked, shoved the gearshift into Park, and shut off her engine.

Swiftly, she exited the car. She held up one hand to stop the traffic coming at her, then hustled over to help the woman. By that time, the traffic on the opposite side was backed up several car lengths. Horns honked. Someone yelled a rather rude suggestion, which he embellished with an even ruder gesture.

Talia glared at the driver who'd flashed the wayward finger. What on earth was the matter with people?

She bent low and scooped up the two oranges, which had strayed in different directions. Together, she and the woman managed to get everything stowed back into the shopping bag. Talia snatched up both bags, looped her arm through the elder woman's, and propelled her over to the sidewalk.

"Are you okay?" Talia asked her.

The woman's faded brown eyes filled with tears. "Yes . . . I think so."

A car screeched past them, and the driver yelled, "Next time use the crosswalk, lady!"

"It really was my fault." The woman's voice rattled. "I should have crossed at the light, but my legs are just so worn-out from lugging these bags. The police won't let my daughter leave the house, and I wanted to make her something special."

The police? Then it dawned on Talia. She slipped her arm around the woman's sagging shoulders. "Are you Crystal's mom?" she asked kindly.

"Yes, I'm Rhonda Flaherty." The woman's eyes, which were a tad bloodshot, widened. "Do you know my daughter?"

"I do," Talia said. She explained how she knew Crystal and then said, "Mrs. Flaherty, I know that your daughter did not kill or harm anyone. The police are way off base on this one. I'm trying hard to figure out who had reason to want Norma Ferguson dead." Talia looked around, afraid that Detective Prescott might be spying on her. She wouldn't be surprised if the woman had installed webcams on drones programmed to follow her. "Can I drive you home?"

"Oh, that would be wonderful," the woman said. Her shoulders drooped in relief. "Are you sure you have time?"

Talia did not have time. She'd already been away from Fry Me longer than she should have. "Of course I'm sure. Stay right here. I'll swing my car around and pick you up."

Once inside her Fiat, Talia sent a quick text to Molly: Slight delay. Be back shortly.

Rhonda and Crystal lived in a two-family home on Posner Street, only three town blocks behind the Wrensdale Arcade. Talia knew Crystal usually walked to and from work, and now she understood why. At best, it was a ten-minute stroll, at least for someone relatively fit. For an elderly woman hauling two bags laden with groceries, the walk probably felt five miles long.

A bag in each hand, Talia followed Rhonda up the wide front steps. One of her dad's favorite songs—"Help Me, Rhonda"—flitted through her head. She shook it away, remembering that it was Rhonda who needed help.

Fortunately, Rhonda and Crystal's apartment was on the first level. A narrow foyer covered by a worn runner led directly into a parlor that was surprisingly open and airy. The furnishings were tidy but worn. In one corner sat a Bentwood rocker, a colorful crocheted afghan folded over its cane seat. In the bay window that faced the street hung a lush philodendron. A small fan resting on a side table sent a weak stream of air wafting through the room.

Rhonda heaved a sigh and waved a hand at the hardwood floor. "You can leave those anywhere," she said. "I'll put it all away later. I do appreciate you helping me, though."

Talia glanced around the parlor. She wondered where Crystal was.

She'd learned from a customer that Crystal had been released after the preliminary hearing, but with a tracking device on her ankle. Burdened with that, how far away could she be? Talia set down the two plastic grocery bags and then peeked into one of them. Among its contents were a container of cottage cheese and a package of hot dogs. "Are you sure I can't at least put away the perishables for you?" she asked Rhonda.

Rhonda looked relieved. She plopped down onto a flowered armchair and pushed a loose strand of straggly gray hair behind her ear. "Actually, that would be helpful," she said. She pointed in the general direction of the kitchen.

The kitchen was another surprise. With all the newfangled appliances Crystal sold at the Fork and Dish, not one of them seemed to have found its way into the 1960s-style kitchen. Talia would swear the two-slot toaster resting on the counter had been around since Neil Armstrong first walked on the moon. A set of vintage metal canisters rested against the backboard, and the sink was the old-style porcelain white. Still, the kitchen had a homey, comfortable feel. It reminded her of the kitchen in her own bungalow, which still had the original glass-front cupboards.

Talia opened the fridge—a throwback to the eighties—and put away all the perishable items. The rest she set on the kitchen table.

"Mom?" The shaky voice came from the end of the hallway adjacent to the parlor.

Talia knew that voice—it was Crystal's. Should she say anything? Let Crystal know she was there?

All at once, Crystal emerged from her bedroom. Her feet bare, she started down the hallway toward the kitchen. Her face was milky white and her blond hair uncombed. Her hands were free of rings, which for some reason made Talia's heart hurt. Clad in a flowered muumuu that floated around her ankles, she frowned when she saw Talia. Talia noticed she wasn't wearing her usual spectacles. Had Crystal even recognized her?

"Talia? Is that you? What are you doing here?"

For a split second, Talia's mind went blank. Then she sputtered, "Oh, I, um—"

"She helped me get the groceries home, dear," Rhonda said. She'd sidled quietly into the kitchen and now stood behind Talia.

"Yes, I saw your mom struggling with her grocery bags and offered to drive her home." Talia knew she sounded defensive, but the way Crystal was looking at her made chills creep up her arms.

With that, Crystal burst into tears. "Oh God, this is all so embarrassing. You coming here, seeing me like this . . ." She sucked in a long, drawn-out sob, then swiped at her eyes with one bare wrist.

Talia rushed to her friend, enveloping her in a fierce hug. "Crystal, you have nothing to be embarrassed about. This is all a mistake, you'll see. The police will find the real killer."

Crystal sniveled against Talia's shoulder. Feeling helpless, Talia patted her on the back. "This will be over before we know it. I promise."

Finally, Crystal pulled away. "I wish I could believe that. Look what they've done to me! Do you know how humiliating this is?" She stuck out one leg. The muumuu fell away, revealing a black device strapped to her ankle. It looked like an oversized watch.

The tracking device.

Oh God. Poor Crystal, having to wear that awful thing. Still, it had to be better than sitting in a jail cell.

"Crystal, I'm so sorry for all of this," Talia said. "It's obvious that someone set you up to take the fall for Norma's murder." She wanted to add that she was trying to find the real killer, but Crystal tended to blab. What if she inadvertently blurted to Detective Prescott that Talia was on the case? Talia would be in hot water up to her eyeballs—that's what.

Rhonda stepped gingerly between them and laid one plump arm on Talia's shoulder. "I'm going to make some tea. Can you stay for a few minutes, Talia?"

She really needed to get back. But here was another opportunity to question Crystal a bit more. Not that she thought for a minute that Crystal was guilty. Maybe, though, she could glean something about her financial situation.

Talia stole a glance at her watch. She'd been playing hooky on and off all day, leaving Martha and Molly in charge. She knew they didn't mind, though. Plus, staying busy helped keep their minds off Lucas. Molly, in particular, would be thrilled to know that she was visiting Crystal. She sent off another quick text—this one only to Molly. Molly texted her a thumbs-up, and she stuck her phone back in her purse.

"Okay, but only for a quick cup," she said.

Rhonda had the tea set up in no time, seating them all at the kitchen table.

Crystal dumped three sugars into her mug and stirred. "It's so good to see a friendly face," she said, and then scowled. "That district attorney didn't waste any time getting a warrant to investigate my finances. 'Course he's running for reelection, so he wants to pin the murder on someone fast and make it stick. He doesn't care if he ruins an innocent person's life!" Her brown eyes filled with tears.

"Crystal's ex is to blame for all of this," Rhonda said quietly. "He left my daughter high and dry. Drained their joint savings account and took off with some floozy he met on a business trip. Horrible man," she added. "Be glad you didn't know him."

Some floozy he met on a business trip. The words made Talia's stomach flip over.

"When I sold my diamond engagement ring," Crystal told her, "I found out it was nowhere near as valuable as I originally thought. He'd bought it at some discount place, not at the Jewelers Building in Boston like he told me. One of the diamonds was real, but the smaller ones were all zircons."

Talia mulled that over, then crossed her fingers under the table. "Crystal, I don't mean to be nosy, but . . . if you were in bad financial shape, how did you get enough money to go into business with Audrey?"

Crystal flushed. She and her mother exchanged glances. "Mom gave me most of it. She still gets a small pension from the paper mill in Pittsfield, where she worked before she retired. She also had some savings. Not a fortune, but it was a big help."

Rhonda nodded, her eyes filled with sadness.

Crystal reached over and grasped her mother's hand. "But it was a loan, not a gift, wasn't it, Mom? I had every intention of paying it back once Audrey and I got the business up and running!"

"Are you and Audrey equal partners?" Talia asked.

"Sixty-forty," Crystal said, her voice wilting. "She put in the larger portion, which was a stretch for her, too. She's helping put Molly through UMass. Her husband died quite young, as you probably know. Kept saying he was going to get life insurance but never got around to it. And then—" She flipped her hand over.

Talia took a sip of her tea. It had a citrusy taste, which she liked. "What did Audrey do before you teamed up to open the Fork and Dish?"

Crystal gave her a wry smile, and a flicker of her old self flashed in her eyes. "Believe it or not, she was a teacher. Seventh-grade history, to be exact. She got so burned out, though. Frankly, I don't think she was cut out for teaching. Audrey sometimes lacks . . . patience."

Interesting. So Audrey owned the larger half of the business. Which, Talia assumed, gave her more power in the decision-making process.

"What about you, Crystal? What did you do before you opened the store?"

"I was a paralegal," she said. "When the economy tanked, my law firm cut back on expenses." She pointed a finger at her chest. "I was the expense they cut back on."

"I'm sorry to hear that."

"After that, I could only get part-time work." She gave Rhonda a grateful smile. "Thank God for Mom, who let me move in after my slug of an ex and I unloaded our house. I'm still paying off the shortage on the promissory note. He, naturally, took off for parts unknown with his bimbo. But we both signed the note, so now I'm stuck. Jointly and sever-ally, they call it."

Well, Talia thought, that helped to explain Crystal's financial troubles. "Crystal, I'm curious," she said. "How did you and Audrey meet? Have you been friends a long time?"

"No, and it's a funny story," Crystal said. Talia was glad to see that she was starting to perk up a little. "I love to cook, as you know, but one night I decided to treat Mom to dinner at this new Italian restaurant in Pittsfield. The server was nice enough, and the place was sort of pretty, but when they brought our food, we nearly fainted. It was absolutely awful. Abominable!"

Rhonda nodded. "The cheese in the lasagna was like glue. I'd never tasted anything like it." She wrinkled her nose at the memory. "Plus, the bread was stale, and they served it with margarine instead of butter or flavored oil. It was all downhill from there."

"So, anyway," Crystal went on, "there was a woman and her daughter seated at the table next to us. They must have heard us talking about the food, because the woman leaned over and said, 'Is it us, or is this the worst Italian food you've ever eaten?'"

Talia smiled. "Was it Audrey?"

"It was," Crystal said. "She was with Molly. After we all paid for that horrid meal, we asked if they'd like to join us for an ice cream. We all went out together, indulged in some decadent sundaes, and the rest, I guess, is history."

"You and Audrey hit it off, I take it?" Talia drained her mug.

"Oh my, we sure did. I realized right away how smart

she was. And how creative. Not much of a cook, but she had business savvy, you know? Together, I thought we made a pretty good team."

"You did," Talia confirmed. "Do," she added quickly.

Crystal's face hardened and her eyes flared. "Then that stupid announcement came in the mail about the Steeltop Foods competition. Audrey was against my entering it from the get-go. She said I'd be competing against some of our own customers and it wouldn't look right. I should have listened to her," Crystal choked out.

"You couldn't have known there'd be a murder, Crystal, so stop beating up on yourself. You love to cook! You had every right to enter that contest." Talia stopped short of saying she wished she'd never entered it herself.

Crystal sucked in a noisy sniffle. "The police claim my prints are on that rolling pin, but I'm telling you, it's impossible!"

Talia bit her lip. That one had her baffled. A similar thing had happened to her friend Bea when she was accused of murdering a fellow shopkeeper. The physical evidence had pointed straight at Bea, but after the real murderer was caught, it all made a crazy kind of sense.

Talia's suspicions ducked back to Wesley Thurman. He was the cause of all this. Had he murdered Norma? Had he come close to killing Lucas in his attempt to cover up his crime? His hatred for Norma could not have been more obvious. Yet the police seemed to be treating him like some sort of celebrity.

And what about Dylan and his Merkur? Had the police even brought him in for questioning?

These thoughts were zipping through her head when she realized that it was nearly six o'clock. She thanked Rhonda for her hospitality, gave Crystal another hug, and then left.

After she hopped inside her Fiat and buckled up, she pulled out her cell again. No text from Ryan. No missed calls.

For some reason, her mind rolled backward to Chet—the man she'd bailed on when she left her job in Boston a year ago. They'd been semi-engaged, without any real plans for a wedding, or even for a formal engagement. Chet was a successful financial planner—a sociable go-getter—who'd pushed Talia to accept a job she felt sure she'd hate. After she quit, and he failed to support her decision, she knew the relationship had to end. But here was the kicker: weeks after she left and returned to the Berkshires, she learned that all along he'd been seeing someone else.

Stop it, she told herself. Ryan was not Chet. He was different in so many ways—so many wonderful ways. Sure, Chet had had a few good points, but they'd been hidden beneath a shell of self-importance that had been nearly impossible to pierce. Ryan was completely different. His personality abounded with humor and kindness and devotion to family. He was the kind of man she'd always hoped to meet. The kind of man she was beginning to think had gone the route of the dinosaurs.

Talia stared at her phone. What was she waiting for? She sent off a quick text to Ryan, asking him if things were okay. She ended by tacking on three blue hearts and hit Send. Almost instantly, she regretted the hearts. Would he think the blue hearts meant she was sad because he hadn't texted her? Would she come off as needy?

This time she tried calling his cell instead of texting. Her call went straight to voice mail. With a sigh, she glanced at the time on her phone. It was an hour earlier in Texas, so he was probably stuck in one of those endless meetings he often complained about. Since she'd already left him a message that morning, this time she simply disconnected.

She bopped her head lightly on her steering wheel, then started her engine. She didn't have time to think about it now. Martha and Molly had been holding down the culinary fort for way too long. It was about time she pitched in and took care of her own restaurant.

18

The best part of Talia's day turned out to be her return home to the welcoming *meow* of her darling calico cat, Bo. Bo was waiting on her usual perch atop Grandpop's ratty old chair. Talia liked to imagine that her grandfather and Bo had been together in a previous life, although in this life her grandparents had never owned a cat. Bo seemed to relish the lingering scent of the old chair—Grandpop's psoriasis cream? The occasional cigar he sneaked?—and was fond of rubbing her face on the seat.

Talia's cell rang barely a minute after she tossed her purse on the sofa. She grabbed for it and slid her finger over it to answer. Bo gave her an indignant look—*you're answering that thing before feeding me?*—then padded into the kitchen. Talia followed.

"Hey, are you home?"

Talia's heart fell. Not Ryan. Rachel. "I just walked in," she said.

"You okay? You sound tired."

"I am tired." *And a little depressed.*

"Can I come over with a pizza? I recently read an article about the mind-healing properties of pepperoni. Quite amazing what it can do. I'm surprised the medical community hasn't picked up on it yet."

Talia laughed. She knew Rachel was joking, but the sound of her best friend's voice never failed to cheer her. "Sure," she said, "but I'm not super hungry. I'd love the company, though." She opened the fridge and peeked inside. "I have half a bottle of chardonnay. Will that do?"

"Works for me," Rachel said. "Be there in a jifster."

Talia fed Bo, adding an extra dollop of savory salmon casserole to her dish for being a minute late with her supper. Bo *brrrup*ed appreciatively and then dove in.

True to her word, Rachel arrived thirty minutes later, pizza box in hand. She'd pulled her dark brunette hair back into a hot pink scrunchie. It was the perfect complement to her rose-colored sandals and pink-and-white polka-dotted sundress. Rachel always looked as if she'd just stepped out of a page in *Vogue*, but her inner beauty outshone all of that.

Rachel hugged her for an extra second or two, then studied her friend's face. "You look upset. It's more than just Lucas, isn't it?" she asked quietly.

Talia felt tears push at her eyelids. She didn't want to cry, not now. Save that for later when she was alone with Bo.

"I'm devastated about Lucas," she said. That much was true—what had happened to her young employee was a crying shame. "But I've also had such a crazy week, Rach. With Crystal under house arrest, Audrey and Molly are going nuts. Plus, that jerk Ferringer is trying to get me to host a campaign strategy luncheon for him on a Sunday, when I'm closed. He doesn't seem to understand the word no."

"That type never does."

Talia sniffled. "All that, plus Detective Prescott keeps threatening to toss me in a jail cell if I keep poking my nose into things. But how can I keep my nose *out* of things when Crystal's been arrested for a murder she didn't commit and Lucas is, you know, lying in a hospital bed?"

Rachel pulled out a kitchen chair for her friend. "Sit," she ordered. She snagged two flowered dishes from the set that once belonged to Talia's nana and set them on the table, along with two wineglasses. Within moments they were tearing slices out of the pizza box and gobbling them down. The combo of spicy cured meat and gooey cheese tasted heavenly. Talia was hungrier than she'd originally thought, and she plowed through three slices in fairly short order.

"Now I see what you mean about the healing powers of pepperoni," she told Rachel, then wiped her lips with a napkin.

Rachel laughed. "The wine doesn't hurt, either." Her smile faded. "Is something else bugging you, Tal? You really don't seem like yourself."

Talia swallowed, then told her about not hearing from Ryan.

"You realize," Rachel said, "that it's been barely twenty-four hours."

"I know, but for Ryan that's a long, long time."

Rachel sighed. "It is, isn't it? But honestly, you're overthinking it, Tal. You're reading too much into his not calling or texting. For all you know, he could have dropped his phone into the hotel fountain and wrecked it!"

Talia smiled, but her heart felt leaden. "And couldn't find another phone anywhere? In the entire hotel? I'm not buying it, Rach."

"You know what I think?" Rachel said. "I think we've all gotten so accustomed to instant communication that we've forgotten what it was like before cell phones. The moment we text someone, we expect an instant response! I do it, too, with Derek."

Talia smiled. That was the perfect opening to turn the conversation away from Ryan. "How are you and Derek?"

Rachel shrugged. "We're good, I think. I'm beginning to see that he's a tad possessive, but I'm trying to work through that with him."

"I'm not sure I like the sound of that." Talia drained her last drop of wine.

For a long moment, Rachel looked thoughtful. Bo jumped onto her lap and rubbed her head on Rachel's arm. "I know what you're saying," she said, stroking the cat absently, "and normally I wouldn't put up with it for a minute. But we've had a few good talks, and I think he's really listening. Plus— and this is a biggie—he's starting to work some serious magic with Noah."

Talia felt her eyes widen and her chin drop.

Noah was Rachel's brainiac brother. Always a sensitive child, he was ten years old when he witnessed a fiery highway crash. A school bus had been involved, and several children had died tragically. It scarred his psyche deeply. His clueless parents had arranged for him to receive schooling at home but scoffed at the idea of any intensive therapy. The trauma from the accident made Noah shrink further into himself, until he couldn't even be dragged out of the house. For recreation he found comfort in various scientific hobbies that would stymy the average mind. Now thirty-two, he worked from their stately home on Milan Drive in Wrensdale, which he shared with Rachel and their mostly absent mother. Talia knew that Rachel would have left years ago if not for the powerful bond she shared with Noah. Rachel also felt a fierce need to act as his protector.

"Rachel, that's . . . really great! Has Derek gotten him to go outside at all? I mean, you know . . ."

"You mean in a car? On the road?" Rachel grinned. "Believe it or not, he's taken a few rides in the patrol car with Derek. But only at night, when the traffic is light. And only on a country road with a thirty-five-mile-an-hour speed limit. Noah knows that most drivers automatically slow when they see a police car, and that helps him relax. Even so, after about ten minutes he gets antsy and wants to go home. Derek never tries to push. The second Noah shows any agitation, Derek drives him home right away."

"But it's progress!" Talia crowed.

"He feels safe with Derek," Rachel added softly. She looked away, as if seeing Noah in her mind, riding shotgun with Derek in the patrol car.

"I'm so glad to hear that, Rach. Back in the day, if you remember, it was Noah who taught me how to play chess. He could still beat me in his sleep, but at least I learned the basics."

"He plays it online now," Rachel said. "The Internet has made such a huge difference in his life. I'm really grateful for it, despite all the bad things having an online presence can cause."

That much was definitely true. Noah had earned online master's degrees in two languages and now worked as a translator for an international law firm based in London.

The Internet had opened up a brave and fascinating new world for Noah.

Talia reached over and squeezed her friend's arm. "That's all really good news, Rach. I'm so happy to hear it." She retracted her hand. "Has . . . Derek said anything about the murder? He's been pretty quiet throughout the investigation."

"Outwardly, yes, but believe me when I say he's working twenty-four-seven behind the scenes. He's developed an excellent working relationship with Sergeant O'Donnell. In fact, O'Donnell's trying to get him to leave the force and transfer to the state police."

"Really?" Talia said. "Is Derek considering it?"

"He's seriously thinking about it," Rachel said, with a trace of a cryptic smile. She bent slightly and kissed Bo's head. "Now, back to Ryan. First of all, he adores you. There's not a doubt in my mind about that."

"Then why—"

Rachel held up her hand. "That doesn't mean he doesn't have problems. His brilliant father is suffering from early-onset Alzheimer's and has to live in assisted care. His indifferent mother carries on with her life as if she's a free agent, without a thought for anyone else. I mean, how many times have you even met her?"

Talia winced. "Twice. Once when she had to attend her elderly aunt's funeral. The other time, Ryan brought her to Fry Me. She picked at her meal as if I'd sprinkled it with rat poison and tore most of the crispy coating off the fish. I guess she only eats fish that's been poached or baked. Poor Ryan. I could tell he was really embarrassed."

"Face it, Tal. She's a snob," Rachel declared. "That's never going to change. But it doesn't have to affect your relationship with Ryan."

Talia rose and stuck their dishes in the sink. "I guess you're right. I know I'll hear from him eventually."

She wasn't fully convinced that something wasn't amiss between them, but she resigned herself to waiting it out.

After Rachel left, Talia curled up on the sofa with Bo. She'd opened the sole window in the bungalow's cozy living room, and now a cool evening breeze wafted in. She knew she should make it an early night, but too many thoughts were tumbling around in her brain. Something Harry said was nagging at her. It crouched at the back of her mind, hidden from view. If only it would spring forward so she could grasp on to it. She felt sure it might be important, but she couldn't remember why.

19

Talia awakened to the sound of rain hammering the roof. Normally that would make her want to curl up and snag a few more minutes of sleep, but today she didn't have that luxury.

She yawned and Bo did the same, releasing a whiff of cat breath in her ear. The little calico then cleaned her whiskers, no doubt in preparation for a hearty breakfast. In spite of her damp mood, Talia giggled. She pulled the cat onto her chest and stroked her furry head. "I guess what they say is true, Bo. There really is no rest for the weary."

They both got up. After feeding Bo, Talia showered and scrubbed her hair. A dreary day like this one made it the perfect time to wear denim capris and her red polka-dot tee. Ryan had bought the tee for her on a whim, knowing she loved polka dots. He'd seen it in the window of a consignment shop in Lee and had ducked inside to buy it as a surprise. First he'd checked it over to be sure it was in pristine condition. When he got home, he rolled it carefully into a sheet of pink tissue and tied each end with polka-dotted ribbon. Talia loved that he took such care with the wrapping. She also loved that he hadn't bought it new. It was so like him to choose the perfect gift from a nontraditional store.

Talia swallowed. Just thinking about Ryan made her heart pound faster. Would he text her this morning, or call? Or would she have to wait until he returned to Massachusetts to find out why he hadn't kept in touch?

Today was Thursday, which meant bank day. Most customers paid with credit cards these days, but there were still plenty of folks who preferred paying with cash. The cash receipts from the past three days had to be deposited. Wrensdale Co-Op—one of the few local banks that hadn't been gobbled up by one of the banking conglomerates—opened at eight on Thursdays. She'd first have to stop in at Fry Me and remove the cash box from the safe that was tucked away in the walk-in storage closet. Her dad thought it was a crazy place to store the safe, but Bea and Howie had always done it that way. And since they'd never had any problem, Talia had continued the tradition.

Still, it had occurred to her on more than one occasion that if someone—a thief—took the trouble to trail her movements, they might take note of her normal Thursday ritual. Was she setting herself up for a robbery? Or was she being paranoid because she'd been inadvertently involved in three murders since her return last year to Wrensdale?

It was something to think about. For today, she just wanted to deposit the cash and head back to the eatery to get started on food prep for the day.

After gulping down a quick breakfast of Cheerios and

juice, she kissed Bo good-bye and headed out to her car. The sky had actually cleared a bit, or tried to. From the morning weather report, Talia knew the reprieve was only temporary. A large chunk of the clouds was still gray and foreboding. A windswept thunderstorm was predicted for later in the morning. She was glad she'd have the luxury of staying inside.

Talia typically chose the bank's drive-through window, but today she noticed a line of about seven cars waiting for the sole teller in attendance at the window. The teller, Gaylene, was a chatty sort who took her time with every customer. While Talia liked the woman, she didn't have the patience today to wait for Gaylene to get to her. She started to circle around to the bank's parking lot at the rear when she spied an SUV pulling out of a prime parking space almost directly in front of the Popover Palace. The Palace, a fairly new eatery with kitschy decor, was across the street from the bank. Talia had heard marvelous things about their bacon-and-egg-filled breakfast popovers but so far hadn't had the chance to sample one.

Without hesitation, she zipped her little Fiat into the slot vacated by the SUV. Smiling at having scored a premier parking spot, she hoisted her purse onto her shoulder and hopped out of her car. She started toward the crosswalk, but as she passed the Popover Palace, she couldn't resist a peek inside the large front window. Tables were lined up along one wall, while vintage wooden booths lined the other. Along the rear wall was a counter lined with old-fashioned vinyl-covered stools. Nearly all the tables were filled, she noticed. The Palace was doing a great job attracting breakfast customers.

A familiar face suddenly filled her vision. Seated at one of the wooden booths was none other than Wesley Thurman.

And he wasn't alone.

She couldn't see the face of the man he was dining with, but she recognized the hair—Dylan McPhee.

What was Dylan doing here at this time of the morning? Shouldn't he be slinging hash browns and eggs at the diner? Or was he acting as an industrial spy, checking out the Palace's breakfast selections so he could copy them for his own repertoire?

Talia instantly chided herself for being uncharitable. Whatever else Dylan was, she couldn't fault his cooking skills. Except . . . well, what if Dylan was a murderer? What if he'd killed Norma in a fit of rage over the minuscule blemish on his precious Merkur?

She peered in a trifle closer. This time she saw Wesley throw his head back and laugh. The two of them seemed to be having a grand old time. For some reason, it made her stomach churn.

Concerned that someone might be watching her—in particular, one Patti Prescott—she turned away and glanced across the street, toward the bank. She shot a look at her watch, hoping it might appear she was waiting for someone who was meeting her for breakfast.

After thirty or so seconds, she couldn't resist turning her gaze back inside the restaurant. Wesley and Dylan were still there, their empty dishes and cups now pushed aside. She saw Wesley lean toward Dylan, as if he were speaking in a low tone. Wesley pulled a white envelope from his shirt pocket, set it on the table, and slid it over to Dylan.

Talia gulped. She wanted so badly to whip out her cell and capture it all on video. It was too risky, though. Standing there like that on a public sidewalk, she was sure to get caught in the act.

Still spying through the window, she saw Dylan take the envelope, open it slightly, and peer inside. If only Talia could see his face, she'd be able to judge his reaction. If only she could see what was in the envelope!

No such luck.

In the next instant, Dylan reached into the pocket of his own shirt. Very slowly, he extracted a slip of paper. From her viewpoint it looked weathered and worn, but maybe she was only imagining that. He handed it to Wesley, who perused it briefly and then stuck it in his shirt pocket.

Some sort of exchange had taken place—that much was certain. Had the two known each other before Dylan entered the contest? They seemed a bit too chummy for Talia's liking.

His expression suddenly sober, Wesley held out his hand for Dylan to shake. He seemed to be thanking Dylan for something, or maybe that was just her imagination running wild.

Without warning, Dylan turned so that he was halfway facing the front window. He did not look pleased. If anything, he looked sad and regretful. He said something to Wesley, who only nodded in response.

Oh Lord, she thought, her knees suddenly quaking. Was it possible? Had the two of them been in on the murder? Had Dylan killed Norma for money, at Wesley's behest? It would have been a double whammy. Dylan got revenge on Norma for sullying his precious car and at the same time got paid for eliminating Wesley's sworn enemy.

Wesley had money; that much was certain. He was a wealthy entrepreneur, with fingers in a lot of successful pies. And Dylan needed money desperately to help his strapped-for-cash mother.

Suddenly Dylan rose, as if preparing to leave. Wesley

handed him a business card, and another short exchange took place. Before Talia had a chance to react, Dylan was sliding out of the booth and striding out the front door of the Palace. She turned her face away quickly, praying he wouldn't recognize her. If he noticed she'd been standing there, he'd probably report her to the police. Even worse—if he was Norma's killer, he might decide he had to silence her. Permanently.

Dylan headed off on foot, away from the direction of the diner. Why wasn't he going to work? Was it his day off?

When Talia dared to turn around again, she saw an aging car—a Saturn—pull up and double-park about thirty feet away. Dylan hurried toward the car and then jumped in on the passenger side. The car pulled away, into the slow-moving traffic. She couldn't see the driver's face, but something told her it was a woman.

Stranger and stranger, she thought. The whole thing was odd.

No, more than odd. It was downright suspicious.

A nutty thought occurred to her. Mercury and Saturn were both planets . . . and they were both cars. It was meaningless, she knew, and yet the silly realization wouldn't stop revolving around in her head.

Shaking it off, she turned toward the Palace again and peeked through the front window.

Wesley Thurman was gone.

Inside the bank, Talia was standing in line, her thoughts reeling, when the familiar chirp of her cell phone interrupted her musings. She saw instantly that it was a text from Ryan.

Heart in her throat, she stared at the words. Lots to tell you, Tal. Have a minute to talk? I'll call.

No pink hearts this time. No Hey, Sunshine! or Good morning, Sweetie!

Her hand shaking, Talia texted the words Call me in ten, then slipped the phone back in her purse. She made the deposit on autopilot, barely noticing the teller's cheery smile and kindly demeanor. When she finished, she thanked the teller distractedly and hurried out to her car to wait for the call.

Something was wrong; she just knew it.

Two minutes later, her cell rang.

"Talia?" Ryan sounded distraught.

She nodded, then realized he couldn't see her. "Yes, Ryan, it's me. Is something wrong?"

He seemed to take a moment to collect himself. "It's my mom," he said.

"Oh my God, is she hurt? Did she have an accident?" Talia blurted the words before she had time to filter them.

"She's fine," Ryan said, his tone flat. "She's filed for a divorce from Dad. My lawyer called me late Tuesday night and gave me the bad news."

Talia allowed herself to breathe. "He called you, not your dad?"

"I'm Dad's guardian, remember? Any legal notices would have to come to me directly."

Closing her eyes, Talia pressed back a tear. Arthur was going to be crushed by the news. He adored his wife, in spite of her long absences. He kept a photo of her in a silver frame on top of his bureau. She was a member of academia, and as a visiting professor, she traveled constantly. When Arthur was lucid, he understood that and respected it. Other times, not so much. Some days, he asked for his wife repeatedly, confused about why they weren't still living together. Ryan took the emotional brunt of his dad's bewilderment. He loved his mom, but Talia knew he was finding it harder and harder to defend her. What saddened Talia most was that the woman rarely visited Arthur. She treated him like a baseball player whose number had been retired. Out of sight and rarely in her mind.

"Ryan, are you okay?" Talia rasped.

"Now that I've had time to process it, I'm better." He blew out a sigh. "The thing that set me off, though, was that Mom called my dad at the assisted-living place to tell him. She actually called and told him she was filing for a divorce! She said they were living two separate lives now, and it didn't make sense for them to be hobbled, as she called it, by a marriage license."

How awful. How insensitive!

"Did Arthur tell you that?"

"Yes, in those exact words. I have no reason to doubt that he heard her correctly."

Talia shook her head. This was terrible news. No wonder Ryan hadn't called her, or even texted. Sheila Collins, apparently, had forgotten the "for better or for worse" part of her marriage vows. If Arthur had been abusive or unkind to her, Talia would have understood it, even applauded her divorcing him. But this . . . this was terrible. Arthur was so sweet, so adoring. Thank heaven he had Ryan.

"I wanted to tell you sooner, honey," Ryan said. "But I was having trouble pulling myself together. I was like a zombie at the meeting with our new client yesterday. It was excruciatingly long, and I couldn't concentrate."

Talia felt hot tears slide down her cheeks. "Oh, Ryan, I am so sorry. Would it help if I went up to the Pines to see Arthur? Should I mention it to Mom? Being the assistant director, I think she'd want to be kept informed."

"I hear you, Tal. But I'll be back late tomorrow, so let's wait and talk to her together, okay? So far only my dad knows. He seems to be taking it well, but I'm not sure that will last. He told me not to tell anyone until I got back from Dallas. Why, I'm not sure. His old circle of friends has pretty much drifted away. But I couldn't not tell you—it was so unfair. Besides, I know Dad wouldn't mind. He already thinks of you as a daughter."

Talia choked over the smile she felt crossing her lips. "And I think of him like a second dad."

After a few moments of silence, Ryan said, "I've been periodically checking the news. I read that the police already nabbed that woman's killer. What a relief. I'm glad they caught up with her so quickly. I'll tell you, though, I wouldn't have pegged her for it. She seemed like such a sweet lady."

"Oh, Ryan," Talia said tearfully. "She didn't do it. Crystal isn't the killer. I just spoke to her yesterday—"

Ryan groaned. "Oh no, not again. Why don't you think she's the killer?"

"Because I know her, and the evidence against her is so flimsy you wouldn't believe it! Besides, I've . . . stumbled onto a few situations that are quite suspect. More than one person had a motive, Ryan. I can't let Crystal take the blame for a crime she didn't commit."

"Honey, please, *please* promise me you won't put yourself in danger. Remember last time? And the time before?"

Of course she remembered. How could she forget two confrontations with two separate killers? The horror of those encounters was still singed in her brain. Talia pulled in a calming breath. "Ryan," she said quietly, "would you want to sit in prison for life for a murder you didn't commit?"

"Of course I wouldn't, but that's for the police to sort out.

I'm surprised Detective Prescott isn't all over you for trying to investigate."

Talia chuckled. "She is, and it's been tricky letting her think I'm minding my own business."

"I'm flying home tomorrow, Tal. Please don't do anything risky, okay? I'll help with anything you need, but you've got to stay safe." Before she could respond, he said in a softer voice, "How's Lucas doing? Any news on his condition?"

"Nothing so far today," she said. That much was true, but she hated deceiving Ryan. After the killer was caught, she intended to tell him everything.

"I have a breakfast meeting in fifteen, honey. I'll call you tonight, okay?"

She smiled and felt her lip tremble. "Okay."

After a slight hesitation he said, "Talia?"

"Yes?"

"I love you."

She started to respond in kind, but Ryan had already disconnected. She pressed the phone to end the call, but a few seconds later heard the familiar *blurrp* that announced a new text. She slid her finger over it to read the message. But there was no message.

Just a long row of pink hearts that seemed to stretch into infinity.

20

Talia sat in her car for a long time, attempting to process everything. Too much was happening. Too much all at once.

Her heart ached like the devil when she thought about Arthur. No wonder Ryan had been incommunicado. Bad enough to learn that his mom had filed for divorce, but he'd had to deal with that in the midst of an important client meeting in Dallas.

In spite of everything, she'd felt a huge wave of relief sweep over her after Ryan's call. Their bond was stronger than ever. He'd actually used the *L* word! In a way she felt guilty for her sudden spurt of joy, but she couldn't help it.

Starting her engine, she glanced down the street toward the next block. On the opposite side of Main, the tired-looking sign for Summers Realty sparked a memory. Harry had said something yesterday that had stuck in her brain. Unfortunately, she still couldn't remember what it was. A nagging voice told her it was important, that she had to figure it out.

Maybe if she had another chat with him, it would pry the memory loose from her head. The problem was, how could she avoid another run-in with Sandra? Was there a way she could get Harry alone?

She sighed. Not really. Besides, it was only eight forty. The realty office probably didn't open until ten, like most other businesses on Main Street.

Talia was trying to concoct an excuse to talk to Harry alone later in the day when a car swerved up to the curb in front of Summers Realty. It was the same car she'd seen yesterday—the one that belonged to Sandra. Sandra didn't get out right away, though. It looked like she might be checking her phone for messages. Finally, Sandra pushed her door open and swung her legs out. She got out of the car, unlocked the door to the realty office, and strutted inside.

No chance to get Harry alone now, unless she called him. She'd think about doing that later, when there was a lull at Fry Me.

Dark clouds were gathering low in the sky. Talia grabbed her portable umbrella from the backseat and stuck it next to her purse so she wouldn't forget it. She'd been caught in a storm once before without an umbrella and had gotten drenched racing to the town lot, where her car was parked. Not something she wanted to repeat.

She inched forward into the traffic and had to stop for the next light. All at once she realized that she was idling right next to Summers Realty. This time she got a closer look at Sandra's car. Something about it bothered her. What?

Oh dear God, what was the matter with her? Sandra drove a Grand Marquis. A *Mercury* Grand Marquis. She felt like an idiot. She should have made the connection yesterday.

A horn behind her honked, and she jerked her car forward. She couldn't find a place where she could pull over to call Detective Prescott. By the time she zoomed into the town lot, her whole body was trembling. She called the detective, but her call went straight to voice mail. Drat!

She'd have to rely on texting again and hope Prescott would read it soon.

Did you know Sandra Summers drives a Mercury Grand Marquis? Call me. We need to talk.

There. It was done. That was all she needed to say. And she hadn't been investigating or poking her nose into other people's business when she discovered it. She'd simply been driving to work. *Let Detective Patti Prescott find a problem with that,* she thought defensively.

One thing bothered Talia. Sandra Summers, as repulsive as she was, had never made it onto her suspect list. Was the Mercury Grand Marquis connection a mere coincidence? A lot of people still drove Mercury models. As for the Wesley/Dylan meeting, she'd have to tell Prescott what she'd witnessed. And she hadn't been spying on them, not really. She'd only been peeking into the restaurant while she was waiting to cross the street.

By the time she reached Fry Me, she was desperate for coffee. She slung her belongings into her assigned locker and immediately fired up the coffeemaker. Martha usually came in early and would welcome a cup. Although, Talia reasoned, the poor woman hadn't been her snarky, witty, wonderful self since Lucas was attacked. Talia missed the old Martha. She wanted the original model back, not the sullen shadow of her friend that had been lurking among them since Monday.

After slugging back a few mouthfuls of coffee with cream, Talia lugged a huge sack of potatoes out of the walk-in refrigerator. She plunked it on the floor next to the newly enlarged worktable. She hoped Molly wouldn't mind peeling again. Or was this the day Molly was going to put up her ballot box and let the customers decide which style "chips" they preferred? If so, then she wouldn't have to peel potatoes today.

Talia was chopping green cabbage for the coleslaw when Martha trudged in. It seemed almost impossible, but she looked even worse today than she had the day before. The gray bags under her eyes hung like gunnysacks, and if she'd run a comb through her hair this morning, she'd missed at least three cowlicks.

"Morning," she mumbled, trudging over to her locker.

"Good morning, Martha." That was all Talia dared to say, at least for now.

Martha opened the door to her locker and lobbed her purse toward the back, scowling when it landed sideways and half the contents tumbled out. She kicked the locker closed with her shoe, then tossed her oversized umbrella in a corner.

Without a word, Talia poured her a mug of coffee. Martha took it from her and plopped it on the small table. "Too hot," she growled out, and then grabbed a blue apron off the shelf.

They worked in uncompanionable silence for a while, Martha punctuating every movement with a huff or a moan. At the point when Talia thought she'd scream, Molly came in, bless her. Talia wanted to hug her just for showing up.

Or not.

Molly didn't make it as far as the kitchen before bursting

into uncontrollable sobs. She bent over at the waist, crying her heart out, while Talia patted her back helplessly. "Molly, what's wrong? What is it?" she kept saying, but Molly continued to cry.

Talia let her cry—for an hour, it seemed—before grasping the girl's shoulders and steering her over to the kitchen table. She shoved a box of tissues at her. "Now tell me what's wrong, Molly. It can't be as bad as all that."

"It is," Molly blubbered, pulling her iPad out of her satchel. "L-l-last night I got another friend request from that Wesley Thurman creep. And I—and I . . ."

Martha's ears perked, and she came over and sat down. "You friended him, didn't you?" she said.

Molly nodded. She wiped her arm over her swollen eyes and then swept her finger over the iPad. "I knew I could unfriend him in a second if he got weird or anything. But I wanted to find out more about him, why he keeps hanging around here. Crystal wouldn't be in jail if it wasn't for him!"

Talia knew she wasn't technically in jail, but she wanted Molly to continue without any interruption.

"Look," Molly said, sniffling. "Here's his Facebook page. Look at the picture on the lower left." She turned it so Talia and Martha could see.

They both looked at the page. Martha saw it right away, and then Talia did. They looked at each other in mute shock, then back at the iPad.

"It says 'Me and my gorgeous baby sister, Prissy, at the county fair, 2004.'" Molly flitted through more images. "There's more of her, everywhere. Everywhere!" Molly shrieked. She flitted through more images, but Talia didn't need to see any more. She squeezed her fingers over her eyes.

"Oh . . . Molly," Talia said softly, her heart sinking. "I

don't really know what to say. Have . . . have you talked to your mom about it?"

Molly swallowed, and her eyes filled again. "No." She looked pleadingly at Talia, then at Martha. "I want you guys with me when I confront her, okay? She'll try to lie. I know she will. But I'm not going to let her get away with it."

Talia rubbed her hands together. She looked at Martha for help, but Martha still appeared shell-shocked. "Molly, I really don't think that's the right approach. Think about it, okay? This is very personal, very private." She slipped one arm around Molly's shoulders. "It should stay between you and your mom."

"No." Molly slammed the iPad back into her satchel. "You guys are, like, two of my best friends. If you're both here, she'll have to tell the truth."

Martha sagged in her chair. She looked worn-out, beaten.

"Molly," Talia said gingerly, "did it ever occur to you that it might be a coincidence?"

"Oh, Talia, are you kidding me!"

Talia threw up her arms. She didn't know what to say. Not for a moment did she believe that the woman in the photo was not Molly's aunt. In 2004, when the pic was taken, the woman was about the same age Molly was now.

She was also her mirror image. A doppelgänger, for lack of a better word. They were as identical as any two people could be.

They could not deny it.

Molly Feldon was Wesley Thurman's daughter.

21

A sudden crack of thunder outside made Talia jump. "Wow, that was a loud one," she said, to no one in particular.

And no one in particular answered.

Martha had gone into silent mode, as if her internal remote was set on Mute. Molly went about the task of peeling potatoes, slicing them with a vengeance that left more potato than peel in the mound of skins that was piling up. Anyone gazing in on the trio would have thought they were getting a sneak peek at some warped silent movie, Talia thought wryly.

The eatery wasn't due to open for another half hour. Talia was tempted to turn the CLOSED sign to OPEN, just to attract some early diners. She'd been, in fact, toying with the notion of opening the eatery earlier in the day and offering some deep-fried breakfast delights. It was an idea that had been percolating slowly in her mind, but so far she hadn't taken it seriously. She already worked six days a week—six long days at that. How could she extend her dining hours even further?

Another crack of thunder sizzled the sky. Talia felt her heart nearly leap out of her chest. This time Martha flinched. "Bad omen," she muttered.

Ignoring Martha's dire warning, Talia scooted around the edge of the counter and into the dining area. She opened the door and peered outside. Large drops fell diagonally from the sky, pelting the cobblestone, sending rivulets of water streaming toward the street. The storm was starting earlier than the weather people had predicted.

She started to close the door when she saw a lone figure, encased in a green raincoat, entering the Fork and Dish across the way.

Audrey.

She watched Audrey jiggle the key and step inside and then close the door behind her. It was only a matter of time now. A confrontation was coming—a showdown between Audrey and her daughter. Talia dreaded it, and yet she knew it might be the best thing for both of them.

Unless it tore them apart.

Audrey had to know that Wesley Thurman was Molly's real father. Talia had noticed the resemblance in their profiles that day at the festival, but she hadn't put two and two together until Molly showed them that Facebook page.

Right now Molly was calm, like the eye of a hurricane. In spite of that, Talia had the feeling that she was building to an emotional explosion.

Talia stood there in the open doorway, mesmerized by the pounding rain. Her mind turned things over. Nothing made sense anymore.

Sandra Summers drove a Mercury.

Dylan drove a Merkur.

Dylan and Wesley were in cahoots over something.

Norma's cabinets were nearly empty.

And Molly had uncovered the secret Audrey had kept all these years—who her father was.

Audrey had wanted her to believe Brad Feldon was her father, but she had to know the truth would come out eventually. She'd probably tried to put it out of her mind, praying it would never happen. Hoping she could keep the truth forever hidden.

A fork of lightning crackled in the sky, followed by a low rumble. A figure suddenly emerged from the bath shop— Sage & Seaweed—a familiar salmon-colored bag hanging from her arm. The figure was decked out in a stunning designer raincoat and a frilly waterproof fedora. Her shoes, which looked expensive, were getting soaked, but she didn't seem to care. An umbrella the size of a tent snapped to life over the woman's head. She marched purposefully toward Talia. Before Talia could step back, the woman grabbed her arm and pulled her out onto the cobblestone.

"Wait a minute," Talia demanded, wresting her arm away. "What are you doing? We'll get soaked."

Jodie Ferringer gave her a look that would have stopped a moose in its tracks. "We won't get soaked under my umbrella," she hissed, clamping on to Talia's wrist. "I want to know why you were asking questions about me. Kasey at the jeweler's told me about you and your spying. What's your gig, anyway, lady? What are you up to?"

"Spying?" Talia swallowed back a tiny lump of fear. Kasey must have gotten her name from her credit card, when she paid for her mom's birthday gift. "I'm . . . I'm not even sure what you're talking about." Another step in that down escalator to a hot place.

"Yeah, right," Jodie said. "Try again. And this time I want the truth. I know it was you who called me yesterday. I recognized your voice. How did you get my private number, anyway?"

Talia ignored the question. And while her head was staying relatively dry, she could feel the canvas of her Keds getting saturated. "All right, look," Talia confessed. "I was only trying to figure out why you and Norma Ferguson were so close. You didn't have a thing in common. Not that I could see anyway."

Jodie's face flushed an unattractive shade of mottled red. She let go of Talia's arm. "That is none of your business. Norma was my friend, my *dear* friend, and she was a huge supporter of my husband. Who, by the way, is going to be *your* next representative." Jodie lifted her pert nose in the air.

"Really? Even though his opponent is heavily favored?"

Jodie's lips turned up into a smug smile. "You're obviously one of those fools who believe the polls. If I were you, I'd welcome the chance to host my husband's campaign strategy meeting. For your information, he could have picked any number of fine local restaurants for his meeting. He wanted to have it here"—she glowered over at Fry Me as if it were an opium den—"because he enjoys helping the little people."

"The little people," Talia repeated, feeling her teeth clench.

"If I were you," Jodie plowed on, "I would call Bruce and tell him that you changed your mind, that you would be more than pleased to open on a Sunday for him and his loyal staff."

"You know, Jodie," Talia said, with a smile as genuine as

Jodie's cleavage, "I might just do that. I mean, why shouldn't I make a little extra money on a Sunday? I could use some extra cash. Maybe I've been way too stubborn about the whole thing. I'll give him a call later today." *Or when the equator freezes over.*

As Talia predicted, Jodie's phony smile instantly evaporated. Her plan to bully Talia had backfired. Talia really hated fibbing like that again, but that time Jodie had pushed the wrong button.

Jodie took a stuttering step backward. "Um, well . . . good," she said. "I'll tell him to expect your call."

Somewhere on the other side of the plaza, the click of a lock nicked into place. Audrey Feldon had just closed up the Fork and Dish and was running toward them. Rain poured off her hooded raincoat as she clomped along over the cobblestones.

Jodie pasted on another faux smile. "Audrey, what are you doing out in this monsoon?" Her fake laugh tinkled across the plaza.

"I saw you talking to Talia," Audrey said, pulling her collar closer to her neck. "I wanted to let you know that your slow cooker came in on Monday. With everything that was going on, I never had a chance to call you."

Jodie slid her gaze over to Talia, then back at Audrey. "Oh, that's wonderful," she gushed. "Can I stop by later to pick it up? Later this week, I mean. It's too soggy out today."

"Sure," Audrey said.

Jodie touched Talia's arm as if they were old pals. "So good to see you again, Talia. Toodles!" She rushed off into the rain, in the direction of the main drag, leaving Talia to get thoroughly drenched.

Talia looped her arm through Audrey's and propelled her toward Fry Me. "Is she one of your customers?"

Audrey nodded. "One of our best, actually. Truth be told, I can't stand the woman, but I'm not going to turn down business. You wouldn't believe all the stuff she buys from us. What a spendthrift."

So Kasey with a *K* was right. Jodie loved to cook. And she loved to spend.

They scuttled inside the restaurant, dripping water everywhere. "Um, may I ask what you two were doing, standing out in the rain like that?" Audrey said.

Talia waved off the question. "Oh, we happened to run into each other and she got chatty. You know how it is." She cringed at the falsehood—she knew it made no sense whatsoever.

Audrey gave her a bewildered look. "I didn't realize you knew her." She shrugged. "Anyway, I assume Molly is here," she said, wiping her shoes on the blue welcome mat. She tugged off her sodden raincoat and hung it on one of the metal hooks near the door.

Talia felt a herd of cattle trample through her stomach. "I, um, Molly is . . ."

"I'm here," Molly nearly spat at her mother. She shot out from the hidden part of the kitchen, holding her iPad out to the side. "You look like a drowned rat, Mother. How very fitting."

Audrey snapped her head toward her daughter. "What did you say to me?"

"I *said* you look like a rat"—Molly's eyes flared with anger—"which is exactly what you are."

Audrey looked at Talia, who felt like melting—Wicked

Witch style—into the floor. "Do you know what this is about?"

"Audrey, sit," Talia said, pulling out one of the dining room chairs for her.

"You'd better have a darn good reason," Audrey flung at her daughter, "for speaking to me that way."

Molly came over and plopped the iPad down on the table. "How's this for a reason, *Mother*? This is Wesley Thurman's Facebook page."

In the solitary moment it took for Audrey to focus, Talia had an urge to run back out into the rain. If the weather hadn't been so horrible, she'd have grabbed Martha and headed outside for a long, bracing walk so mother and daughter could be alone.

Unfortunately, that wasn't an option.

Talia scooted back into the kitchen, and Martha joined her at the small table. For the next several minutes, they listened to a round of cries and accusations that were nothing short of agonizing.

"You're a cheat. A liar!"

"I didn't want to hurt you. I wasn't trying to deceive you!"

"You're lying, Mother. You've been tricking me all my life!"

"How can you say that? Your father adored you. No matter what, you were his child!"

Martha looked at Talia. "I can't take it anymore."

Talia scraped back her chair and went out to the dining room. She stood between Molly and Audrey, both of whom were close to hysteria. "Please, please stop screaming at each other," she begged. "You won't solve anything this way."

Audrey covered her eyes with her hands. "There's nothing to solve," she said hoarsely. "I can't magically turn back the clock."

Her eyes red and swollen, Molly leaped off her chair. "For once, she's right. I'll be going back to school early, Mother. In the meantime, I'll be staying with one of my friends." She scooped her iPad off the table and raced out the door.

"Oh God—she'll get soaked!" Audrey cried.

Feeling helpless, Talia shook her head. Molly would get soaked, but that was her choice. Could things get much worse?

Yes, they could. Crystal could go to prison for a crime she hadn't committed.

The overhead lights flickered just then. Audrey gasped and clasped onto her chair.

"It's only the lights, Audrey," Talia said soothingly. She prayed they wouldn't lose power. She sat down and rubbed her friend's forearm. "Do you want to talk about it? I'm willing to listen, in case you do."

Audrey nodded, her eyes filling with tears. "I have to tell someone. Someone who will understand."

"I'm willing to listen, too," Martha said. She carried out a tray bearing three tall glasses and set down an iced tea for each of them.

Audrey pulled in a long, shaky breath, as if bracing herself for what was to come. "I've known Wesley since high school. I think you suspected that much, right?"

Martha said nothing, but Talia nodded. Vivian had told her much of it, but she wanted to hear it from Audrey herself.

"We were in the same class as Sandra Bosley," she said,

a touch of bitterness in her tone. "Sandra was the pretty, bubbly type. Cheerleader, Pep Club, all that stuff. Boys flocked to her, of course, for the obvious reason. Everyone knew she 'put out'"—she encased the words in imaginary quotes—"as the expression goes, which ensured that she always had a date on Saturday night."

Martha shook her head and scowled.

"At the beginning of our senior year, a new boy moved to town. Smart, athletic, good-looking—but without being too wrapped up in himself. He was polite to a fault. He actually seemed to respect girls, which is why I . . . fell for him."

"Wesley?" Talia said.

"Yes." Audrey cleared her throat. "I turned eighteen in the late fall of my senior year. Wesley was already nineteen. He'd missed a year of school back in his hometown in Illinois because of a bad bout with a strain of meningitis. Luckily, he pulled through it with flying colors. After he moved to Wrensdale, he even joined the track team. Put up some pretty impressive stats." Audrey folded her hands over the table and smiled.

"Sports wasn't his thing, though," she continued. "He had visions of traveling, of seeing the world. His folks were pretty indulgent, and luckily for him, they had a little money. They made sure he applied to all the best colleges."

"Did you have plans for after graduation?" Martha asked her.

"Well, I wasn't really sure what I wanted to do. I was a good student, but not a great one. I thought I'd go to community college and see what kinds of subjects might interest me."

A sudden burst of thunder made them all jump.

"Storm's getting worse," Martha noted.

Audrey continued. "Wesley and I didn't begin seeing each other until after the Christmas holidays. He asked me to the Valentine's dance at school, and after that, we started going steady." She blushed profusely. "For a while, things were wonderful. Our folks, and others, figured it was just teenage infatuation. That we'd forget about each other after graduation. But Wesley and I knew it was the real deal."

"It was Sandra who spoiled it, wasn't it?" Martha said bluntly.

Audrey's gaze hardened. "Sandra had designs on Wesley from the moment we entered senior year. All the boys knew she was easy, but Wesley didn't even like her. She was too brash for his tastes, in spite of her looks."

So far, Audrey had made Wesley sound like a choirboy. Talia suspected that his motives weren't all that magnanimous.

"Sandra didn't like that Wesley ignored her. She tried getting him alone a few times, but she wasn't too successful. Then Wes learned he'd gotten accepted to Northwestern on a scholarship. Excited as he was, he didn't want to leave me. But he knew he couldn't pass up the opportunity. We planned to see each other on school breaks and during the summers. After his college graduation, we could finally get married. I mean, we really were trying to be sensible about it."

"It sounds like you had your futures all planned out," Talia said softly.

"We did." Audrey gave out a tiny sob. "Until I found out I was pregnant." She took a long sip of her iced tea, then pushed the glass away. "It was about three weeks before graduation. We thought we'd been so careful, but . . . well, things happen, as they say. I knew I had to tell Wes, but I was terrified."

"How did you tell him?" Martha asked.

"I passed him a note in algebra class, asked him to meet me behind the bleachers after school at four. I told him it was important." She snagged a napkin from the silver dispenser on the table and used it to blot her eyes. "He didn't read the note until lunch that day, in the cafeteria. He must have dropped it when he was in the food line, because it ended up in Norma Taylor's—that's what her name was then—hands. She immediately gave the note to Sandra, but of course I didn't know it at the time. Norma was a horrible woman, conniving and nasty and petty. She loved causing trouble."

"I don't get people like that," Martha said sourly.

"Anyway, that afternoon I was running a little late. My stomach was gurgling. I'd already thrown up twice. When I got close to the bleachers, Wes was already waiting. Except he wasn't alone. He was with Sandra." She blotted her eyes with a new napkin. "She had her arms wrapped around his waist and her head pressed against his chest. I could tell neither of them had seen me."

"Oh, Audrey," Talia said, imagining how upsetting that must have been, "what did you do?"

"Well, first I dropped to the ground so I wouldn't pass out. It was warm that day, horribly warm. I cried and cried. I finally got myself together and ran inside the school. I managed to keep my stomach intact till I could get to the girls' room. After that, I threw up until my insides ached."

"Didn't Wes look for you?" Talia asked. "He must have wondered why you didn't show up."

"I don't know if he looked for me or not. I broke up with him the next day and told him not to speak to me ever again."

"But you were . . ."

"Yes, pregnant. With his child."

Talia couldn't imagine what she'd have done in Audrey's shoes. Her folks, she knew, would've been supportive—although they certainly would not have been pleased. It was a difficult spot to be in—that's for sure.

"What about your parents?" Talia asked her.

Audrey frowned. "Mom and Dad were very disappointed in me, but they didn't kick me out or anything."

"You must have told Wesley eventually," Martha put in, shoving a napkin under her sweating glass.

Audrey went silent.

"Oh my God," Talia whispered.

Audrey's eyes glistened. "It got around school real quick that I'd dumped Wesley Thurman. It was the talk of the school for the next three days. No one knew I was pregnant, of course, although some of my friends suspected. There was this other boy—Brad Feldon—who'd always had a crush on me, but I'd thought of him only as a friend."

"Kind of like Molly and Lucas," Talia said.

"Kind of, except Lucas was . . . is too young for Molly." Talia saw Martha flinch. "Did Brad ask you out?"

"He did, and he was so sweet that I felt guilty taking advantage of him. At that point, graduation was only about two weeks off. It was clear that Brad was falling hard for me. I couldn't lead him on any longer, so I told him the truth."

"You told Brad about being preggers with Wesley's kid, but you didn't tell Wesley?" Martha looked aghast.

Talia touched Martha's arm. Martha had a habit of jumping onto her high horse when something riled her. Talia wanted to rein her in before she said something she'd regret.

Audrey nodded. "I thought he'd dump me like a hot brick, but instead he did the unthinkable—he asked me to marry him." Her voice grew very soft. "He said no one had to know that the child wasn't his."

"Oh, Audrey." Talia shook her head. One thing still didn't add up. "But the timing was off, wasn't it? Hadn't you been pregnant for at least a few months?"

"Five weeks, actually," Audrey replied. "And Molly was small when she was born. My doctor, and my folks, were the only ones who knew that she wasn't born prematurely."

Talia doubted that. Others must have suspected. People talk, and the news of Wes and Audrey's high school breakup had spread quickly.

"So you accepted Brad's proposal," Martha said, a little roughly.

Audrey lifted her chin. "Yes, I did, and we eloped the following weekend, right after graduation. I have never regretted it," she said defensively. "He turned out to be a wonderful husband and the best father Molly could've had."

But you didn't love him, Talia wanted to say.

"Once Molly started grade school, Brad encouraged me to get my degree. I chose teaching, of all things, and ended up teaching a bunch of seventh-grade monsters." She rolled her eyes. "What was I thinking? I was an awful teacher."

"What about Wesley?" Talia asked, wanting her to backtrack. "How did you leave things with him?"

Audrey's face paled. "Wes and I never spoke again, not even once. When he found out I'd eloped with Brad, he wouldn't even look at me. He went off to Northwestern, and that was the last I ever saw of him."

"Until this week," Martha reminded her.

Audrey's body sagged. She looked as if she might topple over. "When we got that brochure in the mail for the Steeltop

Foods contest, my stomach almost dropped out of my body. All these years, I've lived in fear of him coming back. I was terrified that somehow, some way, he'd find out Molly was his biological child. And then suddenly, there he was. My worst nightmare was coming true."

A host of thoughts tumbled through Talia's head. How would she feel if she were Molly? Would she want to know who her real father was? Or would she be better off thinking that a kind and loving man like Brad Feldon had been her real dad?

Talia didn't have to think long. No matter who her real dad was, she'd want to know the truth.

"I didn't want Wesley coming back here," Audrey continued. "I didn't want him to ever meet Molly."

Talia sighed. "So you tried to talk Crystal out of entering the competition, but she was determined to be a contestant."

"I know it wasn't fair of me—Crystal's an excellent cook. I knew that if she won that prize money, it would help her a lot. But I also knew Wes would try to see me, and that was the last thing I needed."

Talia remembered Molly saying that he'd tried to friend her on Facebook but she'd thought he was just some lech and deleted the requests. "Wesley must have realized Molly was his daughter," Talia said, "when he saw the uncanny resemblance to his sister."

"Resemblance?" Audrey barked out. "My God, they're mirror images of each other."

"At least we know why he wanted that idiotic contest to be held here," Martha said. "The whole idea was goofy and not very well planned. If a woman had been in charge, it would have been far more organized. Thurman only did it because he needed an excuse to see you again."

Talia bit off a smile. Martha thought women should be in charge of everything. But that reminded her of something. "Sandra Summers wanted to help Wes run the competition. Her husband told me about it."

Audrey's small fists clenched. "I'm not surprised," she said tightly. "The woman is like a category five hurricane. She destroys everything in her path. She's been trying to sink her claws into Wesley since the day she met him." She swallowed. "I found out right before graduation that Norma had told her about my note to Wes. I'm not sure how Norma knew, but like I said, Wes probably dropped the note when he was in the cafeteria line. He was forever losing things. Anyway, Sandra told me Norma gave her the note. I knew she had to be telling the truth because she repeated what I'd written, almost word for word, in that witchy, gloaty voice of hers."

Talia thought about the way Sandra treated her husband. "I don't know Harry Summers all that well, but he seems like a decent guy. I can't imagine why he puts up with her antics. I witnessed the way she spoke to him. It was embarrassing."

Audrey's eyes filled again. "I don't care about Sandra. What am I going to do about Molly? She hates me now. She'll probably never speak to me again."

A loud clap of thunder made all of them jump. The lights flickered again, and this time Talia feared they'd go out altogether. She heaved a sigh of relief when the power managed to stay on.

"Audrey, I don't believe for a minute that Molly hates you. But right now she's really, really mad. Her world got turned upside down. I think she's just very confused. Once she has a chance to think it through, she'll want to talk about it."

Audrey sniffled. "Do you really think so?"

"I do."

"Listen, Audrey," Martha said, leaning forward over the table. "I'm going to be real frank here. I've worked with foster kids, and I'm not saying it's anything like your situation. But one thing I learned is that kids want the truth. The worst thing you can do is lie to them, and that's probably how Molly is looking at this. Right about now she's thinking that her life has been one big lie."

Not helpful, Martha, Talia thought.

To Talia's surprise, Audrey sat up straighter. "You're right, Martha. And I appreciate your honesty. I have to make her see that nothing about her life has been a lie. Whatever bad things I've done, they don't reflect on her."

A sudden chill made Talia rub her arms. She stood abruptly and went to the door. She opened it and saw that the plaza was nearly flooded. Rain was coming down in torrential sheets, sweeping over the cobblestone in windblown gusts. The temperature seemed to have dropped twenty degrees since early morning.

Across the way, a solitary figure was peering through one of the windows at the Fork and Dish. Talia could barely make out the person through the downpour, but she was sure it was a man.

"Audrey, did you leave the lights on at your shop?"

"I think so. Why? Is Molly there?" She left her chair and was at Talia's side in a second.

"I don't think it's Molly," Talia said, "but it looks like someone is trying to get in. Do you want me to call the police?"

Just then the solitary figure turned and saw them. He began sprinting toward Fry Me.

"It's him," Audrey said furiously. "Close the door!"

Talia started to close it, but Audrey stood there, frozen, blocking the door's path. "Audrey, let me—" she cried, but in the next instant Wesley Thurman was only a yard away, his expression a mixture of agony and relief.

"We need to talk," he said to Audrey.

We need to talk. Just like the note! He'd been the author of the cryptic note. Talia was sure of it now.

Rain dripped down his face, into his eyes. He sucked in deep breaths, as if the race across the cobblestones had left him winded. Suddenly, Thurman pushed his way inside, spraying rainwater everywhere. He slammed the door shut.

"Mr. Thurman, you are not welcome here," Talia said, trying to keep the fright from her voice. "If you don't leave immediately, I'll get the police to toss you out for me." It was a weak threat, but it was all she could think of.

To her surprise, tears began rolling down his cheeks. "I'm sorry, Talia, but I have to talk to Audrey. Call the cops if you want, but I'm not leaving until I've had my say."

Audrey turned away, her shoulders heaving. "Why are you doing this?" she said raggedly. "Why are you torturing me like this?"

"Because I want some answers," he said quietly to her back. "You owe me, Audrey."

For the longest time, it seemed, Audrey stood there in silence. Then finally she turned, her hands clasped under her chin. "I'll tell you what you want to know, but then you have to leave. And I don't want you *ever* talking to Molly. Is that understood?"

Thurman swept his short dark blond hair away from his face, then shook water from his hand. "No," he said. "It is not understood. I have a right to talk to Molly."

"You have no rights!" Audrey dropped onto the chair she'd vacated and plunked her head into her arms. He went over and pulled out the chair beside her and lowered himself onto it. As if by telepathic consent, Talia and Martha moved away from them, toward the kitchen.

"Wait," Thurman said. "I'm going to say my piece first and then I'll leave, but I want you all to hear this. Please. Sit down." He motioned them back to the table.

Talia did as instructed, but her heart was beating so fast she thought it might fly out of her chest. Martha looked grim, but she seated herself next to Audrey.

"First of all," he began in a soft tone, "I apologize for trying to friend Molly. It was the wrong thing to do. I fully admit that now."

Audrey's face remained hard. "I already told Talia and Martha everything. About us. About our . . . breakup. About Brad and me eloping after graduation. If you have nothing more to add, then I will thank you to leave."

"I still don't understand, Audrey. Why didn't you tell me you were pregnant?"

"I tried to tell you! That's why I asked you to meet me behind the bleachers that day. But you must've dropped my note when you were in the cafeteria line. Norma gave it to Sandra, and she made sure she got there first."

Wesley looked stricken. He stared blankly at the wall, as if seeing it all again in his mind. "Oh God, now I remember. No, I didn't drop the note. I left it on the table in the cafeteria when I was eating lunch with one of the guys. Norma came over to give us more of that gluey beef stew she'd made. She was always flirting with the boys, the old—" He gave a disgusted look and then blew out a sigh. "She must have read it and told Sandra what it said. Those two were always plotting something. Sandra used her, and Norma was dumb enough to go along with it."

"Why don't you just admit it?" Audrey said. "You *wanted* Sandra. I saw the two of you that day by the bleachers. Her arms were wrapped around you, and her head was on your chest." Fresh tears sprang into her eyes.

Wesley groaned. "No. No, Audrey. You've got it wrong." He looked helplessly at her, as the horror of what happened that day washed over him. "Couldn't you see that it was all one way? That my arms were at my sides? That I was trying to avoid even touching her! She knew you'd see us there. She must've had it all planned, that conniving little—" He broke off, and a sob escaped him.

Talia felt stunned. If Wesley was telling the truth, then it had all been one huge misunderstanding. Would things have been different if Sandra hadn't interfered that day? Would Wesley, Audrey, and Molly have gone off into the sunset as one happy family?

"What would you have done if I'd told you?" Audrey said, her voice fading into tears.

Wesley took her hand in his own. She tried to pull away, but he held it fast. "I would have changed my college plans and married you. I loved you, Audrey. I—"

She shook her head. "Your folks wouldn't have let you give up that scholarship."

"They wouldn't have had a choice. I'd have gone to school somewhere else, even without a scholarship. I'd have stayed closer to home, to you and the—"

"Baby?"

Four heads swiveled toward the door. No one had seen or heard Molly come in.

Audrey shot out of her seat. "Molly!"

Talia looked at Molly, then at Wesley. Their profiles were so similar. That was what Molly had seen that day at the festival, when she was staring at the makeshift stage. She was looking at a shadowy image of herself. It must have confused her, even frightened her.

Molly looked a wreck. Her French braid was plastered to her skull, and her colorful tee and denim shorts were soaked. Ignoring her mother, she glowered at Wesley. "By the way, *Mr.* Thurman, I've already unfriended you. I only friended you in the first place to see what kind of crap you were trying to pull. I thought you were a perv then, and I still think you're a perv."

Audrey was trembling so hard Talia thought she might shatter. She looked as if she wanted to talk but couldn't make the words leave her lips.

"Molly, please come in and sit with us," Talia urged. "Let's talk about it, okay?" Even as she spoke the words, she knew she didn't want to be a part of this mess. This was something Audrey and Wes had to work out with Molly—if that was even possible. Talia thought it might be too late for that.

The eatery was going to be opening soon, but Talia doubted they'd have many customers today. The rain didn't seem to be letting up, and the lightning was getting downright scary.

Molly moved away from the door and went over to Wesley, jabbing a trembling finger in his face. "If my dad were alive, he would kick your sorry behind from here to the moon. So why don't you just leave and never come back, because no one wants you here!"

Wesley's jaw dropped, and in the next moment, Molly was gone, slamming the door behind her.

Audrey started to rush after her daughter, but Wesley leaped up and held her shoulders in a firm grasp. "Let her go, Audrey. Give her time to think it through. She's a smart girl. She takes after her mom."

"Then she's in trouble," Audrey said over a ragged sob, "because her mom did everything wrong."

22

After Wesley persuaded Audrey to go somewhere to talk privately, Talia and Martha collapsed into adjoining chairs. "Talk about mental torture," Talia said. "That was absolutely excruciating."

Talia felt surer than ever that Wesley had paid Dylan to kill Norma Ferguson. Now that she understood why Thurman had so thoroughly despised the woman, the pieces had all come together. Seeing the two men together at the Popover Palace had clinched it for her. Payment had been made for something. What else could it have been for?

She wished Prescott would return her call. There was so much she had to tell her.

Martha was looking off in the distance, her eyes flitting from one spot to another. Talia knew her thoughts were bouncing all over the place. She waited for Martha to respond, but her employee seemed to have gone mute again.

"Martha?" Talia prodded. "Wasn't that a nightmare?" She poured them each a mug of hot coffee. Martha didn't touch hers, but Talia added her usual dollop of cream to her own and took a sip.

Martha pushed her mug aside and looked at Talia, a haunted expression in her eyes. "I dreamed about Lucas last night. He was lying in a hospital bed, all hooked up to tubes. I kept screaming at him to wake up, to stop fooling us, but he wouldn't move. Then a man wearing green scrubs came in. 'Please move aside,' the man said. 'We're taking him to the morgue.' I tried to block him, but he pushed me out of the way."

Talia swallowed. She felt fresh tears flow down her cheeks. Then Martha started to cry in earnest—her shoulders heaving—in loud, uncontrollable sobs. It triggered a copycat effect, and before long Talia was blubbering, too. She could barely think anymore. It was almost eleven thirty. Should she open Fry Me? Or should she shut down for the day with a sign proclaiming SORRY. WE'RE CLOSED TODAY?

Then Martha let out one agonized wail and pounded her fist on the table. "If only I could trade places with him—I'd do it in a heartbeat!"

Talia couldn't handle much more of this. She couldn't keep up this deception, and it was unfair of Patti Prescott to expect it. What had she promised the detective?

No one will ever hear it from my lips . . .

Talia looked frantically around the kitchen. Her gaze landed on the sample pack of condiment containers the sales guy from Nifty Squeezables had left her. She'd tossed it on a shelf, figuring she'd deal with it later.

She scraped back her chair, nabbed the Squeezables

pack, and then tore off the plastic wrapper. She grabbed the first one—the plastic mustard container—and unscrewed the cap.

Martha gawked at her. "What are you doing?" she said, and then loudly blew her nose.

Talia held up one finger to signal that she needed a minute. She located a new bottle of ketchup from the storeroom, opened it, and began squeezing it into the yellow container. For once she wished she'd bought one of those runny brands instead of this thick stuff.

"Talia, I thought you weren't going to use those things. They're not even washed yet! And you're putting ketchup in the mustard thingy!"

Talia ignored her. When the container was two-thirds full, she screwed the cap on and then went over and pulled Martha's arm. She tugged her over to the worktable and pointed at the cutting board.

Martha looked frightened. "You've gone over the edge, haven't you?" she whispered.

Talia pressed a finger to her lips, then pointed again. She used the ketchup to spell out the words: *Lucas is okay.*

Martha cried out and stumbled backward. She grabbed Talia's arm and said, "For real?"

Talia nodded quickly and then added, *No one can know,* in ketchup.

Martha nodded, acknowledging that she got it. She understood the reason for the subterfuge. Silently, the two hugged. They jumped up and down like two sisters who hadn't seen each other in twenty years.

Martha snatched up the cutting board and rinsed it off in the sink. She dried it with a bunch of paper towels and plunked it back down. Joy shone in her eyes and tears flowed down her wide cheeks.

Talia went to the front door and opened it. Almost unbelievably, the rain was coming down even harder. Just standing there, she got a face full of rainwater. The cobblestone plaza was deserted. She could barely see as far as the Fork and Dish. If the lights were on inside the shop, it wasn't apparent. Talia couldn't help wondering if Audrey had actually gone somewhere with Wesley to hash things out, or if she'd ditched him and headed somewhere else in search of Molly.

She had to get to Detective Prescott, before Wesley Thurman left town and Dylan stashed the payoff money someplace where it couldn't be found. She called her again. Again she had to leave a voice mail.

Talia turned the CLOSED sign to OPEN. She and Martha were there, and the basic food prep was done, so they might as well open up to customers. Not that anyone was likely to come in.

Still wet from her earlier encounter with Jodie Ferringer, she figured she could at least exchange her damp apron for a fresh one. She reached up to the shelf where the blue aprons with the Fry Me logo were stacked. Martha emerged from the walk-in storage closet at that moment and bumped Talia's arm. The pile of aprons fell to the floor, and suddenly Talia gasped.

"Martha. Oh, Martha, Martha, Martha, Martha, Martha."

Martha raised one eyebrow and gave her a strange look, then bent and began picking up the aprons. Talia squeezed her arm and stopped her. "Oh, Martha, I think that's it." She stared down at the aprons, at the way they'd toppled willy-nilly.

Martha straightened. "You're scaring me—you know that? You're not going cray-cray on me, are you?" she said, almost teasing.

"No. No, I don't think so." She told Martha what Harry had said about Norma dropping her box of supplies and utensils on the way to the temporary cooking stations that day, at the competition.

"Okaaay. So?" Martha said.

"Harry said that he and a few others stopped and helped her pick up her things, but that Norma didn't even act grateful."

Martha frowned. "So? I'm still not following."

Talia waved an impatient hand. "I'm getting away from my point. That day, I'd headed off to my cooking station ahead of the other contestants. I'd gotten a bad feeling about the whole thing and just wanted to prepare my entry, turn it in, and get it over with. According to Harry, he had been trailing behind me, along with Dylan and Crystal and Norma. I'm not sure where Vivian was. She walks kind of slow, so she probably brought up the rear."

Martha rolled her hand in a hurry-up motion. "And . . . ?"

"Martha, don't you see? If Crystal had been the one who picked up Norma's rolling pin, that's how her fingerprints could've gotten on it!"

"Hmmm. It's possible, I suppose," Martha said. "But why wouldn't Crystal have mentioned it to the police?"

"She probably didn't even remember it. I mean, just picture it, okay? Except for Norma, they were all anxious to get to their cooking stations. Norma drops her box and her stuff rolls out everywhere. The others stop in their tracks and start grabbing things and shoving them back in her box. They're really not paying attention to what they're seeing—they just want to get her box repacked so that they can get to their own cooking stations. Crystal was so excited about being a finalist in the contest that it probably never stuck in her mind that she'd been the one to retrieve the rolling pin."

Martha looked doubtful. "Yeah, but wait a minute. Norma made a flaky-top something-or-other for her entry, right?"

"Yes," Talia confirmed. "Flaky-top chicken stew."

"Wouldn't Crystal's prints have gotten obliterated when she used it to roll out the pastry?"

Talia felt her triumphant smile slide off her face. "I . . . um . . . I guess they could have. I don't really know that much about fingerprint technology."

Darn! Martha had just busted her bubble wide open. She'd been so sure she'd stumbled on the solution.

"You'd better Google it before you suggest it to Detective Prescott," Martha said dryly. "Otherwise she's likely to laugh you out of town."

But there was something else. Something that teased Talia's brain like a toy dangled in front of a playful cat. For some weird reason, she felt sure it had something to do with Martha.

A crack of thunder exploded in the sky. The two of them jumped visibly. Talia had an insane urge to yell, "The sky is falling! The sky is falling!" like in that old children's story.

Martha shivered. "It's actually getting chilly in here. It's not even September yet. I hope we don't have another winter like that last one." She scowled, but the old animation was back in her eyes.

It *had* been a bad winter, Talia reflected. Snow up to the rooftops, plus unrelenting cold.

Martha threw up her arms. "Well, we're all set to serve,

and we have no one to serve. I might as well give the tables a once-over. In fact, I should have done it this morning. It was my turn, right?"

Talia nodded, her thoughts drifting off on a tangent. It had been Martha's turn to spruce up the dining room, but in the state she'd arrived this morning, Talia had thought it wise not to remind her.

Martha reached below the speckled counter for the lime-scented cleaner and located a fresh cloth. Talia checked her phone. No text from Detective Prescott. Where was the woman? Could it be her day off? Talia supposed she was entitled to one, but it wasn't like the detective to take time off when an unsolved murder was hanging over the town. Unless, of course, she really did believe that the killer had already been nabbed and tagged with a tracking device.

No, Patti knew something was amiss. She knew the killer had fallen into their laps with far too much ease. Talia had sensed it when they were talking privately outside on the plaza.

"Ugh," Martha bleated from the dining room. She waved a glossy coloring book in the air. "I found this underneath one of the seats. Some sloppy kid got tartar sauce all over it and just left it there." She shook her head in mock disgust. Martha loved kids, but she refused to admit it. Maintaining her curmudgeonly persona was far more fun.

Talia started to give her a halfhearted smile, but all at once she froze. Why did the coloring book remind her of something?

Wrinkling her nose, Martha went over to the trash can and dumped it in. "I hate to tell you what else it smells like. Don't kids have manners anymore?"

And in that moment, Talia captured the memory that had been eluding her. She scurried around the edge of the counter into the dining area, to where Martha was scraping ketchup off the back of a chair. "Martha, remember the day of the festival, when you first sat down at our table?"

Martha stuck a hand on her hip. "Yeah, sort of. Why?"

"Didn't you say Jodie Ferringer shoved one of those political brochures at you, even though you shook your head to refuse it?"

"Yeah, she did. I ended up having to take it so she wouldn't let it drop to the ground." Martha gave an evil grin. "I don't think my attitude pleased her, the b—"

"You brought the brochure to the table," Talia interrupted. "I remember, because you sniffed it before you tossed it down."

"I did?" Martha scrunched up her face, trying to remember. "That's right. I did. It had kind of a pungent smell. No, not pungent—that's the wrong word. It was tangy."

"Tangy bad?"

Slowly, Martha shook her head. "No, tangy good. Kind of like—I don't know—celery salt, sage, and tarragon? It reminded me of Thanksgiving."

Talia felt her heart do a broad jump. She should have seen it all along. How could she have been so blind? Jodie was using the blue cooler to transport Ferringer's political brochures to the festival. But that wasn't all that was in that cooler.

"Martha, I think I know why Norma was acting so weird that day," Talia said. "I think—"

A loud boom from somewhere outside cut her off midsentence.

"Yikes!" Talia cried. "What was that?"

Martha tapped her chest, as if she'd just suffered a heart attack. "That was loud, wasn't it? Sounded to me like a transformer blew."

Sirens wailed in the distance, and in the next instant, the lights went off. The eatery was left in darkness.

23

"Stay where you are, Martha. I've got a heavy-duty flash-light. Somewhere."

Talia fumbled her way back into the kitchen. She'd almost reached the storage closet when she heard Martha bellow, "Ouch, my knee!" A muffled curse followed. Make that two curses.

"Be careful, Martha," Talia called out. "Don't move until I get the flashlight."

She remembered setting the high-powered flashlight, complete with fresh batteries, on a particular shelf in a spe-cific spot in the supply closet. Easy to find in an emergency, right? Wrong. The flashlight had somehow journeyed through a maze of canned tomatoes, jars of mayo, and a slew of condiment cups. By the time Talia located it, she was tempted to let out a curse herself.

Talia snapped on the battery's switch, and a swath of light

swept over the ceiling. "Are you okay?" she asked, swinging the light around so that it illuminated Martha's leg.

"I'm fine," Martha said crankily. "You don't need to shine the light on it."

Talia looked around to ground herself. How could she know the eatery so well and yet be helpless when the lights went out? She should have been able to navigate every inch of it in her sleep.

Whenever a transformer blew, there was no telling how long it would take for the power to come back on. It didn't make sense for either of them to stay there. If the weather cleared up later in the day, they could always come back and reopen.

Talia opened the front door again. The rain was lashing the cobblestones in windswept blasts. She couldn't ever recall seeing the plaza so thoroughly flooded. She turned the OPEN sign to CLOSED and pushed the door firmly shut.

Martha was fairly strong, but she didn't walk fast. Talia hated the thought of her having to trudge to the town lot in this awful storm. They'd both get soaked to the skin. It made better sense for Talia to dash out to her car and then come back and pick up Martha in the service alley behind the eatery.

She told Martha her plan.

"Normally I'd say you were being ridiculous," Martha grumped. "But my knee is throbbing, and I'm not the fastest walker."

"It's a deal, then," Talia said, and handed her the flashlight. "While I'm gone, check to be sure everything is shut down and turned off. Once I'm at the back door, I'll call you from my cell. And lock the front door after me, okay?"

"Sounds like a plan, ma'am. Wait. What about the food? If the power stays off too long, won't everything spoil?"

Talia groaned. Martha was right. "It might," she said, "but there's not much we can do right now. I could take some of it home, but who knows if I'll even have power there? If the rain lets up in a little while and I've got power at my house, I can come back and retrieve some of the perishables."

Martha gave her a weak salute. Talia grabbed her handbag and her umbrella from her locker and seconds later was out the front door. She thought she heard Martha yelling something at her, but she was already being pulled into the storm by the fierce wind. She waved and put her hand to her ear to signal *I'll call you*, but she wasn't even sure Martha saw her.

By the time she reached the sidewalk, her umbrella was inside out. She shivered from the wet and the cold—it was chilling her right to the bone. How could the temperature have dropped so quickly since that morning?

Talia could barely see as she pushed her way along the sidewalk. Water sluiced over the sides of her Keds, and her feet began to feel like ice blocks. The storefronts had all gone dark and the traffic lights were flashing—sure signs that the power outage was fairly widespread. Only a few brave souls were out in the storm, most of them headed toward the town lot.

When she reached the lot, she saw one poor elderly man struggling to open his car door. His hat had blown away, and he looked as if he'd just been fished out of a lake. She slogged over to him and held his car door while he lowered himself inside.

"Ah, thank you, dearie," he said. "Much obliged. Get yourself home safe, now!"

She closed his door and then trod over to her Fiat. At least a bucket of rain followed her inside, but she was grateful to be out of the deluge.

Talia's thermostat was set on AC, but she quickly changed it to warm air and flipped on the defroster. She glanced to her right and spotted Martha's monstrosity of a Chrysler, rain hammering its roof so hard that she thought the sheet metal might cave. Martha had been saving for a new car and hoped to have enough to buy one before the first snowflake of the season fell. For now she was content to cruise around in her old beater, as she called it.

Talia started her Fiat and flicked on her wipers. Even on high, they barely kept the windshield clear enough for her to see. She'd have to drive slowly, very slowly. Since she was picking up Martha in the one-way service alley, she exited the parking lot at the rear, onto Birch Street. That would bring her to the back of the arcade, and from there she could swing into the alley.

Her knuckles white on the steering wheel, she turned out of the lot. Almost instantly, a car was driving right on her tail, its headlights blurred and wavy in the punishing rain. A finger of fear stroked the base of her neck. Was it Dylan in his Merkur following her?

The car behind her turned abruptly onto a side street, and she let out a gasp of relief. Her imagination was going wonky on her. She needed to concentrate on the road in front of her.

She clamped her hands over the steering wheel and kept her grip firm. Even with her headlights on, she was terrified another driver wouldn't see her and would slide into her car.

Finally—the ride seemed never-ending—Talia turned left into the alley. What should have been a two-minute ride had taken her almost nine minutes. When she'd almost reached the eatery's rear entrance, she saw another car already parked there. Had Martha gotten impatient and called someone else to pick her up? The car was gray, possibly a luxury model, and had something stuck to the rear bumper. Stickers of some sort, one on each side. The car didn't appear to be running, and Talia couldn't see well enough to know if someone was inside. Had the driver flooded the engine and just abandoned it there? But why would someone have driven down the alley in the first place?

Talia parked about ten feet from the rear of the gray car and shifted her Fiat into Park. If the other car didn't move, she'd be forced to back her way out of the alley—a near impossibility in zero-visibility weather. It was at that moment that she noticed the license plate. Squinting to make it out in the pummeling rain, she saw that the tag number began with HG7 . . .

Wait a minute. HG7. Why did that jog a memory?

The day of the festival, at the ball field! A young man reading from a slip of paper had asked three people to move their cars, saying they were blocking access. He went on to announce the offending plate numbers over the loudspeaker. The first one began with HG7. . . . She was almost sure of it.

She focused on the gray car again. It was tricky reading the bumper stickers through the heavy rain, especially with her wipers barely making a dent, but she was almost sure the stickers read: GO FAR WITH FERRINGER!

Ugh. Another Ferringer supporter.

But something else was sticking in her memory. What was it?

And then she got it, and her insides morphed from a solid to a liquid. High school chemistry. The periodic table of the elements.

That day, when Lucas mumbled "mercury" to the EMTs, it wasn't because the killer drove a Mercury. It was because the killer drove a car with a tag number that began with HG. On the periodic table, Hg was the atomic symbol for mercury. And Lucas had just bought those book covers at Queenie's Variety, so the periodic table of the elements had been fresh in his mind.

She scrolled the wheels of her mind backward in time, to the start of the festival. After the young guy had made the announcement, she remembered seeing Bruce Ferringer toss his car keys at his wife. Jodie had looked quite put out that he'd expected her to move his car. She'd stalked off toward the parking lot, pouting like a spoiled child.

But that hadn't been Jodie's only trek to the parking area that day. She'd had to go one more time so she could pull off her underhanded ruse.

Her fingers trembling, Talia pulled out her phone and rang Martha's cell. It rang and rang and then defaulted to voice mail. Darn! Martha had probably gone to the ladies' room and left her phone in the kitchen. She'd have to try again in a few minutes. She wanted to tell Martha to stay inside with the doors locked and also to call the police.

Never mind. She'd have to call them herself. Prescott still hadn't returned her calls, so she started to dial nine-one-one. She'd gotten as far as the first "nine" when her passenger-side door was suddenly wrenched open. A bulky figure in a dripping wet raincoat bent low and then rushed inside. The intruder dropped onto the seat, then slammed the door shut. He plucked her cell roughly out of her hand.

Talia gasped. Her throat closed with terror. Without a word, the man disconnected her call and then ripped the battery out of her phone. Talia noticed he was wearing tan leather gloves. Water trickled down his face, and his eyes shone with fury.

Ferringer jammed her cell phone into the pocket of his raincoat and pulled out another object—a small handgun. He pointed the gun at her heart. "Hands away from the steering wheel," he ordered. "Turn off the wipers and shut off the engine."

Cold shivers racking her limbs, Talia did as instructed.

Ferringer laughed, a grating sound that shredded her nerves. "By the way, if you were trying to get ahold of your Martha, you can forget about it. I sent her on a wild-goose chase."

Talia stared at him. "But . . . but how did you—"

"I was driving down Main when I spotted you struggling against the storm to get to the parking lot. I watched where you went. I planned to follow you and get rid of you once and for all. When you turned left out of the parking lot instead of the other way, I figured you were headed back to your restaurant. You were driving at the pace of a turtle, so I quickly made a call to your eatery and pretended I was the police. I told Martha all businesses in the downtown area have been ordered to evacuate immediately. I even told her what route to take home, since some of the roads have been closed. She wanted to wait for you, but I put the kibosh on that notion. Told her you weren't even going to be allowed to drive back to the arcade because roads were being blocked off. Right about now, she should be sitting in traffic backed up halfway to Mars, trying to get over the bridge on Railroad Avenue." He chortled at his cleverness. "Oh dear, I guess I didn't tell her the road is all washed out and traffic is at a standstill. Plus, there's a fire at the abandoned coat shop, so no one is going anywhere too quickly. By the way, my call to Martha will prove untraceable. Every smart politician keeps a disposable phone or two on hand."

You're not smart. You're evil, Talia wanted to say. She wrapped her arms around her stomach, trying to stanch the shaking in her body. At least Martha was safe, even if she was sitting in that big old Chrysler of hers, cursing at the traffic.

"After I hung up with Martha, I whipped onto a side street, took a shortcut to the arcade, and parked here. My Avalon handles like a dream, you know. Too bad you'll never own one."

Stay calm. Play dumb, she told herself.

She tried to avoid looking at the gun. "Um, Bruce, I'm still not sure why you're so upset with me. Can't you put the gun away so we can talk? Is it about that political luncheon? If it is, you should know that I've already changed my mind. I decided to let you have it on a Sunday after all. If you don't believe me, you can ask Jodie. We talked about it only a short while ago."

"Cut the crap," he said in a dangerous tone. "You've been asking way too many questions about my wife. It's time I put an end to your interference before you ruin me."

"I . . . I'm sorry," she said, trying to act confused. "I'm honestly not following." And then, pretending the light had suddenly dawned, she widened her eyes. "Oh, is it because I asked about her new pendant, the one from LaFleur's? Oh my, that was gorgeous, wasn't it? So generous of you to buy that for her. I wanted to get something similar for my mom, but the price was way out of my league."

Talia knew she sounded like a babbling boob, but she was trying to keep him distracted.

"You are one pain in my behind. You know that?" Ferringer's eyes flashed with fury. "You and my wife, you're like two bedsores on opposite sides of my butt. Her with her uncontrollable spending and you with your constant spying. What's the matter with you, anyway? Can't you leave well enough alone?"

Talia murmured a silent prayer, and then her ire flared. "Does 'well enough' mean letting Crystal Galardi go off to prison for a murder you committed? And leaving Lucas to languish in a hospital bed?"

Ferringer's face reddened, and he swallowed. "I never wanted to hurt that kid. He saw me open my trunk with the rolling pin in my hand, so I had no choice. As for Crystal . . ." He shrugged. "I have nothing against the woman, other than the fact that she's always peddling expensive cooking crap to my wife. Apparently she thinks I'm rolling in dough, and I don't mean cookie dough."

"Jodie has a shopping addiction, doesn't she?" Talia said.

A harsh laugh escaped Ferringer. "My wife has what the experts call a compulsive buying disorder. Sounds fancy, doesn't it?"

"Then it's a sickness," Talia sniped. "Maybe she needs help."

"Yeah, everything's a sickness these days. Everyone's got a handy excuse for their lousy behavior."

And what's your excuse for being a monster?

Ferringer ranted on. "I'm trying to run a campaign, and she's wasting money on clothes and jewels and all sorts of other trash she doesn't need!" He curled his lip in disgust. "She finally confessed to me this morning that she's been running up two secret credit cards in her maiden name—and I use the word 'maiden' loosely. Between the two cards, she owes about thirty-nine grand, plus interest up the wazoo."

Talia stared through the rain-coated windshield. With the wipers off, it looked as if she was sitting under Niagara

Falls. Ferringer had murdered Norma and had come closing to killing Lucas. He wouldn't hesitate to kill again.

She was in bad trouble. Detective Prescott was right. The third time would not be the charm.

"That's why Jodie needed the prize money from the Steel-top Foods competition," Talia said. "Twenty-five thousand, minus whatever cut she was giving Norma, would've gone a long way toward paying off those cards before you found out."

"So you figured out about Norma. Goody for you. Everyone said you were nosy but smart." His grin mutated into a scowl. "It wasn't just the credit cards. I found out she'd been tapping into my campaign account. The witch was even cleverer than I gave her credit for. She listed things under expenditures—a few hundred here, fifty bucks there—nothing to raise any red flags. Treated herself and her friends to a couple nice lunches at the country club. She made out the check stubs like they were for campaign events. Even Stacey didn't catch on right away."

"I still don't understand," Talia said. "Why did she need Norma? Why didn't she just enter the competition under her own name?"

"Are you freakin' nuts?" he railed. "Can you imagine how it would've made me look when she won? Everyone would think I'd paid off the judges or rigged the contest. I've got an election in less than three months, and I need to look squeaky-clean! She didn't enter under her own name because she knew I'd kill her. You're not as sharp as I thought."

"Her chances of winning would've been one in six," Talia said.

"Wrong. Technically she won, didn't she? And you've obviously never tasted my wife's cooking. Absolutely out of this world. No way she'd have lost. *No way.* My wife is a prime example of why women should stay in the kitchen and leave the business world to the men."

You unenlightened creep.

"She's been overspending for at least a year, racking up charges like she's some kind of princess. She even had that dizzy dame at the jewelry store making up phony receipts so it would look like she was getting some real bargains."

Talia's mind darted back to what Dylan had told her, how he'd heard the radio go on in Norma's cooking station that day. That had to be the moment when Jodie sneaked in to deliver her chicken stew. Her casserole must have been hidden in the zippered cooler, under all those stacks of brochures. That was the scent Martha had detected on the brochure—the aroma of Jodie's delectable chicken stew. Jodie had either brought, or instructed Norma to bring, a radio, to cover up the sounds of their voices in case they drifted into the other cooking stations.

Talia's voice rattled. "I still don't understand why you killed Norma."

"After the competition she came looking for me, said she had something urgent to talk to me about. I couldn't imagine what the old biddy wanted that was so important, but I agreed to meet her in her cooking station. Luckily no one was around when I got there. Otherwise I'd have been screwed. By then everyone was watching the softball game. Jodie had toddled off to meet up with a couple of her gal pals who were watching the game. I think they just wanted to ogle the ballplayers. Anyway, when I got there, the first thing I saw was the box of utensils sitting on the floor. At first I thought maybe she wanted help getting it to her car. But then she dropped a bombshell on me."

"Let me guess," Talia said. "She told you about the ruse and wanted more money. Whatever Jodie agreed to pay her wasn't enough. Or maybe she wanted to keep it all—the whole twenty-five thousand."

Ferringer shook his head. "No. It was worse. Much worse. Dear old Norma came down with a sudden attack of conscience. After she told me about the stunt she and Jodie had pulled off, she said she was going to confess to her role in the whole mess and forfeit the prize. She blamed it all on Jodie, said my wife nagged her until she agreed to do it, but she'd never felt good about it."

Norma's sister, Ethel, had been right. She'd sensed that something serious had been weighing on Norma's mind. Despite her unpleasant and conniving ways, Norma had probably never done anything quite so devious. So she'd decided to confess—and signed her own death warrant.

Talia rubbed her arms. They were nearly numb from fear and cold.

"I flipped out," Ferringer said. "My political career would've been over, flushed straight down the chute." He turned to Talia, his eyes glazed. "I looked down at her utensils. She'd never even used them because Jodie had made the stew. Ironic, right?" He laughed, an awful sound that frightened Talia to the core. "When she turned to leave, I snatched up the rolling pin—it was right on top—and smashed her on the back of the head. The second she fell, I knew she was gone. Her eyes—" He swallowed. "There was a pot holder in the box, so I used it to wipe off the handle and bring it out to my car. I figured I'd toss it all in my trunk and get rid of it later."

"Why didn't you just wipe off the handle and leave the rolling pin there?"

"For the obvious reason, dummy. It's harder for the cops

to solve a murder if they don't have the weapon. I didn't get the idea about planting it in that Dumpster until later, when I found out the cops were focusing their sights on Crystal. Anyway, that day, I was at my car when—" He broke off and shook his head.

Talia knew what came next and felt her stomach clench. "When you saw Lucas, the one person who could tie you to the scene."

"Cripes, I never wanted to hurt that kid! But the look on his face . . . I knew he'd seen enough to nail me to the wall. I've got plans, Talia. Big plans! My career is finally going somewhere. Mark my words. I'm going all the way to the statehouse. I just couldn't have that kid . . ." He covered his face with one hand, but the gun in his other remained straight and steady. "I had to do it. Can't you see that? I'm glad he's in critical condition. With any luck, he'll pass quietly, and I'll be off the hook. I'll attend the funeral, of course, and be right there consoling his parents."

The urge to reach over and punch Ferringer was almost irresistible. Talia clenched her fist in her lap to keep it steady. "You won't get away with this, Bruce," she said softly. She knew it was hopeless, but she had to try. "Why don't you let me drive you to the police station and we'll hash it out there?"

Ferringer looked at her through crazed eyes, sending a fresh batch of shivers down her spine. "Are you freakin' kidding me? You seriously think I'm going to turn myself in?"

From somewhere in the distance came the wail of competing sirens, whether from police cars or a fire truck she couldn't be sure. Both, probably. To her dismay, they seemed to be traveling farther away.

"I can't sit here with you all day, chatting like we're at a tea party. Sorry to say it, but you deserve what you're getting, Talia. You should have kept your nose out of things and stayed in the kitchen, like a proper woman is supposed to."

The rain was still coming down in sheets. Tears stung her eyes. What would her folks do without her? Ryan would probably take Bo, but—

Without warning, Ferringer shoved open his door and got out. Could she make a run for it?

No time like the present, she decided. She opened her door and stumbled out into the rain. Almost instantly, she felt a powerful hand clamp over her upper arm and drag her toward the other car. She went limp to keep her feet from cooperating, but he dragged her along the pavement as if she were no heavier than a scrap of cloth.

A sob erupted from Talia's throat. *Don't cry,* she told herself. *Scream!*

She opened her mouth and let out a shriek that should have pierced the average eardrum.

Ferringer slapped his hand over her mouth with one meaty hand and crammed her head under his arm. He dragged her toward the Avalon, using his key to click open the lock to the trunk. Talia saw the lid rise and started to cry.

In one swift movement, Ferringer hefted her upward and dumped her inside the trunk. Her left leg hadn't quite made it in, so he grabbed onto it. She kicked at him, grazing his shoulder, and he called her a charming name. He grabbed the leg again, and this time managed to thrust it into the trunk. "You're toast, Talia," he said with a final rumble of laughter.

Somewhere, a siren whined. This time it sounded closer, almost as if—

Ferringer started to close the trunk, and in the next instant,

...is face contorted. He let out a shrill, agonized cry and col-
...apsed to the ground. And then a second, even louder cry.

Talia sat up to see Martha standing there, drenched to
the bone, a triumphant smirk on her face. Wielding her new
umbrella like a weapon of mass duck feet, she pointed it at
Ferringer. "I wouldn't try to get up if I were you, Ferringer.
Like you just found out, these duck feet pack a punch."

Red lights flashed behind Talia's Fiat, and a siren whooped
and then died. From the other end of the alley, in front of the
Avalon, a state police SUV roared up and screeched to a halt.
Two men hopped out and raced over to Ferringer, who was
writhing on the pavement.

"Oh God, please get me to a doctor," Ferringer moaned,
while his hands were being cuffed behind him. "It hurts
so bad."

Sergeant Liam O'Donnell quickly checked him out.
"You'll be fine," he said with a slight wince, aiming his gaze
below Ferringer's belt. "Probably could use an ice pack
down there, though. I'll see if we have one handy." He read
Ferringer his rights and then led him to the SUV.

Detective Patti Prescott sprinted over to where Martha
was standing, and then she saw Talia trying to clamber out
of the trunk. She helped her out and made sure she was steady.
"Are you okay?" Prescott asked.

Talia nodded. "I am now. A little shaky."

"Never a dull moment with you, is there?" Prescott said,
and then turned her gaze on Martha. "You got him good,
Martha. Right on the money!" She gave Martha a light, playful
punch to the shoulder. "I guess he couldn't *duck* your swing,
could he?"

"Actually I got him twice," Martha said with a sly smile.
"Just in case the first one didn't take."

Prescott laughed. "Double whammy!"

Talia wiped rainwater and tears away from her face. She ran over and hugged Martha. "He said you'd be stuck in traffic all day, and I believed him."

"Yeah, well, his directions for evacuating the downtown area made about as much sense as his political platform. I might not be a native, but I wasn't hatched in a bird's nest. When he told me to turn left on Bramber, I knew he was sending me in the wrong direction. I probably would've ended up in the Housatonic River." She looked at Talia. "I waited inside for a while, and then I started to wonder if you might be in trouble. I peeked out the back door and saw you sitting in your car. I couldn't make out much through the rain, but what I saw didn't look good. I called the cops, grabbed my umbrella, and"—she shrugged—"you know the rest."

"He told me everything," Talia said. "He killed Norma and hurt Lucas because Norma and Jodie cheated on the contest and he didn't want it to ruin the election and—"

Prescott made a time-out sign with her hands. "You can tell me when we get to the station," she said. "O'Donnell needs to hear it, too."

Talia turned and hugged Martha again. "You're my hero," she said through a round of sniffles.

"I hate to break up this little reunion," Prescott said. "But we're standing here in the pouring rain, and you both have to come to the station with me to give a statement. Why don't you both get inside the unmarked car and—"

"I don't think so," Martha interrupted. "I'm not going to the police station until I've seen Lucas, so I suggest you drive us straight to the hospital."

For one agonizing moment, Talia held her breath, waiting

for Prescott's reaction. Had she caught on that Martha knew the truth about Lucas?

The detective gave Talia a stony look, and then her nutmeg-colored eyes softened. She waved both women toward her vehicle. "You don't have to go to the hospital. Lucas is home. We were going to arrange for round-the-clock protection, but now it looks like we won't need to."

Talia looked down at her sodden clothes and made a face. "Only one problem. Unless the waterlogged look is in vogue this season, I don't think we should show up at the Barto-linis' house looking like this."

"Good point," Prescott acknowledged. "How about if I drive each of you home to change into dry clothes? Then I'll pick you up and we'll head over to Lucas's folks' house. You can have ten minutes with him, and that's it. After that, you're both coming to the station to give a statement. And for heaven's sake, don't maul the poor kid! Even though he's going to be fine, he's still recovering from a head injury."

Talia let out a tiny hoot of joy, and Martha gave the detective her coolest of smiles. "Anything you say, Detective. You're the one in charge."

24

"Oh my, Talia, I think I am just going to burst! I can't believe we're really doing it!" Crystal Galardi wrung her hands, her brown eyes beaming from behind her ruby-tinged eyeglasses. She looked like her old self again, her fingers decked out in colorful rings and her nails glimmering in a sparkly shade of pumpkin. She'd had a beauty treatment the day before, and her blond curls positively bounced around her face.

Talia glanced up from her task of setting up her student stations and smiled at her friend. "Well, we're doing it," she confirmed. "I think it's going to be so much fun. I only hope I won't mess up my demonstration!"

"Oh, good gravy, don't even think such a thing." Crystal clomped over to Talia on her floral-print peep-toe pumps and gazed over the counter along the far right-hand wall where Talia was preparing for her deep-fry demonstration.

"Don't worry. I'm teasing," Talia assured her. She hoped.

Talia herself was wearing her usual blue Fry Me a Sliver apron and her cozy new pair of Keds. When she cooked she had to be comfortable, and that meant wearing soft soles.

With Audrey's help, Crystal had come up with a syllabus for eight cooking demonstrations, one per week, starting on the Saturday following Labor Day. The first one would be today, and Talia had agreed to be the visiting chef. Seven other local chefs, including Dylan McPhee and Harry Summers, had agreed to take a turn at the teaching gig. According to Crystal, Harry had actually gushed over the opportunity, while Dylan had merely shrugged and said, "Sure."

Along the far right wall of the Fork and Dish, an oak counter, along which six stools had been lined up, formed the somewhat informal classroom. Talia had set up her deep fryer and a convection oven on the work space behind her. It was a mite cramped, but she could make it work. Plans were in the works for a more functional teaching space, but for now the temporary setup would do just fine. She'd heard a rumor that Wesley Thurman was going to help with funding the renovations, but so far that was only hearsay.

Audrey appeared from the storeroom, looking comely in a pale blue sheath and navy ballet flats. Her eyes bore a touch of coppery shadow on the lids, but the sadness in them couldn't be concealed. "Are we nearly all set?" she asked, looking over Talia's work space.

"We are." Crystal slipped her arm through Audrey's. "Thank you for agreeing to do this, Audrey. I really do think it'll help bring in more business. It'll get our name out there, and when the time is right, we can think about expanding."

Audrey removed her arm and slipped it around her friend's waist, her pale brown eyes clouded. "I'm sorry I've been so

awful these past weeks. All I could think about was Wesley
coming to town. I was terrified he'd find out about Molly,
but it's obvious he'd already gleaned it. The drawbacks of
social media, I guess."

"Did he tell his family about her yet?" Talia asked.

Audrey nodded. "His dad's dead, but his mom knows.
She's so anxious to meet her only granddaughter. And his
sister, Prissy, went crazy with joy when she learned she has
a niece. They're both going to fly up here to meet her, once
Wesley can arrange it." Her eyes watered.

Talia walked around the oak counter and hugged her
friend. "You doing okay?" she asked.

Audrey blotted one eye with her finger. "Molly barely
spoke to me before she left for school. She wouldn't let me
drive her, but she let Wesley do it. Oh God, I miss her."

Talia and Crystal exchanged glances. "So they're talking,
at least. That's good, isn't it?" Talia said.

"I guess so. But I feel as if I've lost her . . ."

"You haven't lost her," Talia assured her. "I know Molly,
and I know she adores you. Give her a little space, Audrey.
It'll all work out. I promise."

Crystal gave Talia a tiny wink and went back to busying
herself in the shop.

"Wesley's thinking of giving Molly the Merkur he bought
from Dylan," Audrey said. "It's a classic. He said he coveted
that hunk of metal from the moment he saw Dylan driving
it into the parking lot that day." A tiny smile quirked her
lips, and her expression grew distant. Was she remembering
their younger days together?

Talia had heard all about the car purchase. It had happened the day she saw Wesley and Dylan having breakfast
in the Popover Palace. Wesley had given Dylan a check for

the car, and Dylan had reluctantly handed over the Certificate of Title. No wonder he'd looked so glum when he'd shot out of the restaurant!

"Dylan worshipped that car," Audrey said, "but he was willing to sell it to help out his mom. Wesley gave him an excellent price—more than it was worth. He promised to help Dylan find another one, when the time is right."

Talia cringed when she thought about what she'd witnessed that day at the Popover Palace. She'd totally misread what she'd seen and pegged both Wesley and Dylan as killers.

"I can totally picture Molly tooling around in that car," Talia said with a laugh.

"I can, too. But before Wesley gives it to her, he wants to have it thoroughly vetted by a mechanic to be sure it's in good shape. Old cars have issues. He doesn't want Molly breaking down on the highway, or worse."

Audrey wasn't the only one who missed Molly. Talia missed her, too. The young woman was a hard worker and fun to be around. A week after Ferringer's arrest, Molly had set up her ballot box for customers to vote for either skin-on or skin-off French fries. For an entire day, the eatery served only skin-on fries. The locals voted overwhelmingly for the original fries, nixing the ones with skins. Molly was disappointed, but she took it in stride. She'd hugged Talia and thanked her for letting her test her theory.

"It looked to me like Dylan took excellent care of the Merkur," Talia said. "I saw the clip in the paper about him a few days ago. I'm so glad for him. He's been taking care of his mom for a while. It's his turn to get a break."

According to the director of media relations at Steeltop Foods, the company had offered Dylan a contract to develop a minimum of three recipes a year, subject to approval by the board of directors. The recipes would be widely distributed and used to market a new line of products. Dylan had accepted the deal, subject to his attorney's approval of the contract. Talia could not have been happier for him. Maybe with a little outside help he'd take the time to polish his manners a bit. He might be a decent guy, but he came off as a grump.

"Did you hear about the Flavor Dial?" Talia asked Audrey, trying to take her mind off Molly.

"It was supposed to be hush-hush," Audrey said, "but yes, I did hear the news. It was a total embarrassment to the company, so it's gone the way of the pterodactyls. Good riddance, I say."

"I think I'm going to hang on to mine," Talia said. "Steel-top Foods produced a limited number of them, so they might be worth something someday."

Crystal giggled from the adjacent aisle. "Maybe you can retire on it."

The door to the shop opened, and in stepped Harry Summers. His handsome face glowed, and his smile lit the room. He waved a sheet of paper in the air and then summoned them over to where Talia stood at her work counter. "I couldn't wait to tell you all," he said. "Look."

The three women crowded around and stared at the photo of a charming old house. Below the photo was a purchase and sale agreement.

Talia recognized it immediately. "You bought Hainsley House!" she squealed, nearly leaping out of her Keds.

Harry beamed. "The owner accepted my offer. We close in ninety days, subject to a satisfactory inspection, of course." He slid a shy glance over at Audrey. "Mr., um, Thurman is helping me with the financing. He's giving me a much better deal than any of the banks were able to offer."

"That's because he has faith in you, Harry," Audrey told him. "Remember, it's an investment for him, too, and he's hoping to see a return on it."

"I'll do my best not to let him down."

Talia couldn't help herself. She rushed over and gave Harry a solid hug. "Is everything else okay, Harry?"

His brow furrowed and his face flushed. "Sandra and I are splitting. Her choice, not mine. Even the idea of owning Hainsley House didn't excite her, so we're calling it quits."

"I'm so sorry," Talia said quietly.

"Don't be. I really think it's for the best. Everything happens for a reason." With a wave and a grin, Harry headed toward the door. "Good luck with your class, ladies! I'm looking forward to taking my turn at it!" He closed the door, but then opened it again and popped his head in. "Oh, I forgot to tell you—my new restaurant has a ghost!"

They all beamed at the announcement. Talia felt sure Harry would make the most of his newly discovered specter.

"He's such a sweet man," Crystal said after Harry left. "That Sandra woman didn't deserve him, anyway. I'm glad she's bailing."

Audrey paled and sat on one of the stools. "I don't think Sandra ever knew what she wanted. In a way, she was a lot like Norma. Two peas in a venomous pod." She gave an ironic smile. "I'm tempted to feel sorry for her, but I don't think I can muster the emotion."

"Speaking of Norma, have you heard the latest on Jodie?" Crystal tittered.

"Yup," Talia said. "I saw the interview with her on the news a few nights ago. Now she's saying she suffered mental abuse at the hands of her husband."

Jodie Ferringer, whose accusations against her spouse

had been lighting up the local papers, claimed she hadn't been surprised at all to find out he'd killed Norma Ferguson and harmed that "poor young man." She was anxious to finalize their divorce so she could move on with her life.

"She's lucky," Audrey said. "Wesley agreed not to press charges against her for the scheme she tried to pull off. You heard he's giving the prize money to local charities, right?"

Talia and Crystal both nodded.

"But she might not be so lucky," Talia added, "if she gets investigated for mishandling campaign funds."

Crystal looked thoughtful. Talia wondered if she was thinking about her own ex and how he'd stolen their joint savings, leaving her nearly penniless. At least now she was on the right path, trying to get her finances back in order.

As for Jodie, in a crazy way Talia felt bad for her. Ferringer had used her as a trophy wife, never guessing she had a spending problem until it blossomed out of control. It was a marriage doomed from the start.

Besides, he wasn't a very nice man.

Lucas made a full recovery, which would work in Ferringer's favor. Ferringer admitted to killing Norma but claimed it was an accident. He'd retained a well-known attorney to represent him, but Talia doubted the ex-politician would see the light of day for a very long time.

But as the cliché goes . . . stranger things have happened.

Talia gazed at the six eager faces poised to witness her demonstration. Two men, both somewhere in their thirties, three fortysomething women, and a teenager in pigtails and braces. All looked excited to be there. Was she seeing future chefs in the making?

"I want to thank you all for being here today. I haven't done this before, so please bear with me if I bobble something or if I drop cheese on my shoe."

Everyone chuckled, and she started her spiel. The mac-and-cheese recipe she'd decided to use was the "busy woman's" recipe Ryan said his mom always made. Still furious with Sheila Collins for her callous handling of the divorce announcement, she'd almost ditched it at the last minute. She realized, though, that it contained the perfect shortcut for the hectic pace of today's homemakers. Plus, Arthur had been pleased to hear she'd be making the mac and cheese that he and Ryan had always enjoyed at home.

The demo went without a hitch. Talia showed everyone how to layer slices of sharp cheddar with cooked macaroni shells in a casserole dish. She prepared a mixture of whole milk, dried mustard, and a smidge of nutmeg and then poured it over the layers. She stuck the whole thing in the convection oven and started the baking process.

Since the deep-fried mac-and-cheese squares had to be prepared from a chilled casserole, she retrieved from Crystal's mini-fridge the one she'd already prepared and baked. The tricky part was the deep-frying. It wasn't foolproof, by any means, but through trial and error she'd come close to perfecting it.

She cut the cold casserole into workable squares, then showed them how to prepare the panko crumb mixture she'd created on her own. By the time the golden-fried squares emerged from the deep fryer, everyone was itching for a taste test.

"They look fabulous!"

"Oh, I'm just dying to taste that!"

"I can't wait to try this at home!"

After their appetites were sated, they all left, promising to return for another cooking demo. Talia gave each of her students a Fry Me a Sliver magnet, figuring a bit of advertising might go a long way. Crystal was thrilled that three of them—one of whom was the teenager—walked out with newly purchased deep fryers. The teenager had used her babysitting money to buy it.

Crystal did a tiny jig in the center aisle. "Oh, I just knew this was a great idea! Thank you so much, Talia!"

"Hey, don't thank me. It's good advertising for my place, too."

Audrey smiled, but it was clear that her heart was heavy. "It's been a good day," she said wistfully. "I think I'll do a little bookkeeping. I'll be out back if you need me."

"Audrey, wait a minute," Talia said. She looked at Crystal.

Crystal went over to the cash register station. She reached below the counter and brought out a silver laptop. She set it down and began tapping at the keys.

Talia took Audrey's elbow and led her over to where Crystal was booting up the computer. "There's something you need to see," she said.

Audrey wore a look of concern but said nothing. All at once Crystal grinned, and she turned the laptop so that it faced Audrey. The smiling visage of Molly filled the screen.

"Molly!" Audrey cried.

"Hi, Mom," Molly said softly, offering a sheepish smile. "Hey, look, I know things haven't been great with us the past few weeks, but I was wondering if you'd mind coming here next weekend and staying over for a night. Wesley and I have been talking about a lot of things, and . . . well, we want you to be included. You can stay at that little bed-and-breakfast you always liked. Wesley kind of, you know, already took the liberty of booking you a room. I told him you liked the one in the corner, overlooking the pond."

Tears sprang into Audrey's eyes. She choked out a smiling sob—Talia and Crystal's cue to get the heck out of there and give her some privacy.

Talia removed her apron and folded it on the counter. "Let's take a walk around the arcade," she suggested. "It's gorgeous out."

They walked outside, over the cobblestones, in the direction of Sage & Seaweed. "It's weird, isn't it," Talia said, "the way Audrey and Molly both forgave Wesley but then couldn't talk to each other?"

Crystal nodded. "He wasn't really guilty of anything . . . well, except for getting her pregnant. But they were both responsible for that."

"They were over eighteen," Talia said. "In the law's eyes, they were adults. In reality . . . ?" She smiled and let the thought dangle.

"I wonder if they'll work it out," Crystal mused. "Audrey and Wesley, that is."

Somehow, Talia doubted it. But then—

"You're seeing Ryan today, aren't you?" Crystal asked. Her voice sounded odd.

"You bet. In fact, he should be coming by anytime now. We're taking that fresh-baked mac-and-cheese casserole up to the Pines for Ryan's dad. The chef, Tina, is going to reheat it for us, and then we're going to indulge ourselves in some good old-fashioned comfort food. Mom is having a private area set aside in the dining room just for the three of us. Why do you ask?"

"So Martha and Lucas are covering for you?"

"Of course they are. I told them I'm taking the whole day

off and leaving Fry Me in their capable hands! Why are you so curious?"

Crystal blushed. "Oh, look," she squeaked, striding over to Sage & Seaweed. "Suzy has her fall display set up. Well, it's about time, I say. Oh, glory, look at those vampire bath salts!"

Suzy had indeed rearranged her front window. Summer was out. Pumpkin-flavored lip glosses and ghoulish accessories were in. "Shall we take a peek?" Talia said.

Crystal glanced all around. "Um, no, not now." She looked distracted.

"Is everything okay, Crystal?"

"I'm sorry," she blurted. "It's just that I saw him—I mean, yesterday, coming out of the—" Her hands fluttered. She looked stricken with panic. "Oh God, I'm not supposed to say anything. Don't pay any attention to me, okay? Forget I ever mentioned it." She leaned over and gave Talia a fast hug. "And thanks for today. You're a doll. A lifesaver!" She rushed off as if a mad bull were chasing her.

Baffled, Talia could only shrug and watch her friend toddle off in the direction of the Fork and Dish. She was hurrying so fast Talia was worried she might twist an ankle on the cobblestones.

Shaking her head, Talia turned to go into Fry Me to wait for Ryan but then spied a man with a familiar face strolling along Main Street toward the arcade. Her heart gave out that little blip it always did whenever he came into view. Ryan waved and broke into a huge grin, and then he picked up his pace. Something dangled from his left hand. A bag of some sort. Gold. Shimmery.

Talia swallowed. That bag—it looked like the one Jodie had strolled out of LaFleur's with a few weeks earlier.

She wanted to move, to run toward him, but her legs were welded to the cobblestones.

Talia remained where she was. She would wait. Whatever was in that bag, she would find out soon enough.

And soon enough would suit her just fine.

RECICES

TALIA'S DEEP-FRIED
MAC-AND-CHEESE SQUARES

Ingredients for Casserole:

2¼ cups small shells, uncooked

1½ cups whole milk

⅛ teaspoon black pepper

¼ teaspoon ground mustard

nonstick cooking spray

10 ounces very sharp cheddar, sliced about ⅛ inch thick

Deep-fry Coating:

1 egg

1 tablespoon milk

½ cup plain panko crumbs

1 teaspoon Parmesan cheese
a few shakes of cayenne pepper (optional)

Mac-and-cheese casserole:

Boil shells according to directions and drain. Combine the milk, black pepper, and mustard in a measuring cup. Coat an 8-inch-by-8-inch pan (preferably a glass pan) with nonstick spray. Spoon about ⅓ of the cooked shells into the pan. Top shells with ⅓ of the cheddar slices. Pour about ½ cup of the milk mixture over it all. Repeat two more times to complete the layering. Bake in an oven preheated to 350 degrees F for 45 to 50 minutes or until firm and the cheese is golden on top; allow to cool, then refrigerate overnight.

Deep-frying:

From the refrigerated macaroni cheese, cut about ten bite-sized pieces, about 1- to 1½-inch cubes (you'll have some mac and cheese left over for reheating). In a bowl, blend the egg and milk. In a separate bowl, combine the panko crumbs, Parmesan cheese, and cayenne pepper. Dip each square into the egg mixture, making sure all sides are coated. Then place each square in the panko mixture and coat thoroughly, pressing the crumb mixture into the squares. Chill in the refrigerator on a tray lined with parchment paper or nonstick foil until you're ready to fry (this can be done ahead of time). Once you're ready to fry, in a deep fryer or heavy-bottomed pan, heat vegetable oil to 350 degrees F; if using a pan, a candy/deep-fry thermometer will help you gauge the temperature. Using a slotted spoon, carefully lower each mac-and-cheese cube into the oil, no more than three at a time (the oil will sizzle if you do so). Fry only about a minute, until golden,

then remove and drain on a plate lined with paper towels.
Serve while still warm.

*Note: If you have any left over, they can easily be reheated
in the microwave.*

TALIA'S MINIATURE DEEP-FRIED
APPLE PIES

Dough:
2 cups flour, plus a little extra for coating
½ cup vegetable oil, plus additional oil for frying
¼ cup milk

Filling:
4 Cortland apples, peeled, cored, and sliced
1 tablespoon butter
¼ cup white sugar
¼ cup brown sugar
½ teaspoon cinnamon
¼ teaspoon nutmeg
⅛ teaspoon vanilla
powdered sugar

Prepare the dough:
Blend the flour, vegetable oil, and milk with a fork, then
form into two separate balls. Coat each dough ball with
flour. Roll out the first one onto a floured cutting board until

it's ⅛ inch thick. Cut out rounds that are 4 inches in diameter. Repeat with the second dough ball. Set aside the rounds.

Prepare the filling:
In a large frying pan, combine the apples, butter, sugar, cinnamon, nutmeg, and vanilla. Cook gently over medium heat until apples are soft, about 15 minutes. Remove from heat and cool.

Deep-frying:
Place a heaping tablespoon of the cooked apples in each dough round. Moisten the edges of the dough with cold water and fold in half over the apple mixture. Press the edges with a fork to crimp and seal. Repeat with the remaining rounds. Place pies on a tray or cookie sheet that's been lightly sprinkled with flour, then chill for 15 minutes.

In a deep fryer or heavy-bottomed pan, heat vegetable oil to 350 degrees F, using just enough oil to cover the pies. A candy/deep-fry thermometer will help gauge the oil temperature. Lower the pies into the hot oil with a slotted spoon, frying only a few at a time. Fry about 2 minutes on each side, or until both sides are golden. Remove and drain on paper towels. Sprinkle with powdered sugar and serve warm.

The Deep Fried Mysteries

By Linda Reilly

Talia Marby brings a little bit of the South up to the Berkshires with her fabulous deep-fried restaurant—and her sleuthing skills.

Find more books by Linda Reilly
by visiting prh.com/nextread

"Quirky characters, a darling small-town New England setting, and a plucky heroine...Reilly cooks up a perfect recipe of murder and mayhem in this charming cozy."
—Jenn McKinlay, *New York Times* bestselling author

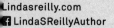
Lindasreilly.com
LindaSReillyAuthor

Penguin Random House